PENGUIN BOOKS

# LITTLE LOVELY LILY

Ahmad Rizaq lives in the skyscraper-fenced compact community in Jakarta. His wordsmith journey started as a digital storyteller with a focus on crafting marketing pitches. He has bent all multimedia elements, from blogs and social media to e-commerce and visual copywriting. His childhood dream was to become a fiction writer, and on one reflective night, he rediscovered that dream. He is now making his debut with *Little Lovely Lily*.

Connect with him on Instagram: @ahmadwrizaq

T0244845

# Little Lovely Lily

Ahmad Rizaq

**PENGUIN BOOKS**

An imprint of Penguin Random House

PENGUIN BOOKS

Penguin Books is an imprint of the Penguin Random House group of
companies whose addresses can be found at global.penguinrandomhouse.com

Published by Penguin Random House SEA Pte Ltd
40 Penjuru Lane, #03-12, Block 2
Singapore 609216

Penguin
Random House
SEA

First published in Penguin Books by Penguin Random House SEA 2024

ISBN 9789815204704

Typeset in Adobe Caslon Pro by MAP Systems, Bengaluru, India

www.penguin.sg

*For the first step of this journey,*
*this is for Mama.*

*Thank you for teaching me how to walk.*

# Part I

First Semester

# Chapter 1

## June

'Why was June made?
Can you guess?
June was made for happiness!'

—Annette Wynne,
'Why Was June Made?'

Lily's sweet seventeen had come, and all she wanted was for it to not go miserably, like her sixteenth had. Simply because there is no such thing as a 'sweet eighteen'. It was her now-or-never chance to rewrite the end of her Diary of a Not-so-glam Teen.

Yet, in the wild realm of classroom drama, her classmates seemed to be wishing, 'Today's her birthday, let's throw a party—for her death!'

The party itself was a masquerade ball. A festivity just for her, and yet it felt like a contest for who was the best at looking away or pretending to not see her. So, the moment of unmasking carried even more thrill than exposing what lay under Darth Vader's helmet. The faces hiding beneath weren't the kind who would politely knock on one's door—their rudeness left one tingling and lost for words.

The Lily-is-pretty-meh attitude they wore with such finesse was their personal comedy, but for her, it was a heart-wrenching tragedy. And the audience's conscience remained untouched for as long as they partied it up with their popcorn and belly laughs.

Once again, the party took place at Bloementuin High School. On a typical, scorching June day, defying all expectations, the elements seemed to align favourably. It was the day of the Physical Education exam—a relay swim race taking centre stage. The girls, wrapped in the embrace of synthetic garments, pulsated with excitement. They were all set for the aquatic rodeo.

Lily blazed with an inner fire, stoking the flames to incinerate all the diminishment she had endured; a blazing manifesto that declared, 'I'm no loser!' She had gone over this in her head a million times, putting on a show, trying to get them to see her in different scenarios. Even then, it felt like no one was really buying tickets to her show.

She was wearing a swimsuit that perfectly matched her skin tone—a tropical island tan. It was hugging her body so closely, it felt like a second skin. The fabric stretched across her midsection. An audacious choice, especially since it was that time of the month—also known as 'Let's Make Lily Feel Like a Volcano Inside'. But the sanitary pad-shaped bulge on her swimsuit was her way of saying, 'Who cares? I'm still making it look good'.

And let's be honest—no one really cared.

In that locker room—a hallway lined with lockers that looked like metal troops in a parade—the party finally revealed itself. It was either a masterclass in pretending to forget or a grand performance of 'Oops, Lily, who?' Everyone masqueraded, making Lily feel as invisible as a silent fart in a noisy room. She had slammed the door like a gunshot in a silent movie, practically begging for the spotlight, but their chatter rolled on like a river that had zero interest in a rock along its way. The room echoed with mindless chit-chat.

'Guess what? Miss Drama Queen apparently has a thing for Mr Chemistry Whiz! I mean, who knew?'

'Did anyone catch that lunchtime interaction? I swear, if they were any cheesier, we'd be in a romcom ourselves!'

'All right, change of topic—spill the beans, who's your current all-time favourite artist? I'm low-key obsessed with their new songs!'

'So, my brother's at a whole new level of laziness. Seriously, I've seen sloths move faster than him—it's like the couch has his name on it!'

The noise pollution of teenage girls' babble, complete with insidious gossip, infected the room. The stories left hanging were resumed with new plot lines, like a line of dominoes falling in succession, their voices mixed together in a medley of high-pitched laughter and proliferating rumours. Meanwhile, towels, swimming caps, goggles, and torn pieces of plastic packaging from care products were scattered on the floor.

The girls put on bright swimsuits, each one a riot of colours—bright pinks, bold blues, and vivid greens; patterns ranging from bold stripes to intricate floral designs. The cloth stuck to their bodies and made them gleam as they moved with a carefree confidence. Some girls fixed their swimsuits awkwardly, pulling the material, then putting it back in place, even though they had been doing so for almost an hour now.

The air was thick with the sweet smells of many different perfumes. It formed a cloud of smells that you could almost touch. There were scents of fruits and flowers mixed together. The sugary scent of strawberry, reminiscent of cotton candy, intertwined with the delicate fragrance of jasmine tea, the refreshing sweetness of watermelon—bright, playful, and endlessly joyful.

And then there was Lily, parading down the hallway, still wearing a today's-my-birthday-folks grin. The girls were excited and energetic, so they pushed each other playfully, probably part of some secret teenage Morse code. But only Lily didn't seem to get the message. It was like she had shown up to a music festival wearing earplugs.

Perched in the corner like the last cookie on the platter at a party, Lily's locker resided in the eh-it's-okay-I-guess section of the room. It looked decrepit, paint peeling off it and rust forming abstract art on it. It even smelled a bit musty, like old clothes. When she opened it, it made a loud creaking sound.

All sorts of things—books, sports gear, and clothes—lay jumbled together inside. She skilfully navigated her locker's contents, finding her swimsuit and towel tucked away under a pile of notebooks and a water bottle. The noise of the locker room buzzed around her as she focused on getting ready as quickly as possible.

Dressed and about to slam the locker shut, Lily's eyes settled on an unexpected intruder in the locker—

an item that had no business being there. This was no mere misplacement; it was a full-blown invasion of her personal space.

And what was this invader? A red box with a white ribbon that screamed 'GIFT ALERT!' in big, bold, capital letters. But did Lily engage in a philosophical debate with herself, pondering the deep mysteries of its existence? Did she launch into a series of inquiries like 'Who sent this?' or 'Why is it here?' Nah, she skipped the monologue and headed straight to the point: someone remembered her birthday!

She didn't need to be a detective; she wasn't about to let this golden opportunity slip through her fingers. With the excitement of a child on Christmas morning, she unleashed herself on that ribbon and opened the box like it held the secret to eternal happiness.

*Pandora's box!*

She stood there; her face caught in a perfect snapshot of shock. Teeth gnashing, hope vanishing, her expression turned to despair. It was like time had hit the pause button, freezing her nerve endings in a collective gasp of 'Oh no!'

She didn't need a degree in detective work to observe that whatever she was seeing was a total mess. Her gasp was so loud, it could've triggered a car alarm. In a knee-jerk reaction, she slammed the box shut. The sound it made when it kissed the floor was loud, like something crashing or breaking. Things inside the box tumbled out, scattering around her in a disorganized heap on the floor.

The contents of the box were like a recipe gone horribly wrong. Her mind told her to not even think about it as she tried to make sense of the mess she was seeing. If she had to sum it up in one word—SICKENING! The whole thing stank like a dumpster on a hot summer day, and her gag reflex woke up from its nap to join the party.

Lily's eyes did a tug-of-war between wanting to see more and wanting to unsee everything. The rotten smell was piercing, and its vomitable looks made it feel like her food was coming back up her throat.

A single glance was enough to grasp the crime scene: a thick, crimson fluid that looked like it had had an intense argument with hygiene, and hygiene had lost. The smell screamed 'blood', but the source was shrouded in mystery. And that's not all! Alongside this bloody circus were a doggy's special souvenirs, veggies that had given up on life, sewer water (because why not?), and a motley crew of critters in various states of distress: squashed frogs, flattened rats, pancaked cockroaches. Just a whiff of it made her question life choices, and the smell of stale pee joined the birthday celebration like it was time to blow candles and make Lily wish she'd lose her sense of smell.

The rest of the contents? Oh, you don't even want to know. It was the stuff nightmares are made of, starring your weirdest fears as the main cast. Or maybe it was a reflection of how much the sender sucked.

Lily's mood plummeted, setting a new record and hitting the deepest depths of despondency. But because of that damn box, Lily was thrown into the spotlight. She was the centre of attention now as everyone watched her stunning performance of being perplexed and her valiant struggle to keep her stomach from revolting.

Who would've thought that a box of horrors could make you a star? Maybe, just maybe, Lily should send a thank-you box back to the sender.

But the gazes locked onto her weren't the gazes she'd been daydreaming about while staring out of classroom windows. Nope, they were the kind of gazes that had the power to make their eye-rolls felt from miles away; the kind that whispered, 'Look at her, the queen of awkwardness'. They were not gazes of care, recognition, jealousy, or even an ounce of sympathy. They were the kind of gazes that could curdle milk, drenched in a mix of disdain, unpleasantness, superiority, and the special ingredient: mockery. Their unrelenting gazes were soon coupled with raccoon-like laughter.

It wasn't like this was the first petal being plucked from Lily's self-esteem—her tormentors had made a hobby out of that. Her fingers were practically begging for mercy from counting the many instances from the past. Another petal had fallen away today, adding to the grand total of torment that had begun almost a year ago.

Sure, it might appear as if today was a major chapter in Lily's ongoing saga of misery, but the truth was stranger than a circus freakshow. The sheer variety of sadistic tricks up her tormentors' sleeves made today's horrific incident seem like a harmless tea party. Today was just a sampler offering a teeny-tiny taste of the full buffet of evil they had to offer.

On Teacher's Day, her heartfelt letter to Miss Van der Mey, her English teacher, had been sabotaged and rewritten as a mean note of mockery. Of course, the school had chosen to act like a drama queen and made a big deal about it. Cue her suspension and more of her petals falling.

Then came the cruel chapters. She had once fallen asleep in class and her T-shirt had been defaced with doodles and mud had got into her shoes and stained their holy white colour. Gum, like an unwanted guest, had found its way to her hair while the things in her locker had either been stolen, hidden, or destroyed in this campaign against her. They had broken her from the stem, so she couldn't grow anymore.

Friendship felt distant, making her feel like an alien from an isolated planet. Even when she was minding her own business, peaceful in her solitude, a menacing half-circle would often form around her like a trap. Hurtful insults and mocking words would be hurled at her, everyone eager to join the cruel spectacle.

The constant torment crushed her fragile self-worth and self-esteem, making her feel worthless. These negative thoughts and feelings were like a ridiculously huge and useless pistil in her mind. It made her constantly seek the approval of her tormentors—an attempt to be the centre of attention again. This pistil wasn't a glistening crown but a cursed mark on her mind. Long ago, before this growth had marred her sense of self, she had been the centre of attention—the most beautiful flower in the world, so enchanting that even Aphrodite, the creator of all things pretty, had felt insecure. It almost felt as if Aphrodite had conjured up this monstrous pistil of worthlessness—Lily's most glaring imperfection—out of jealousy. This big, gross limb acted as a stark reminder of her scary desires and mindset.

Whispers spread around Lily—an electric undercurrent of gossip that struck her like lightning. The cacophony was deafening, a swelling tide of hearsay. Murmurs darted around her like shadows, weaving tales of her character that, in hushed corners, told a different story.

'Damn, Lily had it coming! That's one way to celebrate a birthday!'

'Whoa, Lily sure knows how to throw a birthday bash! Poop-themed presents, anyone?'

'You mean that pile of shit is worth more than her, right?'

Laughter, the main act, entered the scene.

'Oh, come on, Lily! Hurry up and deal with your "gift", you clueless fool! The stench is unreal! Seriously, it's rotten enough to make me puke!'

'That girl, seriously, what's her problem? She's beyond gross!'

'Lily has reached peak DISGUSTING levels!'

Insults were flying around like Regina George tossing pages of the Burn Book around in *Mean Girls*. Specifically, the page that stated Lily was a look-at-me girl.

'And the award for the most dramatic entrance goes to . . . Lily, again!'

'Lily, do you ever just chill, or is it always about making sure everything's about you?'

'Watch out, Lily's here. Bet she's got another wild story just to grab our attention.'

The news was spreading like wildfire. Inevitably, someone from the locker room grapevine said, 'There's Lily, putting on a performance as usual. Who is she trying to impress today?'

'Umm . . . no,' Lily tried.

Laughter had never caused such a degree of misery.

'NO!' Lily just couldn't handle it. 'Please, stop!'

But the more she asked them to stop it, the more uninvited participants joined the party.

'Please! Please! Please! JUST STOP!'

Oh God, what was she even thinking?

I mean, if you look at it technically, Lily was one of the tallest kids in the whole school. She could've just taken them out, one by one. Popped those snarky mouths with a single punch and scared the living daylights out of them! They totally deserved that. Come on, Lily, they need a reality check!

But nope, that just wasn't her style. She decided to let their verbal jabs peck her, like seriously? Was she at an all-you-can-eat buffet for toxic words? Or maybe she had just developed selective deafness for it all without realizing?

About a million times—seriously, it's easy to lose count—those words had ping-ponged their way through Lily's ears and stuck in her mind like they had found the perfect spot to hang out, without bothering to leave.

And who could forget about the inventor who coined these taunts? It was Rosy—the favourite flower of poets. Crafted by the divine fingers of Chloris, the OG flower deity, she was like a floral phoenix reborn from a nymph's ashes in the wild. Aphrodite herself took a break from matchmaking to sprinkle Rosy with fairy dust, while Dionysius poured in a little liquid charm over her. Zephyrus, the wind god, like a paparazzo, parted the clouds to give Apollo, the sunshine deity, a prime view of her growth spurt.

'Happy Birthday, Lily!' Rosy chirped. Yup yup! That was her. And gods and goddesses agreed, she was the Queen of the Flower Garden.

'Yo, how's the party going? Quite the circus, huh?' Right next to Rosy was her mistletoe—a classy parasite that had decided to dedicate her entire existence, heart and soul, to serving as Rosy's eternal sidekick. It was Missy, the mysterious goth chick and Rosy's private satellite. They were like a duo of darkness, besties bound by the shadows.

Their friendship was like a movie—a horror flick directed by Missy with Lily in the leading role as the unwilling victim. Lily couldn't help but wonder if Missy's brain was a twisted script factory, churning out plots inspired by her favourite collection of thriller movies to determine the path of Lily's horror show life.

And now, in the jungle of Lily's thoughts, thorny vines of suspicion and grudge were taking root. Her heart seethed with hate for Rosy. It felt as though it would be trapped with this feeling until it withered and perished. The vines infected Lily with self-doubt and threatened her sanity.

So, today's main agenda was knocking Rosy's crown off.

Lily's and Rosy's fates entwined like two kooky characters' in a sitcom. They had made no ordinary bet—there were fireworks and confetti cannons going off in the background because of it. Their bet had transformed today's exam into something of a Wild West showdown, with Lily saddling up for justice and Rosy, the outlaw, facing off against Lily in a moment of reckoning. Lily aimed to cash in big—collecting her dues for every toxic vine Rosy had planted, every slight and scar Rosy had inflicted on her.

It was like Lily's victory was a foregone conclusion—a win so necessary, it was etched in stone.

* * *

June turned the indoor pool into a cauldron of chaos, like a witch's brew on steroids. Now don't let your imagination run too wild—it wasn't actually bubbling like a witch's brew, but the ceramic pool, just 1.5 metres deep, did resemble simmering stew. The air was so hot, you could almost feel steam wafting off the water's surface.

The boys, fresh off the exam battlefield, were just finishing up with their fun in the pool when the girls jumped into the watery fray. The pool's embrace left them with a sensation as refreshing as the touch of a light summer rain.

Then, out of nowhere, BAM! Something wet hit Lily right in the face, drenching her in an instant. The offending object was a white, tattered towel marred by stubborn yellow-brown stains. This wasn't unusual for her; things often landed on her—paper balls, basketballs, or oddly enough, animal waste shaped like balls.

Every finger pointed in one direction, towards a boy with pallid skin whose grin resembled that of a Derbidae bug ready to nibble on Lily's petals. The persistent pest in her life—Derby—completed his trio of torment with his loyal sidekicks, Timmy and Billy, who were never far behind him.

Derby and Rosy were like two peas in a bully pod. Rumour had it they were distant cousins, part of a grand lineage of troublemakers and sneaky schemers, reigning as the classroom's supreme tyrants. The two shared the same spooky look—they were practically twins separated at birth, sporting a similar deathly pale complexion, straight blonde hair, brows that were medal-worthy arches, cheekbones you could cut cheese with, and smiles that oozed wickedness.

The only real difference? Derby's shirtless escapades unveiled a tiny pink wart on his chest, looking like a third nipple that had lost its way.

All right, now let's dive back into the pool party! The girls were divided into four squads, each comprised its own Fab Four. The A-Team, basically the school's 'golden kids', including Rosy and her girls.

And then, there was Lily's team, the leftover crew, the ones who probably got matched with the wrong partners on a friendship app. They were like a bouquet of ugly flowers; you know, the ones that don't get to star in perfume commercials. One girl stuck out like a monstrous sunflower with petals the size of satellite dishes—Rafflesia, whose scent was ghastly. Then, there was the deadly nightshade—Dean, pronounced as 'D-N' almost like 'the end'. Nobody wanted to touch her. And amid this floral folly, Lily harboured a tiny hope—the Cactus (not her real name, of course), whose nickname was owed to the galaxy of ripe, prickly pimples decorating her face and back. Poised on the starting block, she clung to the railing with an iron grip, her feet set against the pool wall, ready for the imminent dive.

*TOOT!* Mr Verwey, the P.E. teacher, blew his screeching whistle. Get ready for the splash!

Cactus dove in and broke into a front crawl. Don't you doubt it, her form was an A-grade masterpiece and she led her pack effortlessly. Five metres behind her, Rosy's girl struggled against the waves, her strokes erratic, legs flailing. In under five minutes, Cactus claimed the first round, leaving Rosy's girl trailing by nine metres.

Round two, Dean dove in, the water seemingly propelling her petite frame with newfound speed. Victory Island beckoned, its sweetness within reach of Lily's senses. Yet, the aftertaste turned bitter. Dean's control slipped, her body swaying uncontrollably. Lily's shouts and curses fell on deaf ears. She watched in disbelief as the second girl from Rosy's team caught up with Dean. This round was a different story; Dean garnered no admiring glances. Worse, she ended up third in the second lap of the race.

Rafflesia dove in without a moment's hesitation, conjuring an unexpected tsunami of energy that crashed into Lily, drenching her head and cleansing her thoughts. Lily's expectations from the formidable Rafflesia were swiftly swept away; there was little hope left for her.

Thankfully, the third member of Rosy's team was Missy, deemed the weakest link in the team, perhaps even in the entire class. If not for Rosy's intervention, Missy might have been the class's underdog. The curious question lingered—why had a rose chosen a mistletoe over a lily as her companion in a bouquet?

In a twist of fate, Rafflesia turned her performance around and exceeded all expectations, potentially even proving herself in front of everyone. She navigated the water with grace, her strokes propelling her like an arrow. Surprisingly, she outpaced members of other teams, closing in on Missy, who struggled with proper arm movements. Rosy mirrored Lily's frustration, cursing and shouting at Missy like a football coach hopped up on too many energy drinks. As only three metres separated Rafflesia and Missy, they crossed the finish line together, concluding the third lap.

Lily and Rosy took a leap of faith, propelled by a stubborn determination to outshine the other. Lily was as agile as a dolphin, while Rosy was as strong as a frog. Their water play was more like a mermaid marathon. They stirred up froth that floated towards the pool's edge. The water's movement was untidy and turbulent, causing it to spill over the pool's rim, wetting and slickening the surrounding floor.

On the other side of the watery stage, the remaining two girls floundered like cats learning to swim backstroke—their efforts barely managing to create a ripple, let alone a wave.

Amid the rippling water, Lily caught glimpses of the raucous cheers from her classmates, engulfed by the rush of water and the subsequent wave of applause. In her trance, she almost believed the adulation was exclusively for her. Suddenly, a realization dawned upon Lily that Rosy was trailing by merely three metres. Flipping a mental switch, Lily turbocharged her limbs, turning into a human jet engine as she charged towards the finish line, which was merely seven metres away.

And for those who underestimated her, Lily emerged as the unsinkable victor, proving that when the chips were down, she could swim circles around her sceptics.

The plot thickened. Rosy managed to catch up, her face was a mix of disorder and disbelief. History had been made, a legacy-defining moment had taken place, someone finally reduced Rosy to a state of defeat and humiliation. Lily grinned, mimicking Rosy's signature taunting expression. It was as if she was saying, 'See who's the big loser now?'

Lily was ready to soak up the applause like a beach towel in the sun, but she was thrown a curveball. Those smiles the spectators would undoubtedly have showered upon Rosy if she had triumphed, evaded Lily. But why?

Ah! Why should Lily even care? She wasn't playing their rigged game anymore. She knew the drill and was familiar with their patented masks of indifference. They probably didn't want her to enjoy the spotlight of victory. So what? Let them marinate in their pool of envy! Lily had a ball at the show, delighting in their discomfort as she outshone their favourite flower.

Strangely, their expressions defied the condescension she often encountered in moments of humiliation, and they didn't mirror the earlier locker room scene either. Instead, their faces seemed to be marinating in a cocktail of shock and mild disgust.

And then, with the subtlety of a cannon blast at a tea party, Derby screamed like he'd just seen a ghost: 'OH GOD! THAT'S HER PERIOD BLOOD!'

Lips parted in surprise, yet no sound escaped. Eyes opened wide and breaths were held tight.

Suddenly, all the girls from the other teams, with hysterical disgust, climbed out of the pool, leaving Lily standing alone, like a little island of disbelief. Her gaze was like a lost boat floating aimlessly in a sea of perplexity.

The classic Lily plot twist! She had mastered the art of playing the protagonist in her own tragicomedy, but this time, she found herself a script she hadn't seen before. In her new role, she had transformed the pool into a murky soup of mortification—she was an octopus with unexpected secretions, releasing a slick fluid.

She shivered, not from the chilly water, but from the all-too-familiar sensation of humiliation running down her spine. Because, as you know, humiliation just isn't complete without a chorus of giggles and finger-pointing. In fact, some documentarians even whipped out their phones to capture the historic moment, preserving it for future generations as the 'Oh no, Lily!' incident.

It was bedlam all around her. The whispers, Lily knew what they were about. The walls themselves seemed to resonate with the audience's pointed words, striking her repeatedly.

TOOT!

'Enough, everyone. Let's show respect and kindness to each other! The exam is over, time to clean up!' Mr Verwey's whistle pierced through the commotion. 'Lily, just give me a moment. I'll go get Miss Van der Mey, okay? You can towel yourself off meanwhile.'

The children's silhouettes slowly vanished from the room as the gaping maw of the doorway consumed them one by one. The bustle of voices subsided. The reverberations of their very existence vanished completely. The room now gave in to the soothing sound of rippling water once more.

Yet, in this tranquil environment, Lily lingered in the pool's embrace, motionless, feigning an air of resilience. Beneath the surface, a tempest of emotions swelled in her, threatening to spill over in a flood of tears. But she held them at bay, for in her world, shedding tears would be an admission of defeat, a victory for her tormentors.

Her fingertips now bore a delicate, prune-like web from the cold water immersion. A wave of nausea hit her. It was self-directed disgust, tangled with the splashy silliness of it all.

Agony, torment, fifty shades of dreariness—when would this circus fold its tent? The crystal ball had gone foggy about what sick stunt they had queued up for her next.

Lily felt worry brewing inside her. She believed the only escape from this dark chapter was to end her life's book, leaving its pages empty and untouched by any more colourful tales. But she refused to let the cruel ones write her final words, no.

No, no, revenge is a dish best served cold, right? Time to whip up a dish that would make diners come back for seconds. A savoury revenge soufflé, baked to precision, sprinkled with the pepper of pent-up rage, and seasoned with pure payback. Take cover, you tormentors—Lily's about to serve her secret recipe, and guess what? It's going to be extra spicy!

Roses might have thorns. But haven't they heard lilies are poisonous too?

# Chapter 2

## July

'July is proof that even Mother Nature needs
a summer vacation.'

—Unknown

'Phew, you wouldn't believe how hectic it's been, coming
to school in the holidays to get everything set for next
month's summer camp. It's been non-stop!' Miss Van der
Mey leaned in, looking really concerned. 'By the way, can
you fill me in on what happened during the P.E. final in
the pool?'

'You mean to that girl with the curly hair from Rosy's
class?' Mr Verwey scratched his chin, thinking.

'Lily, right?'

'Yeah, Lily,' he confirmed, looking into the distance.
'She's usually so quiet, kinda flies under the radar. But that
day, she was like a whole different person; seemed like she
really wanted to get noticed, you know?' He stopped for a
second, trying to figure out how to say it. 'She even beat

Rosy in swimming, which nobody saw coming. But she was overdoing it, totally ignoring how much it was taking out of her. It was like watching a tragedy unfold in slow motion.'

'Was she getting picked on again?' Miss Van der Mey looked even more worried.

'Picked on? What do you mean?' He looked confused. 'No, she just . . . she kinda blew the P.E. test, that's all.'

Miss Van der Mey sat back, her mind racing to piece the puzzle together.

'From the get-go, I've had this rule in my class that everyone's gotta join in on all the sport demonstrations, practices, and exams, except for a few cases. And the girls are allowed sit out during their period. They just need to let me know. But Lily, man, I have no clue what she was thinking. She just kept to herself, went all out and dove into the pool. Next thing, it was like watching ink spread in water,' Mr Verwey explained.

Miss Van der Mey remained quiet, clenching her teeth in disbelief.

'I was just as shocked. Maybe it was a really bad day for her,' Mr Verwey added, sounding a mix of puzzled and worried.

'What was your reaction?'

'I told her to get cleaned up right away. I even tried to get help from another teacher in the office. Thought you'd be there, but nope, ended up dealing with it all by myself. When I got back, there she was—still in the pool, crying and shaking, wouldn't get out. It took forever to get her to come out.'

'Yeah, that's pretty common,' she nodded slowly. 'But what about the other kids?'

'They were totally taken aback at first, then started cracking up. Typical teenage stuff, I guess. But it got so loud, I had to step in and shut it down,' he added with a shrug.

'No, Mr Verwey. That's not just humour; that's terrifying.' Miss Van der Mey's expression hardened.

'Yeah,' Mr Verwey admitted, his brow furrowing in confusion.

'You know, after teaching for over seven years, I've seen all kinds of student behaviours. But it's funny, they always seem to fall into the same patterns, no matter the generation. It's like a farm, you know? You've got your queen bee, a male goat, and then there's Lily—the black sheep. She's the one who is different, the odd one, either not getting or not wanting the same attention from others.' Miss Van der Mey theorized.

'Wait, are you saying there's bullying happening in our school?' He looked worried.

'Exactly. Often, the black sheep just keeps quiet. What we need to do is catch this bully,' she said, her eyes shining with determination.

'But the whole pool incident, wasn't that just self-embarrassment? It turned into a show, but do we really need to punish anyone for that?'

'Definitely, it's a must. The problem's deeper and more complex than it seems. You might not have noticed but that was the bullies' perfect chance to make Lily's life even harder. We need to punish them to teach them tolerance and respect. Did you see who started laughing first or who took it too far?'

'They all started laughing at the same time. But I heard someone call her "squid". Pretty sure it was Derby, but Billy or Timmy could've said it too; they were all sitting together,' he remembered in an 'aha' moment.

'Those three again? Can't say I'm shocked. I *just* had to discipline them for not handing in their final poetry projects. Made them write a 2,000-word essay about what they had learned in my class.'

'All right, I'll figure out the right punishment for them.' Mr Verwey sounded determined.

'Good.'

The school was peaceful and quiet, which was quite different from how busy it got during normal hours. It was almost like it was taking a slow, deep breath to prepare for its residents to come back.

'Apart from them, I often hear about someone else who dislikes Lily, someone maybe you and the other teachers wouldn't even suspect. It's hard to believe, but it happened in my class. Such behaviour isn't ideal, especially from your favourite student, our school's star athlete.' Miss Van der Mey folded her arms, her face expressing her disappointment.

'Rosy?' Mr Verwey leaned in, looking surprised. 'What did she do?'

'On Teachers' Day, remember how we had the students write letters to their favourite teachers? Who did you get one from?'

'Rosy.'

'I guessed as much. I received letters from Susan, Bella, Levy, Max, and Lily. Lily's letter was pure white and had a lily's fragrance.' She paused, a distant look in her eyes. 'I didn't know her well back then; she's always been quiet. "Just another silent student," I thought.'

'That's true in my class as well. She can't even do twenty push-ups in a minute,' Mr Verwey shrugged slightly.

'But Lily's actually got some serious talent in English. I never expected her to write a letter to me,' her voice softened, 'but the letter I got was neither celebratory nor affectionate. It was blasphemous.'

He chuckled. 'Sorry, but that's a bit funny. Did she criticize your straight hair? Or your insistence on speaking with a British accent in class?'

'Shut up.' She was lost for a moment. 'I forget the exact words. But I told the principal and he suspended Lily. I had no issue with that, until I reread the letter. Lily always writes her 't's like a cross and her 'g's with a single loop. But the letter had 't's with tails and 'g's with double loops. The only one who writes 'g's like that is Rosy. I matched the handwriting, and that's how I found out who the bully was.'

'So, you're saying someone tampered with Lily's letter, and it was Rosy?' His eyes widened in disbelief.

Miss Van der Mey nodded firmly.

'Wow, I never would've thought Rosy could do something like that,' Mr Verwey said, running a hand through his hair, clearly stunned.

'That's because you're not watching your students closely enough,' she said, sounding a bit accusatory. 'We were kids once too, stuff like this happened all the time. But it's tough for teachers to notice these little things. Better to catch on late than never, I guess.'

'Okay. Starting today, I'll keep a closer eye on Rosy. And Lily too,' he resolved, straightening up. 'Was the pool incident a result of their rivalry?'

'I believe so. But there's something more complex about Lily.'

'Like what?'

'I can't quite put my finger on it. She's very private.' She frowned slightly. 'The kind of kid who says everything's fine when it's not. She's my first student like this, so I guess I need to be more patient and try to understand her better.'

'All right. How much do you really know her?'

'Better than other problematic students I've handled,' her gaze drifted away, contemplative. 'I mean that's just how I feel.'

Miss Van der Mey handed Mr Verwey a stack of papers.

'What are these?' He looked at the papers, puzzled.

'Her poetry assignments. Because she barely speaks, I have been trying to understand her through these.' She gestured towards the papers, her eyes deeply curious.

Mr Verwey began flipping through the stack of Lily's poetry assignments, each page offering a glimpse into her world. 'She moved here when she was thirteen, right?' He looked up briefly.

'Yes, her mother's a diplomat. She came here after her parents separated, and she hasn't seen her father since. Or so it seemed, at first . . .'

Mr Verwey's interest was piqued as he continued scanning the papers.

'Where do I start?' She paused, collecting her thoughts. 'Well, take a look at this.' She pointed to a specific poem, her finger tracing the lines as if they held a hidden message.

## Carnival Night

At the town's edge, where night lights flicker
through the wild,
I roamed alone through the carnival, a place you always
told me not to.
Once, this ground was a myth for my childhood, a realm
where laughter rang,
a haven for dreamers, where fantasies unfurled
their wings.

But that night, after endless spoiled daughter's pleadings,
when you led me there, far surpassing these solitary
evenings, setting it apart.
With you, the carnival's magic was real, more than
just a dream.

No heart-pounding rides—that was your first rule.
It made you question life, you'd say; was the act of a fool.
Their cries called me, your hands big enough to shield me.
In the safety of your shadows, I felt so small.
No games of chance, you think they're too tricky.
Their siren song was silenced, so contagious.
While those vibrant booths, tapestries of dreams,
untouchable, unseen, like the moonlight in the distance.
And the treats, oh the treats,
cotton candy, sugary drinks;
part of a plan, a colourful ban.

Maybe it's because you were always so firm, so resolute,
sticking to dad things, where you naturally took root.
Like your dad jokes, or barbecues.

I was your little girl, in your protective gaze,
but the carnival's wild whirl—that was a phase.
You should've left the chaos of lights and laughter to me,
while you watched, cautious, just letting me be free.

But now, here I am, no voice to say no, I'm free.
Riding the whirlwinds, letting the dice roll.
Tasting the sweetness of a forbidden land,
with no guiding hand, no reprimand.
Atop the merry-go-round's peak, I stand,
you should see that.
But yes, it's frightening, like,
like teetering on death's boundary.
Now I feel cold,
without your big hands,
I feel blue.

This freedom has its charm, a taste of sweet delight,
yet it pales beside your hug, holding me tight.
In every cheer, I find a hidden abyss.
The lights don't shine as bright, the laughter rings hollow.
The rides, the games, the candied delights,
all feel empty; like distant, faded lights.
I realize now, it wasn't the thrill I sought,
but the care of your rules, the battles with my ego
you fought.

I spent all my coins playing darts,
with no arcade prizes, just the pieces of my heart.
I just wish you were here to win me those baby dolls,
Dad.

'I'm not big on poetry, but this is about her father quite literally,' Mr Verwey looked puzzled as he glanced over the lines of verse.

'If you read it carefully, you'll see her father is depicted almost like a first love. It led me to think that perhaps her issues began with being separated from that love,' Miss Van der Mey said thoughtfully, her eyes scanning the poem.

Mr Verwey was still trying to piece together the deeper meaning and looked up, slightly confused. 'Wait a minute . . . Is this her father's shopping list or something?' He held up a paper, squinting at the words, trying to make sense of the seemingly mundane list among the poetic lines.

### Dad's Florist Shopping List

Red rose means Dad loves me very much.
Yellow viola means Dad misses me very much.
White clover means Dad knows that I miss him too.
Pink camellia means Dad really wants to see me.
Purple hyacinth means Dad is sad.
An orange anemone means Dad is sick.
Purple salvia means 'get well soon' when I'm sick.
Sunflower means Dad admires me.
Carnation for Mom.
And white lily, of course, for me.

'I think her father was super busy with work and often left her alone for long periods, so he taught her how to communicate using flowers.' Miss Van der Mey's voice carried a hint of empathy as she shared her insights.

Mr Verwey was silent, not sure how to respond or what to ask next, his confusion apparent.

'But, Mr Verwey, do you think her mother didn't move here just for work? Maybe it was also to keep Lily away from her father,' Miss Van der Mey pondered aloud.

'How did you get that?' He looked up, his curiosity rekindled.

'Oh, which one . . .' She started rummaging through Lily's assignments, the sound of shuffling papers filling the room. Unable to find what she was looking for, she moved to a drawer in the right corner of the room. Returning with a paper adorned with an A+ on its top left corner, she handed it to Mr Verwey. 'Here, take a look at this. This is her final assignment.'

### I'm My Mother's Child

My father's wife now sees it all brightly,
that is a bad idea, isn't it?

I'm my mother's child,
I know she cries all night.

The man my mother wed, no longer here,
I know she couldn't make it without him.

The woman my father wed can't hide it,
still sees me as a child who knows nothing.

Her mother's son-in-law, he has no desire to meet,
that's what she said, her answer bittersweet.

Her mother-in-law's son, he called, again and again,
I overheard their talk, unveiling her deceit, so apparent.

Her daughter's mother doesn't know it's a bad idea,
to separate her husband's daughter and her daughter's
father, it's her idea.

'Maybe you should read these for a better understanding.
I've arranged them for you.' Miss Van der Mey suggested,
emphasizing the importance of the poems. She passed a
carefully arranged pile of papers to Mr Verwey.

**How the Ending Begins**

. . . and I will tell you every sequence in order and full,
can you believe how, in just three days, my world turned
utterly upside down? It's like strolling under blue skies,
then suddenly, a storm hits town. So gather 'round,
let me spill the beans, the whole crazy spree, it began
with Mom and Dad, their voices wild across the sea,
they had this mega fight, over the phone, it was like a
megaphone; their words crashed and clashed, like waves
upon the shore, glass smashing into stone, or maybe
the other way around, the air thick with tension, their

angry sounds, I couldn't grasp all they yelled, but the
air was heavy, dense, thicker than Gramma's gravy,
the atmosphere intense, then, after that bizarre day, it
all spiralled out of control, Dad's flowers and messages,
our family's heart and soul, suddenly, they just stopped,
the silence deafening, stark, no blooms, no texts, like
lights gone out in the dark, I was praying, hoping it
didn't mean the end of visits, of seeing his face, in this
sudden quiet, our family rhythm lost its pace, I tried to
get the scoop from Mom, but she kept it all locked tight,
'It's better if you don't know,' she said, shrouded in the
night, I was in the dark, just a kid caught in the fray,
in the midst of grown-up mysteries, in a world turned
grey, those gloomy days painted everything a sombre
shade of blue, and deep down, I sensed this topsy-turvy
was far from through.

**No More Magic in Fairy tales**

So, you know how Mom's a super cool diplomat;
        Europe-bound and all that jazz?
She moved me to this country, a name at first as elusive
        as a dream;
was it Windmillia, perhaps Tuliptopia, or Clogland?
        Maybe the United Flows of Canals?
Yes, you nailed it—it's that fairy tale land!

Once upon a time, in lands of endless fantasies, fairy
        tales spun magic, or so it seems.
My adventures here, oh they started like tales of old.
Exploring ancient streets where stories untold,

weave through canals like ribbons of silver,
and windmills stand like sentinels, but prouder and taller.
In fields of tulips, colours burst alive,
each petal a painter's vivid archive.
I biked under skies, a canvas so vast.

But can you believe, it just took me one full moon to
unravel every corner of this kingdom,
until the charm of fairy dust faded into the ordinary?
The thrill was a bubbling fountain, now seemed like a
drying well.
The adventure was an old storybook, its magic now
fading, left me in a longing spell.

Gone were the days of dragons breathing fire,
of brave knights and quests that never tired.

No happy ending in tales we chase after,
when in real-world hurts our hearts are plastered.
Like Peter and Wendy lost in their flight,
in a world of make-believe, escaping reality's plight.

Now I miss my home, that familiar comfort's hug, my
room a pink paradise.
And Rex, my feline confidant, his purrs and cuddles, oh,
how they haunt.
The sunflowers in my yard, how I long for their sunny
face, they were rays of joy.
And Daddy, my hero in every tale, our moments together
now a longing veil.

Where fantasies wane, and reality assails, there's no more
magic in fairy tales.
Now I have ended up like Rapunzel, in a castle haunted,
a boring cell.

## You Won't Be Home This Christmas

When you said you won't be home this Christmas, this
festive season,
my belief in Santa and fairy tales and miracles faded for
that reason.
The lights lost their twinkle,
the tree stood untouched, no gifts beneath,
in the quiet of the snow, I felt the chill,
in each flake that falls, a wish unspoken,
so now, beneath the mistletoe, I stand alone.

When you said you won't be home for a month,
I feared I couldn't survive the emotional drought, so blunt.
Yet, surprisingly, two months passed, I endured the thirst,
by the third, I almost forgot the rituals, the firsts.
But in the fourth month, you returned, a sudden rain,
quenching my longing, easing the pain.
Your presence, a brief respite, not lasting through five,
a fleeting rain, barely enough to keep hope alive.
Then, you left again, and time became a blur,
counting months turned pointless, memories stir.
I ran out of numbers, in your absence so stern,
each season without you, a lesson hard-learned.

When you said you were coming home, a spark lit in my
heart, so clear.
Then, you left, and I waited, counting days until
you'd be near.
Each time, you'd rekindle the spark, a promise to return,
but the flame I had to nurture, as your delays I discern.
Again, you'd ignite hope, yet the wait was unsure,
apologies, but keeping that fire alive became a
task obscure.
Now, when you say you're returning, my hope doesn't
spark, doesn't ignite,
that flame doesn't flicker any more, in the endless,
waiting night.

## The Lonely House

The Lonely House where a dark fantasy began its tale.
The Lonely House lost in shadowy forest reels.
The Lonely House slouches, oozing dampness, an
old-school frame.
The Lonely House, the aroma of decay and weathering
wood—its claim to fame.
The Lonely House, of wood, carved flowers its only dress.
The Lonely House stands naked, rain-gnawed,
termite-gobbled in distress.
The Lonely House blurs the borders of the town.
The Lonely House, a solitary crib, a kilometre from
civilization, wears a gloomy crown.

The Lonely House, down a dirt path, tyre tracks its
guide, sunbaked grass patches leading to where its
shadows reside.
The Lonely House, my mother sent me there, her work
calling her away.
The Lonely House of Uncle Toby, a man with no wife.
The Lonely House, Toby's, but all mine after the church
calls for his service.
The Lonely House, small and humble, in my eyes, a
haunted mansion.
The Lonely House where my young life lacked
thrill or truth.
The Lonely House where I wait for my mom, for her
return I yearn,
The Lonely House where I dream of rescue, for
love I burn.
The Lonely House, a silent witness to my waiting game.

'Wait, "The Lonely House" refers to her actual house? Does
she live in some sort of prison?' Mr Verwey looked perplexed.

'No, the house is on Bosrandweg Street. It's somewhat
isolated from other homes and surrounded by trees, hence
the nickname,' Miss Van der Mey clarified.

'I'm worried about her. The poem implies she's living
there all by herself, doesn't it?'

'Actually, the house belongs to a distant relative of her
mother's, a man named Toby. Her mother trusts Toby to
look after her while she works. But Toby, with all that work
he's got at the church, ends up spending more time at the

rectory than in his own home,' Miss Van der Mey explained. 'Lily wrote about it, but I can't recall where I put that piece.'

'So she's essentially alone most of the time?' Mr Verwey's eyebrows furrowed.

'That seems to be the case.'

'But is her mother aware of this? I mean, if she were my mom, leaving the house to me would've set off alarm bells. She'd rush back not to check on me, but because she'd be more worried about her antique fine china. "Did you feed the cat? Is the china okay? Oh, and how are you, by the way?"—in that order!'

'I believe her mother has always thought that being a successful career woman equates to being a good mother to Lily. But that could be because Lily has never expressed that this isn't the type of mothering she needs.' She handed a paper or two more to Mr Verwey to read.

### A Dutch Braid with a Ribbon Bow

Look at that little girl,
her mother wove her hair into a Dutch braid so fair,
her father, with a gentle hand, tied a ribbon bow, light as air.
Look at that little girl,
she got love from her mother and father,
it's fair, it's beyond compare.

Look at that little girl, so naive and small,
unaware of how the tables turn, unaware of it all.
A twist of fate, silent, no time to behold.

For the little girl, realization came slow,
her Dutch braid unravelling, beginning to let go,
the bow loosened its knots, ready to blow.

But look at her mother,
braiding her hair, tying a ribbon, struggling to keep it together,
both roles to play, till it really hurt her.
Look at that little girl, looking at her mother,
striving to fill a father's space,
yet in her haste, motherly love's trace fades without grace.
Look at her mother, never looking at her daughter,
forgets the gentle touch, the braid's artistry,
while her hands, entangled in ribbon, struggle to be free.

Now look at that girl, older, growing each day,
her hair untamed, no braids, no ribbons in sway.
Her mother's touch with the braid she lost,
her father's love with the bow, a line uncrossed.
A silent toss,
a total loss.

## Mama, Look at Me Now

Mama, look at my long hair now,
I've seen photos of you as a teen,
your hair was long, very beautiful,
I hope you see your younger self in me.

Mama, look at my eyes now,
they've grown wise, seen the world somehow.
I remember your stories, bright and bold,
I've lived some new ones, yet to be told.

Mama, look at my hands now,
capable and strong, I've learned to stand alone, and how.
They're no longer those of a little girl,
I've held onto a life of pain, longer than I've known.

Mama, look at my smile now,
life is hard, but I can still maintain the curve.
It looks like Dad's, do you see it?
I hope you see it, and it stops you from trying so hard,
like Daddy's did.

Mama, why don't you look at me,
see the changes; the woman I've come to be?
I'm not just your twelve-year-old girl anymore,
I'm seventeen now, with a new world to explore.

'I've tried to get Lily to explain the meaning behind her poetry, but her answers are always the same. Either "I just wrote what was in my head" or "It's just nonsense, nothing really."' Miss Van der Mey sighed in frustration.

'Is she really that closed off? You're doing great, by the way, Miss,' Mr Verwey offered his support.

'Thanks, but I still feel like I'm missing the bigger picture. But do you know how far I've gone?' Miss Van der Mey looked at him, seeking a response.

'Nope.'

'I reached out to her mother via email about her talent in poetry. I even sent her the poems, hoping she'd see her daughter's distress. It took her a long time to respond to my email. And she just thanked me for praising her daughter's skills.' Her voice carried a hint of disappointment. 'But Lily kept writing in the same vein. It seems her mother still doesn't grasp what her child is going through.'

'So you're trying to say Lily's mother is oblivious?' he enquired, trying to understand the situation better.

'Not oblivious but I think she's a bit misguided about how her daughter needs to be loved. Lily doesn't want to be loved like she is being loved, but her mistake is that she never expresses it,' she explained sadly.

'That's tough. Maybe we should inform the other teachers. The school might offer support, like psychological counselling.'

'I agree, but first, I want to understand Lily's needs better. For now, we should ensure her peers don't make things worse for her.' She seemed determined to find a solution.

'Got it. But does any of her poetry talk about her friends? The ones causing her trouble? Maybe we can learn more about her situation from those.' He wanted to look for more clues.

'There are these two poems,' Miss Van der Mey said, picking up a couple of sheets, 'One seems to be about her, about self-esteem and validation. The other, I think, hints at a crush—something about her "Daffodils". But I'm not sure who she's referring to.'

## Who's the Most Beautiful Flower?

When someone asks, who's the most beautiful flower?

Tell me it's not that Sunflower!
That flamboyant show-off,
flaunts its sun-worshipping ways like a true sunbeam
groupie.
Well, that's practically more like a fan-made romance plot,
except without reciprocation from the idol!
She seriously needs to channel her inner Clytie,
absorb some tragic wisdom,
slap on some sunglasses for her incessant star-stalking
from now on.

Tell me it's not that Aster!
A single petal of hers does a solo performance that
steals the show.
These petals are Astraea's sob story-turned-stardust,
a glimmering constellation of sorrow,
something even more valuable than the celestial twinkle.
Now, as much as those petals have charisma,
there is a teensy problem in the olfactory department.

Tell me it's not that Hyacinth!
Wafting in is the most enchanting scent,
enough to stir up a love triangle between her, Apollo
and Zephyrus.
But, here's the kicker:

planting her requires a green thumb, like being a
heart surgeon.
Her bulbs are fragile,
like a Jenga tower after a particularly aggressive
game night,
and she has more health issues
than a bunch of hypochondriacs at a health spa.

Tell me it's not that Anemone!
Flaunting a dazzling array of hues,
shades that will make Aphrodite herself shed a tear,
her colour palette is like a love letter to Adonis.
But this vibrant being has one catch: like
solar-powered gadgets,
she needs sunlight to shine.
In the shadows, it is like her beauty takes a hiatus,
just like Adonis did from the world.

Tell me it's not that Lotus!
Gliding on the lake's surface, singing a swan song,
she embodies nature's serene beauty.
Gaze at her long enough,
and you may just drift into a peaceful snooze,
like those mythical lotus-eaters.

Tell me it's not that Poppy!
She smells like sleep and forgetfulness,
a product of Demeter's grief.
But watch out, these delicate petals pack a punch—
sure, they smell dreamy,

but they're also the botanical version of a lullaby,
ready to knock you into a sleeping beauty.

When someone asks, who's the most beautiful flower?

Tell me it's another than Lily!
Born in a time when purity graced the earth,
she grew from Hera's milk, holy and fertile.
In times when savagery soaks to civilization's core,
her pristine essence can cleanse it once more.
Just like Uncle William said,
'A rose may enchant, but its thorns deter herds.
Even the whitest sheep bear horns dark as the sod,
yet your beauty, hornless, thornless, wins our
hearts, awed.'

## Daffodils

Everyone knows his name,
but I call him my daffodil.
He stood amid golden fields,
the first time I saw him at the bus stop in wait.
His smile, a summertime breeze
in the quiet humour book nook in a freezing library.

But the way he was speaking,
was like a springtime song.
I watched, silent, feeling I belong.
Our paths crossed, at a glance, in a busy school hallway,
and I hate that I missed the opportunity.

His happy petals touched my white pistil,
his hair a golden dance,
his corona brings light to anyone's day,
and in his presence, my heart comes undone.

Still, he's unaware of my quiet adoration.
I cherish these moments, simple and few.
My daffodil—if only I could call you that someday.

He's my spring,
my sunshine,

My daffodil's making everything right.

As Mr Verwey continued to peruse the poem, Miss Van der Mey reached for another sheet. 'Oh, there's another one here. But I'm not sure it'll be clear to you. She's quite metaphorical in this one.' She extended the paper towards him.

'Okay, hold on to that,' he declined, placing the poem he was reading on the table. 'I need to step out for a bit. There's an issue with our basketball collection mysteriously shrinking. I have to find out who's been taking school property home.'

He got up from his seat, preparing to leave.

'Just keep at it,' he called out as he left. 'I'm certainly going to see this case through to the end.' He exited the room, leaving Miss Van der Mey alone.

She settled at her desk in the quiet room, immersing herself once more in Lily's latest poem. She scrutinized every stanza and line, her expression gradually changing, as if she were uncovering new layers of meaning within the words.

## There's Something in Your Lovely Garden

Sorry for interrupting your tea party,
but there's brutal natural selection going on in your lovely garden,
and I don't think you know that.

See, roses have a harsh side, hidden under their beauty,
And mistletoe, a parasitic thief, not really that cutesy.
Then there's the lily, wilting away, getting hurt quietly.

Sorry for interrupting your tea party,
but there's a wicked food chain playing out in your lovely garden,
and I don't think you know that.

The stingy Derbidae beetle, it drills holes in her petals,
Those nectar suckers, they just drain her; it's on another level.
And now, poor lily, no one wants to pick her, you know?

Sorry for interrupting your tea party,
but there are naughty pests in your lovely garden,
and you punish them with pesticides, not sending them to their natural predators,
and they just breed oppression again that punishes their prey for their punitive account,

and you punish them again and they punish their prey for
their punitive account, again and again.
and that's how you create a never-ending toxic
natural cycle,
and I don't think you know that.

\* \* \*

'Your mother should have listened to me and sent you
to a Catholic boarding school. Then this would not
have happened,' Toby's words echoed his firm beliefs,
and though well-intentioned, to Lily, they seemed like a
band-aid on a wound that required much more care and
attention.

She remained silent, sitting across from him. Her eyes
reflected a mix of emotions. In her mind, she questioned
his narrow perspective, wondering how he could see the
world in such black-and-white terms. *Is life really so simple
as to be solved by changing schools?*

'In a place with proper moral guidance, you wouldn't
face such trials,' he continued, oblivious to her inner turmoil.

Mistaking her silence for agreement, he nodded to
himself. 'I'll speak to your mother soon. It's not too late
for a change.' He exited the room, clutching his phone.
He dialled a number, and soon, a woman's voice answered,
sounding strikingly similar to Lily's mother's.

Lily stayed in her chair. Her thoughts went back to
when she was first put under Toby's care, deprived of her
mother's embrace. That was supposed to be enough to

make Lily a saint, yet in truth, his holy rhetoric had only pushed her closer to hell. It all started when Lily came to him heartbroken after her mother's sinful abandonment of her. There was a huge gap between Toby and his cousin sister, Lily's mother, in terms of their beliefs and morals. While Lily's mother was interested in learning about the world, Toby moved to the Netherlands to study religion. Although their different perspectives had led to them sharing a somewhat awkward relationship, Lily's mother had had no choice but to leave her in Toby's care. And ever since, Lily had been the one constantly subjected to his endless sermons.

The main room of the Lonely House was enveloped in silence. Abruptly, the door swung open and Lily braced herself, expecting another one of Toby's stern sermons. Instead, he stepped in wearing a different demeanour.

'Your mother wants to talk,' he said, extending his cell phone towards Lily.

Taking the phone, she held it to her ear but remained silent. Her eyes met Toby's, conveying a wordless message: this was a private moment between a daughter and her mother. Understanding flickered in Toby's eyes, and without a word, he turned and quietly exited the room, closing the door behind him.

'Hi, Mom,' Lily said, her voice tentative.

There was no clear answer; the distant murmur of a crowd told her that her mother was busy with other things. The background noise made her think of how hectic her mother's lifestyle must be.

'Hello, Mom,' Lily tried again, a bit louder this time.

Her mother still didn't answer. Instead, a German voice spoke through the phone, but it wasn't talking to Lily. Short bits of Dutch followed.

Lily gave up trying to get her mother's attention. She started feeling down. The phone was still at her ear, its screen starting to warm up. The static noise began to whisper, the silence consuming the room.

'Umm, hello? Darling, are you there?' Her mother's voice finally came through, sounding distant yet warm.

Lily was the one who remained silent this time, her thoughts swirling in a quiet storm.

'Hello, Mom. Yes, it's me,' she finally replied, her voice barely above a whisper.

'Oh, darling. I'm glad to hear your voice again. How's life?' Her mother's question was routine, yet it felt heavy.

Lily didn't respond. The pretence that everything was fine had become too exhausting. She had played that part too often.

'Eh,' her mother hesitated, as if sensing something was amiss. 'Not feeling well, huh? I heard about it from Toby.'

Lily stayed silent, her heart sinking. She could almost predict her mother's next words—an apology for her absence, a reminder of her busy schedule, a promise to be home soon, followed by an abrupt ending of the call. It was a pattern that had become all too familiar. Each repetition chipped away a little more at Lily's hope to have a different kind of conversation; one that didn't leave her feeling more alone than before.

'Are you really okay?' Her mother's voice, unexpectedly tender and concerned, broke through the line. It was different this time; warmer, more present.

It wasn't the usual cold, hurried tone that Lily had grown accustomed to.

'Yeah, there was a bit of trouble, but it's nothing major,' Lily found herself replying, but why did she just say? This was her chance, a moment where her mother seemed genuinely engaged. She could share the true depth of her feelings, not just the recent incident but the accumulating hurt and loneliness. Yet, she chose words that masked her inner turmoil, even as she nervously twirled her hair around her finger. It was a nervous tick she had developed.

'That's good to hear. I just wanted to make sure everything's okay. I've been really busy here,' her mother continued, not catching onto the unspoken plea in Lily's voice. And so, the opportunity to unearth her buried wounds slipped away, leaving them to fester in silence. 'I trust that you're handling everything well. You've always been independent and strong . . .'

Her mother's words flowed on, but it wasn't really too late for her to open up about her loneliness, her yearning for attention and care. But instead, she replied, 'Yes, I'm managing. I always do,' her voice a steady façade.

She gazed out of the window and her heart echoed her unvoiced desires: *But I wish you could see that sometimes— maybe not now, but sometimes—I don't want to be strong.*

'That's my girl. Just remember to stay focused on your studies, okay?' Her mother's voice dispensed the usual advice. 'Anyways, did I promise that I would come home in September?'

'Actually, August, Mom.'

'Oh, really? Well, I'm sorry I have to break my word again then. But I'm trying to come home in October.' There was an apologetic tone in her voice. 'I'm working on building a new foreign policy, and it requires a lot of research, meetings, and deep collaboration. Visiting countries, negotiating treaties . . . It's all very complex and time-consuming. You understand, right?'

'I understand.' Lily's response was brief, a habitual understanding, but a surge of disappointment swept through her. The constant postponements had become a familiar tune.

'Thanks, darling. I'm so lucky to have you as my daughter.' The affection, which used to make Lily feel better, now made her feel empty. 'By the way, I'm worried about the supplies. Do you have enough groceries? I can have some essentials sent over. And the utility bills? I've set them up to be paid automatically, but just double-check, will you?'

'Yes, I took care of them. That's fine.' Lily hid her feelings at being ignored behind a mask of competence.

'Great. I just want to make sure everything is all right while I'm not there. You're doing an excellent job managing everything, Lily.'

'Thanks, Mom,' her voice was calm and normal. On the inside, though, she was struggling with doubt and rising resentment—it was hard for her to understand why her mother was always more interested in these mundane things rather than in her own daughter's emotional needs and problems.

She was still on the line, but she had switched to German as she talked to someone else. She turned her attention back to Lily and said, 'By the way, why don't you go outside and have some fun? I think it would be helpful.'

Lily took a moment to answer. 'I can't, Mom.'

'Why not?' Her mother sounded really confused.

'Outside . . . Uh, it's . . . you know, not exactly the paragon of safety.' Lily's voice was a little shaky, and her words didn't quite make sense.

'What do you mean it's not safe, honey?' Her mother sounded worried.

Lily felt a knot of anxiety as she tried to come up with a good excuse.

'Lily, what's with the "not safe" talk? Why is it not safe? Do the mean kids at school bother you outside of school hours too?'

'No, it's not that. Umm . . . you know, Toby's been hanging out with this group of old men who've started coming to our town. I don't know who they are or where they have come from. It's weird, I've never seen them before. And get this—they all wear these old-fashioned, all-white outfits, like they're stuck in the past or something. They look like they're from another era, Mom!'

Her mother didn't respond and Lily thought she might have been left alone on the phone again. Nonetheless, she continued speaking, pouring out her thoughts into the void, hoping her mother might still be listening on the other end.

'Also when these guys come in, they go about setting things on fire—like, they're obsessed with it. And on their way out, they toss flower petals or scented water. I'm pretty sure they're saying some weird chants too. But who they are or where they come from doesn't really matter to me. What's really strange is what they're doing here. You won't believe it, but the people in town are actually welcoming them to do some sort of—wait for it—*exorcism* extravaganza!'

'The Ghostbuster Gramps?'

'Yeah, that's right. They talk about getting rid of evil spirits. There's been a lot of rumours lately about people claiming they've seen a ghost causing trouble around town. Have you heard about it? It's the famous scary story here . . . of the . . . the "Heartbreaker".'

Before she could shut her mouth, the atmosphere in the room suddenly darkened, like a scene from a horror movie just before something spooky happens. But let's not overthink it. It was just a cloud briefly covering the sun that caused the light coming in through the window to dim.

As the cloud moved away, Lily's mother seemed to mirror the meteorological phenomenon. She suddenly burst into laughter like a thunderstorm on the phone. 'Wait, hold on, do you actually believe these myths?'

'But they've been telling it like it's the gospel truth, Mom.'

'Gos . . . what? Okay, fine. What's the gossip?' her mom asked, her tone revealing her scepticism.

'Okay,' Lily began, ready to tell her story, 'the Heartbreaker, he's not your typical ghost. And by "not typical", I mean he's not a regular, scary ghost. People say he looks really handsome: sharp jawline, long blonde hair that shines like gold, blue eyes like the sea, very pale skin, and he's always holding a flower as if he's about to propose to someone. But!' she quickly added, 'don't be fooled by his good looks, okay? He's not some Hollywood heartstopper. He's more like a "Halloween Heart-attacker" who brings curses upon his victims. Speaking of which, people say this ghost is really into flowers, but he's no anthophile—he's more like a hummingbird. He's on the hunt for innocent lilies, maiden daisies, unmarried orchids, and he steals all those chaste blooms away to be his companions in his afterworld garden. Some people think he can be summoned by playing a creepy game, and others think he's the ghost of a Dutch nobleman. But everyone who tells these stories agrees on one thing: one should stay away from this ghostly charmer, even if they've been single for a while.'

'What happens if a girl becomes his target?'

'Oh no! Did I really just say all that!?' Lily suddenly realized. 'No, no, no! Forget I said anything. We shouldn't talk about it, Mom.'

'Scaredy cat, huh? Believe me, dear, it's all just silly superstition. There's nothing to fear.'

'But you're not here when I feel scared!' Those words were spontaneous; Lily had finally blurted out one of her frustrations. But her mother left her hanging again, turning away to talk to a French guest who spoke English with a heavy accent. She likely didn't even hear what Lily said.

'Okay, Lily. Sorry that you're scared,' she finally said, returning to their conversation. 'Let's talk about something else. How about an update on your teenage life? Have you met your first love yet?'

'There's a guy I've been noticing.'

'Oh, really? Tell me more! Who is he? Is he good-looking?'

'He goes to my school. I've liked him since the beginning of high school. I remember seeing him on our first day, and I just knew. And yes, he's really handsome. I doubt any girl at school would disagree.'

'What's his name?'

'His name's Daffy. I like to call him—'

'Sorry, hon—'

'My Daffodil . . .' Lily trailed off. Her mother's French guest had stolen her attention again.

'. . . *il faut le traiter avec la plus grande attention* . . . Ummm, sorry honey, I have to go now, but we'll talk again soon. Take care of yourself, Lily.'

She hung up before Lily could even say goodbye. She was left holding the silent phone, feeling the familiar sting of their incomplete conversations.

Lily put the phone down. She hadn't even learned about her mother's opinions on her crush or got any advice on how to deal with her fears related to these ghost stories. More crucially, her mother's words had failed to bring any warmth or comfort to Lily's world, which was once again drowning in a sea of darkness.

A sudden noise from outside the room broke the silence. It sounded like something had fallen and broken. Lily walked towards the door, the rusty hinges groaning as she pushed it open. She was intrigued and scared. The weather outdoors was calm; it was easy to see what had caused the noise. Their yard, which had carefully been set up to look like the Hanging Gardens of Babylon, was a mess. The pots were broken and their contents spilled all over the ground. Flowers and plants had been pulled out—a scene of floral chaos.

The first thing Lily thought was that it might have been Toby's calico cat, which he had abandoned to roam as a stray after he had moved into the rectory. She was surprised, however, to find that Toby himself was standing in the middle of the chaos.

'I bet your school didn't teach you about the Dutch Tulip Bubble of the seventeenth century,' he said, launching into an unexpected speech, 'and how tulips turned into signs of luxury and indulgence. This was because their prices were so high, there was a boom of speculation around them. They were treated as signs of foolishness and greed because they were so pretty and hard to find that people did crazy things to acquire them. Such is the sin of seeking joy and material things in this world . . .'

Lily didn't have to listen to all of Toby's preaching. As he talked, she looked down, and a larkspur caught her eye. It had been standing upright, full of happiness and positivity, but was now lying in the dirt, very sad.

By now, Toby had come to the point of his monologue. Lily was all ears. 'So, this ghost's love of flowers signifies his attachment to material things and pleasures of this world. This obsession is what keeps him from finding peace in the afterlife. His spirit is still around and longing for the beauty and charm of earthly pleasures. It is tied to this world and can't rest.'

# Chapter 3

## August

'GET READY, GET SET, GET SHOPPING!
Back-to-School Saturday Extravaganza
Kicking off in August!'

—A Back-To-School Campaign Ad
at a local stationery store

Just like that, the new semester had begun. Neither was Lily looking forward to the new semester nor was she missing the previous one.

Girls whispered behind her. Lily tuned in like a secret agent as always. They were all thrilled, except Missy, who had shifted gears to supernatural sagas, including the currently trending ghost lore of the Heartbreaker in town.

It was just that the Rosy incident occurred at 8.00 a.m. Her eyes shot daggers like she was privy to Lily's grand secret: that secret social media hate account Lily had created, lovingly crafted to topple Rosy's reputation. They also whispered, 'Lily's got it coming'. A kind of punishment that can only be described as harrowingly humiliating.

It was also just that things were going smoothly after until someone initiated a paper ball assault on her. Of course, Derby masterminded this. Some things never change, except that he now had a hairdo that could be his villain origin story. There was an evil aura in his eyes, too, as he stared at Lily in silent fury. The last time she had seen that look, he had been banned from the basketball club for three months for stuffing a frog in Lily's lab coat. However, his current look was even more menacing and Lily expected to face twice the trouble as before.

When his fists clenched, Lily braced to get caked in the face, but today wasn't the day. Lily strolled home unscathed in the blossom-filled outfit she had started the day in. Not a single petal plucked.

It was just that, Lily tried to convince herself, it was a 'just that' day. She seemed to be having a lucky day so far. But she had a hunch this semester was gearing up to be a thriller. It was just that one more thing had happened: news that didn't exactly light up Lily's life, though the other kids treated it like a fireworks display. There was going to be a summer camp in August. For Lily, it was just another triviality to roll her eyes at because every day felt like a military camp to her.

\* \* \*

The morning on the first day of camp was very humid, and it felt sticky as they stepped outside.

The kids were full of energy, running and jumping around in a lot of excitement. Their little shoulders sagged under the weight of their backpacks, bulging with food and drinks in cans and cartons—essential tools for surviving in the wild.

But the heaviest load these kids carried wasn't in their backpacks. It was their wild expectations about the campsite—all these weird scenarios formed in their heads.

'I heard Tina practising her "screams of joy" in case she meets a squirrel ...'

'Oh, absolutely! I haven't seen everyone this thrilled since we discovered chocolate chip cookies!'

'I hope the forest animals don't mind us crashing their "woodland spa". Imagine squirrels giving us tiny massages and raccoons offering us mud facials!'

'I overheard Mr Verwey saying something about marshmallows. I'm expecting there will be a cozy campfire with s'mores or karaoke or ...'

*Or zip it and lock it!* Lily thought.

They thought the forest was like a huge amusement park! Yeah, it was called 'BranchLand' and the line for the squirrel carousel was nuts! But the woods were not going to be as fun as they thought. Nobody had a closer kinship with the forest than Lily. She was betting money on the other kids' exciting plans turning into cries for a taxi home. The thought of seeing how things would turn out was the only thing making Lily look forward to the camping trip.

Townie kids were like intricately crafted porcelain dolls. They came adorned with a warning: 'Fragile Contents. Handle with Extreme Caution. Keep Away from the Elements.' Snoozing on the forest floor might result in them waking up as human pretzels. Their skin had been pampered with the kind of care usually reserved for royal tapestries, and they had been confined to temperature-controlled chambers for ages. Their notion of 'fun' could very well lead to spontaneous burnout, only for them to realize that reclining on a soft couch and binge-watching TV was a far safer bet.

Lily grinned, picturing their thin bodies writhing and shivering in the chilly forest dawn, then the midday sun burning their flesh and them jumping at the nocturnal sounds of both the unseen and the seen in the dark. She couldn't wait to see it. But she would have to wait. A boring game awaited her. They, the kids, were all over the place, laughing, tumbling, sweating, yelling, and making the quiet forest feel like a noisy playground.

So, in the midst of a game that felt like hide-and-seek, Lily slowly disappeared. Ironically, no one cared or even realized that she was missing. No one even knew that Lily had joined the game. With or without her, the game remained enjoyable. If asked, they might have even chosen to play without Lily. Thus, they wouldn't be blamed for why Lily wasn't having fun.

Adding to Lily's already waning fire was the fact that the campsite forest was feeling increasingly claustrophobic, like an over-soaked sponge cake. And it was not just any forest, mind you—it was the twin of the forest that surrounded the Lonely House, with the same oak trees, pine trees, beech trees—all probably trees that just wanted to be left alone.

Local legends shrouded these twin forests, seen as two sisters with different personalities—a dichotomy of beauty and scarring, peace and horror, heaven and hell. People here had drawn a paved line to separate these twin forests and called it the 'main road'. The first sister, being closer to the town, befriended humans, and the Lonely House resided there. The other sister, where this camp was taking place, was less friendly to outsiders. It was where the dark side of the forest grew, bred, and dwelled. Many had gone missing in this forest.

The camp served as a gateway between reality and mystery, and Lily was now on its edge. She honestly wasn't there to test her strength or to confirm the scary stories; she just found the camp itself more frightening. So, feeling all pumped up, she was flexing those leg muscles, gripping her shoes firmly, and there was no need to worry—the local advice was, 'As long as you stick to the main road, you'll find your way home.'

* * *

In the heart of the forest—the one that guarded the Lonely House, earlier, and now this one they were camping in— Lily stood alone, and it had always been like that; a lonely audience of one. She listened to Mother Nature's playlist— 'Birdsong Symphony', 'Leaves Dancing in the Whistling Breeze', and 'Moss-Covered Melodies'.

A dramatic plot twist lurked nearby. Just as it found the right time to attack, a new song injected an off-key note into the harmony of nature: the crisp crackle of dry leaves and branches, orchestrated by someone's less-than-elegant footfall.

Lily's gut told her to hide, and fast. She quickly hid behind a pine tree, her go-to spot for getting away from it all.

A teenage boy, the cherry on the cake of Lily's misfortune, it was . . . well, of course, it was Derby. But how did he always find a way to ruin her peaceful moments? Why couldn't he find something else to do, like raking leaves or literally anything else that didn't involve bothering her?

There he was, poetically swearing at the leaves in his way. His words hit Lily's ears like a choir of dying goats: 'Damn these leaves! I'm gonna give that bitch a taste of her own medicine.' It suddenly dawned on her that the so-called 'bitch' was none other than her.

But hold up, it was not the usual circus trio this time. Timmy was there, next to Derby, clutching a basketball, but where the heck was Billy?

Out of the blue—or rather, green—someone grabbed Lily from behind, muffling her cries so it sounded like she was gurgling underwater.

'Shh, quiet down!'

'What the—?' Lily started thrashing about, only to realize it was none other than Billy, peek-a-booing his friends from behind a tree.

'Listen up, Lily! They're cooking up something seriously messed up for you!' his face twitched nervously, his eyes darting around as if he were on the lookout for danger. 'You must stay at the campsite and not wander off like this or it will get worse . . .'

This whole 'plotting against Lily' thing again? Lily said, 'Huh?' but she knew one thing for sure—she was not about to take orders from Billy. As soon as he glanced away, she figured it was her chance and gave him a swift kick where the sun didn't shine, and he fell to the ground, moaning.

The trees suddenly seemed to part like they were in a dramatic movie scene. Derby and Timmy were caught off-guard, 'Seriously, dude, can you be any louder? Now she's definitely going to hear us!'

And you bet she had. She was starting to realize that perhaps Derby was the one with the least brain cells. Meanwhile, Billy, still reeling from the pain and trying to come up with an explanation for where he was, exclaimed, 'Hey, over here! She's right here, behind this tree!' Yeah, real helpful, Billy.

*Wait, seriously?* Was this how he planned to help her? To send her sprinting when she was not ready for it? The clock was ticking, so she went, 'All right, fine!' and burst out from behind the tree, whizzing past Derby in a neon haze, as if spelling out 'Catch me if you can!' in her trail.

'Oh, there she goes! Catch her! No one escapes on my watch!' Derby exclaimed.

Now, the forest had been awakened from its nap. Its peace had been broken—no more of the days when only the sound was of the rustling wind and the soft chirping of birds filled the air.

A rowdy hunt ensued with Lily as the prey. It grew more intense with Derby hurling animal insults at her as he chased her around the forest. But this time, Lily was no defenceless rabbit—she was a foxy fox eluding her hunter with ease.

The leaves hindered the townie kids' movement. Their faces started to look more tired and their panting footsteps became slower and slower, while their clothes got drenched with sweat. What's more, Timmy slipped and fell twice. All the while, Lily pranced around as if in her element, convinced she'd got this. No need for leg day at the gym. No sweat, literally.

The tables had turned and Lily was calling the shots this time. She plotted whether to set some bees on her pursuers or take them on a slip-and-slide adventure by the river. Choices, choices.

But as usual, life threw yet another curveball at her. There was a bunch of logs in Lily's way. They tripped her like a sneaky schoolmate in a crowded hallway and it sounded like a coconut had fallen from a tree, accompanied by shooting pain. Derby and his gang made their grand entrance, sealing Lily's fate like a villainous posse in a movie scene. She lay half-conscious, the world spinning before her, while the Reaper hovered behind the trees, slowly moving towards her.

'This time you're just begging for a beatdown, aren't ya?' panted Derby. His breath wheezed in and out dramatically.

'HE'S A TRAITOR!' Lily yelled, pointing her finger at Billy with desperation in her eyes. 'Billy was about to reveal your plan to me behind the tree, earlier!'

For a moment, all you could hear were the sounds of the forest again. Derby, confused at the unexpected plot twist, gasped like a beached whale, looking at Billy. He was the image of a thief caught red-handed, twitching eyes and all, searching for an excuse. Timmy seemed as out of place in the scene as a clown at a black-tie event.

'She's crazy!' Billy's voice pierced the air, his dog-ate-my-homework sort of excuse echoing from the tree trunks. 'Don't believe her, Derby! She's making up stories.'

'Liar, liar, pants on fire!' Lily interjected.

'YOU'RE THE LIAR!' Billy cut her off, trying to play his get-out-of-jail-free card with his friend. 'Well, um . . . I was sorta . . . kinda . . . tryna trick her. You know, to fool her into staying put, so she couldn't hightail it.' He sounded like a bad actor. 'Helping her? Yeah, right. Not my style. Derby, you know that's not possible, right?'

Derby stayed mum. But, come on, a guy with his intelligence level would believe that.

'Now, for your brave accusation and, oh yeah, for that kick from earlier too,' Billy's grip tightened around the basketball under his arm that he'd snatched from Timmy, 'Eat this!'

He threw the ball with all his might at Lily's face.

She clamped her hands over her face in defence. She had played 'catch the basketball' more times than she'd like to admit, so this time, she was ready for the showdown.

But strangely, it never came. Did the ball never arrive or was her face now numb to the impact? But that was impossible, right? Maybe it had been transported to another dimension?

Fingers trembling, she removed her shield. She surveyed the dim scene—trees, leaves, and . . . something else was in her path. Lily blinked and blinked again, rubbing her eyes. The basketball was nowhere to be found. Instead, there stood between her and her bullies a human form. Its head eclipsed the sun's glare; a luminous halo casting a veil over its features. Lily squinted at it like a mole who had stumbled into daylight. Then, slowly, his face, radiant as a sunrise, and his smile, the kind that could warm the coldest heart, sharpened into focus.

That smile seemed familiar—it had that effect; it could make the world seem like it was in eternal springtime at every glance. Who could it possibly be but her daffodil?

'Seriously, can't you guys keep your weird antics confined to the school?' his voice had a stamp of authority. It was Daffy; he was her favourite flower. He stood cradling the basketball that had been hurtling towards her nose.

'You got a problem with that, buddy?' Derby demanded.

'Oh, absolutely. It interrupts my enjoyment of nature, you matchstick heads!' Daffy snapped back.

'Who you callin' a matchstick head, huh?' Timmy threw down the gauntlet. He hoped it was not him.

'All of y'all.'

Lily felt like a fight was about to break out.

'Now, will you get back to the campsite or should I light you on fire?'

Strangely, the trio didn't throw a tantrum. Not even a peep of protest. Even though they could've probably easily tag-teamed up against Daffy, three-to-one, it turned out they were behaving with Daffy as if he was Mr Verwey. Maybe it was Daffy's blue-belt-level karate skills or maybe it was because Daffy was taller than them. Was it the matchstick label that had finally burned them? Or perhaps . . .

Lily no longer cared why. She just couldn't stop thinking about how Daffy had saved her today.

And he was her daffodil; his DNA had traces of Narcissus's—that handsome hunter from the land of Thespiae. A guy so good-looking, he could woo nymphs without a love potion. But here's the catch—despite the potency of his spell on all the goddesses, he loved himself above all; more than a kid loves candy.

'What's with those troublemakers? Aren't you wasting good camping time with them?' blurted Daffy. Lily was still on the ground, hoping Daffy would lift her like a superhero or something. But he hadn't even touched her hand, and she knew she'd have to get up herself.

'Those rascals never know when to quit. It's like second nature to me now, trying to get rid of them. Oh, and Daffy, you're a lifesaver—thanks a million!' Lily responded.

But her dream still felt unattainable: to lock eyes with Daffy. Oh, those eyes. That's where Medusa's spells may have lived. Every time she looked at them, her body was rooted to the spot like a statue; her thoughts turned to stone, and her words disappeared like dust in the wind.

'Well, lucky for you I showed up just in the nick of time,' Daffy said, saluting her. 'But why hang out with the trio? Camp's full of a lot of fun, you know?'

His questions, she never knew why, always blanked every space in her mind. It was like answering a cruel Sphinx's riddle. If she got it wrong, a plague of bad luck would befall her. She had to channel her inner Oedipus to find the right thing to say.

'Um, hello?' Daffy's voice zapped Lily back to Earth. 'You're an odd one, you know? I've never had a girl turn me down for a chat.'

'Huh? Oh, yeah, um . . . I was just . . . bored of the game,' Lily fumbled. 'So I decided to go on . . . a private nature walk. I just got caught off-guard by Billy, Timmy, and Derby as it always happens.'

'Oh.'

*Really? That's all?* Did he not see the epic quest Lily went through to come up with an answer to his question? Couldn't he at least throw in a consolation prize of his empathy for her? To her, this was building up to the moment she would ask him to occupy the permanent role of her guardian angel against Derby. But silence hung in the air, and she with it.

'Be a part of my club!' Daffy broke the quiet. 'Yeah, I'd suspected that camping with them would be like watching paint dry. And the games? Ugh! As someone who worships nature, it's such a travesty to spend one's time in the woods like that! I decided to break free too. I want to forge my own camp trail.'

Lily jolted upright.

Suddenly, he said, 'Oh, how about we embark on an adventure together?'

*Hold up! Did Daffy just challenge me to a life-or-death quest?* Lily's heart whined. But she refused to turn him down. 'Sounds like a wild ride!'

'Or, how about I take you to my secret place?'

'To . . . where?' Lily's mental compass spun in confusion.

'I guarantee you, this place—listen, for a homebody like you, this spot's like an oasis in a desert. Nobody dares to camp there. And guess who holds the title of "First Discoverer"? Yours truly. Safety? No sweat! I'm an experienced camper. This spot will redefine "camping" for you. No more lame games and sing-alongs . . .' Daffy grinned.

And so did she. That smile of his, it was like a Pavlovian trigger for hers. This was routine—she always grinned when he grinned, but this time she was still in the dark about the secret reason behind it.

'Trust me, once you witness it, you'll think of me as your personal Indiana Jones.'

\* \* \*

Lily strolled deeper into the forest along the main road, confirming the rumours about there being a desolate, moss-covered, deserted, and unsettling side to the woods. The trees along this road were not the same as those at the campsite. These were colossal and fearsome. Their roots stuck out of the ground like the muscles of a strong athlete. From tree to tree, creeping vines formed a web and the path looked like a strange tunnel, a portal leading into another world.

There was a stillness in this part of the forest. There were no happy birdsongs or the soft, tapping sounds of squirrels' feet. Sunlight had a hard time getting through the thick canopy, making it look like the world had gone dark; the air was quiet and grey. Lily couldn't figure out what time it was.

All along the journey, Daffy remained quiet, merely guiding her towards the enchanting destination he had described. Lily noticed that they were going farther and farther away from safety and comfort. The path went on and on like an excited puppy wagging its tail until it finally gave up and sat at the base of a wall.

It was a huge wall that stood there like something out of a horror story. It seemed to be concealing something terrifying behind its two and a half metres of broken, disorganized bricks. Vines crowned its top as if it was a prince of darkness.

This wall—it wasn't just old architecture; it seemed to have come to life, whispering scary tales to Lily. She squinted in the pitch-black darkness, feeling a mix of uncertainty and unease.

'Is this where you keep your secrets? The lovely place you were talking about?' Lily asked.

'Is there supposed to be a specific definition of "beauty"?' Daffy responded.

Lily's brow furrowed in confusion. Daffy ran to a nearby tree to take an emergency leak. 'Well, kind of!' he continued talking, 'The real spot is past this wall. Just a few more steps and we'll be there.'

Lily was confused. How was Daffy's face so calm? Also, wouldn't the forest spirits on the prowl be angry to see someone urinating on their house? Lily's eyes remained fixed on the wall and the Halloween vibes of the forest sent a chill down her spine. The wind caressed her through her clothes, playing an eerie tune in her ear.

'Lily, let's move it!' Daffy's voice, loud and abrupt, snapped her out of her reverie. She blinked in surprise, realizing that he had already started walking ahead. She quickened her pace to catch up with him, driven not by a desire to stay close but by the strange, cold sensation on her skin.

They drew nearer to the wall whose ghastliness was remarkable. Stains of black adorned the bricks aged by time; it was an abstract artwork worthy of a place in a haunted museum. Cobwebs, like hair, hung from the top edge; a layer of dust clinging to them. They performed a ghostly waltz whenever the wind blew. The cement had started to crack and the paint had resignedly peeled off and settled at the bottom. Spots of dried mud decorated the scene in the shape of wild beasts' claw marks, hinting at the terrifying creatures lurking in the forest and adding yet another layer to the wall's spooky charm. In the distance, a gap half the height of the wall caught Lily's attention, which is where Daffy seemed to be guiding her with unswerving determination.

Was that really the way across this daunting barrier? Indeed, it was, unless one was Spiderman. Daffy gestured for Lily to lower her head to dodge the cobweb cascade, which somehow snagged her hair anyway, causing her to launch into a frantic effort to disentangle herself from it. This hair-raising episode managed to distract her momentarily from their utterly unsettling surroundings—a temporary reprieve from her faltering courage.

However, as her awareness of her environment returned, she stared in utter shock and her mind went as blank as a fog-covered cemetery. The words she wanted to say remained stuck in her throat. Her tongue twitched, but she kept silent. But her eyes, oh those eyes—they embraced the role of silent storyteller, capturing every intricate detail of what lay before her.

There was an assortment of abandoned Dutch-style architectural gems standing there, each mauled by the relentless maw of Mother Nature. Tattered, their grandeur had faded into obscurity under the tapestry of vines. The walkways lay hidden beneath a carpet of grass, a witness to the decades of abandonment it had suffered; cracked walls, shattered windows, and corroded iron bearing the signs of time's toll.

The detritus of its past residents still clung desperately to what remained—furnishings, ornaments, and artefacts from a bygone prosperous era. They littered the landscape, which was now home to an unholy alliance of insects, reptiles, and rodents. The buildings, aged yet resolute, still wore an antique Art Deco flair as an ironic tribute to a time when they stood for dignity and class—a mere ghostly façade now.

The place struck fear in Lily's heart. She felt the urge to about-turn and make a quick escape. It looked like the backdrop of every apocalyptic scene. Oddly enough, Daffy's expression showed no terror—none of the emotions that had settled in Lily's bones, causing her to glue herself to his side, playing a hesitant game of shadow as she mimicked his every step.

For some strange reason, Daffy's attitude seemed a lot like Alice in Wonderland.

'Daffy, are you for real with this place?' Lily asked him, inching beside him, using his jacket to hide her horror-struck face.

She had even turned her neck in a way that she avoided the sight of the nightmarish buildings as she passed by them, but she couldn't help but feel like an ominous pair of eyes was peering at her through those dilapidated windows.

'Not entirely, no. But hey, this spot has its own unique charm that I wanted to share with you.' Why Daffy had chosen her to unveil this particular secret remained a mystery to Lily. 'Look, the forsaken haven of the Dutch nobles!' he proclaimed with the enthusiasm of a dedicated tour guide showing an underwhelming tourist spot. 'Or maybe we can call it the "Disused Duchy Den" or "Regal Relic Residency"?'

*An abandoned, gated neighbourhood of the Dutch nobility?* Lily's mind vaulted back to the gossip circulating around the town about some sort of a grand clean-up project involving an abandoned luxury housing complex. Could this be the place that had sent all the tongues wagging?

'This swanky place was once occupied by fancy-pants Dutch folks back in the day, and boy, was it the crème de la crème of living areas in its prime!' Lily couldn't help but notice that Daffy had a real knack for history. He seemed like he was completely obsessed with the place, as if he'd struck gold amid old and shabby ruins. 'They even brought in some of the best architects to design these buildings, and let me tell you, it was quite the sight. Check out that building! And that one over there! Oh and don't miss that hexagonal gem! Did you see that asymmetrical roof there?'

Lily played her usual role—zipping her lips when history was being taught.

'But hey, have you heard those ghost rumours?' Lily was suddenly captivated by Daffy's words, her focus sharpening. 'Guess where his hideout is? Right here!'

Something seemed to crumble inside her—maybe her nerves, who knows? A jolt of electricity ran through her and she had goosebumps. She was spooked and almost involuntarily, snuggled closer to Daffy, her face half-buried in his shoulder. She clung to him not only for emotional support but also for his profound warmth to melt away her cold nervousness.

'Daffy, seriously! Spare me, okay? This isn't the place for ghost stories!'

He caught his breath, halting abruptly; naturally, Lily's steps followed suit. He shot her an odd look, a mixture of surprise and amusement on his face.

And then, out of the blue, he burst into uproarious laughter, shattering the eerie hush that hung around the place like a clingy ex. 'So you've been hanging out with witches, huh?' Daffy just wouldn't quit chuckling, 'Classic sceptic move, oh my god! Like, really? You believe there's a haunted hunk with a crush going around? That's like the world's weirdest fantasy. Ghosts and good-looking? Knee-weakening? Seriously?'

Lily's cheeks turned a bright red, and she grinned like the Cheshire Cat. Her smile showed that she was innocent. She slapped herself mentally for believing that load of nonsense. She would not have fallen into the pits of gullibility if she had just listened to her mom.

But Daffy's laughter was like a sweet melody in the midst of all the grimness. It looked like he had let loose a huge group of fireflies, turning the dark into a party with twinkling fairy lights.

'But here's the kicker: the "Heartbreaker" is no myth. Dude was real and kicking, back in the day—you know, like during the whole "colonial era" that historians talk about.' Daffy snapped back into his storyteller mode. 'Imagine this Dutch aristocrat slash sugar tycoon, strutting back and forth on business for the Dutch East India Company—he was practically swimming in cash. He was also a botanist by day, obsessed with plants. He imported Dutch flowers and transformed Dutch colonies back then into an experimental ground for flora,' he continued. 'The history books say he had a garden here, a green paradise, but it vanished into thin air. *Poof!* Only a mention of a park named after a local woman he made his *njai* survived.'

Lily felt a little ruffled at that bit of information.

'Know what a njai is?' he quizzed.

'Javanese girls the Dutch made their concubines,' she replied.

'Yes!' he grinned, 'And most ended up living a crappy life after being ditched by their Dutch masters, since the position didn't exactly come with a pension plan. But the Heartbreakere's njai had a different story. This local lady worked her magic and charmed him into marriage.

That was a big deal, especially with his uppity European background. His family wasn't too happy about him marrying someone "brown". It was like a cultural coffee stain on their lineage. But guess what? He still went ahead and tied the knot with her, saying goodbye to his inheritance and family. He chose love over sugar,' Daffy grinned. 'But here's the bombshell. No fairy tale ending here. Cue the tragic twist.'

Lily was hooked—part spooked and part entertained.

'Just when they were ready to say "I do" to their own version of paradise, *bam!* The Japanese invasion happened, kicking the Dutch out of their own party.'

He paused.

'Yeah, yeah, the World War II part. They were all arrested, jailed, even tortured. It was all in the history book. Snore,' Lily said.

'That's what you don't get, Lily. The school history books have lied to you. More precisely, they've been spreading bad gossip, which was either incomplete due to censorship or deliberately changed to make it sound more palatable,' he reasoned. 'Because not all Dutchies met that fate. Some packed up and headed back to the Netherlands, including our Heartbreaker. He took his girl sailing across oceans and continents to his homeland, but she wasn't exactly welcomed with open arms there. She was shunned and, well, things got even more messed up because he couldn't handle losing her—'

Suddenly, a house with a trapezoidal roof let out a confusing symphony. Lily's jaw dropped as she saw a cluster of creatures fluttering out of a window, with two cats chasing after them.

'So, the dude's legacy has a confusing ending. Some say he was ghost-zapped into oblivion, others reckon he's still pulling pranks around the 'hood. Whatever the case, the result is the same: he's the bogeyman of this area. His heartbreak hung like a curse upon this place and it gradually turned into a state-of-the-art jungle gym for nature,' Daffy summed up. 'And the guy is still on the hunt for his bride, even today. So we got the "Heartbreaker"—sounds like a contestant on a Halloween-themed reality show, doesn't he?'

Lily didn't understand. She didn't understand why Daffy knew all this or would even be interested in finding out about it.

'Wait, there's more . . .' he went on. 'So he's got this other quirk—he's a fan of messing around with kids. And his favourite game is—well, I can't quite get the pronunciation right, because it's in Javanese folks' language—but it is turning into a taboo around here. They say if you play it, he might just show up . . .

'The game is a traditional one, with a song and all that. But the Heartbreaker is said to have treated the lyrics like a tribute to his njai. It was like their love song or something. Anyway, it's a simple game where a girl stands in the middle of a circle and the others in the circle chant a mantra. They put fragrant flowers on her head and sprinkle petals everywhere as an invitation to the ghost because he's a big fan of flowers. So, essentially, it's like this "proposal ritual" where the girl is offered up to the ghost as his potential bride. And then, guess what? Apparently, she's haunted by the ghost until she accepts his so-called proposal. Wanna hear the chant?'

'Nah, I'm good,' Lily said firmly. But Daffy was already belting out the song:

'Garden breeze, blow it all,
Who's the fairest flower of them all?
In a garden so chic,
Which flower to pick?'

'Hold up!' Lily pleaded. All conversation hushed. 'I mean we could totally play that song back at the campsite. You know . . . it'd really bug the other kids, and they'll probably start bugging Mr Verwey to let them go home . . . that'd be hilarious!'

'Brilliant idea!' Daffy chimed in.

It seemed that his tale had reached its end. As had the complex of ancient buildings. A sense of relief washed over Lily. It felt the same as spotting a rainbow after a storm. The pot of gold at the end of the rainbow was the view that awaited them at the end of this mystical journey.

'See the beauty I was talking about?' Daffy boasted, puffing up his chest. 'This, my girl, is what we call "camping".'

In front of her was a beautiful scene: a massive concave meadow full of wildflowers and a few trees, here and there, with a calm lake in the middle. Even though it was August, a time when things tend to dry up and colours fade, this place was bright and vivid. The gladioli stood tall like a guard. As butterflies and bees flew from flower to flower, they gently touched each petal on the lovely tapestry of reds, pinks, creams, and purples spread out before them.

'Could this be the Heartbreaker's lost garden you were talking about?' Lily wondered aloud.

'And *I'm* the one who found it!' Daffy answered in a definitive tone and Lily decided not to say anything more.

Also because he shushed Lily. He locked his fingers with hers and pulled her to run through the waist-high blossoms with him. The leaves shook behind them, causing the butterflies and bees in their nectar feasts to scatter at this disruption. He led her to the lakeside, which on closer inspection, looked less like a water body and more like a colossal mirror, reflecting the trees, cerulean sky, vivid gladioli, and Lily's awestruck visage in perfect likeness.

Oh, and Daffy's face, though Lily couldn't help but notice a quirky twist in his reflected image. He lowered himself, bowing towards the mirror-like water's edge. Bringing his head almost near its surface, he smoothed his hair with theatrical flair after dipping three fingers in the water.

He then sprang up and ran to a tent that had been set up in a small clearing of sorts. It was evident that the tent belonged to him. Or maybe it was the secret basecamp he had been bragging about all this time.

As Lily stood there speechless, her eyes as wide as saucers, she realized she'd been wrong all along. The forest she'd known had been a dreadful snoozefest, like nature's unkempt backyard. Who would've thought that behind those boring trees lurked a secret paradise, ready to dazzle her senses?

She found herself lost in a daydream, utterly spellbound by the magnificence around her. The perfection of the moment was enhanced as music began to weave through the air. It bridged the gap between Lily's soul and the essence of nature.

'Love My Way' by The Psychedelic Furs. So '80s. So rhapsodic. The sound was a captivating mix of electric guitar, bass, and synthesizer—a symphony so enchanting it could get even the least rhythmic person moving. The source of this magical melody—Daffy's tent. She glanced at him and that sly grin revealed what was up.

As if in a sugar rush, Lily dashed toward him. Flower fields parted, a few petals fluttering to the ground dramatically, like snow. The agile butterflies' wings keeping time while the bees' buzzing resembled a romantic saxophone melody. The wind joined in. The music intensified, beckoning Daffy and Lily to join in the euphoria and sway like wildflowers in a meadow.

A daffodil and lily, both stars in this botanical ballroom dance. As it turned out, the daffodil ruled the dance floor. Limbs swaying side to side—legs swinging like joyful pendulums; arms arching like petals, forming ripples as serene as the lake waters. He spun, his rotating corona more breathtakingly than the sun itself.

The lily, however, was more reserved in her movements as if restrained by invisible vines. Her stiff pistil and trembling petals—the daffodil noticed it all. She was shy, avoiding the daffodil's gaze, for her tendrils seemed to curl up whenever their eyes met.

And just when the music drew to a close, there was a second beat that Lily was wholly unprepared for. The intro played out, a call to action. Daffy briefly disappeared into the tent, reemerging with two items—one for him and one for Lily.

*Clink!* Liquid refreshment. Just what the doctor ordered. Lily gulped it down, assuming it was merely water in an eccentric glass vessel. Except, it wasn't the bland hydration she had expected. It tasted peculiar and she felt almost like she'd involuntarily grimace and spit it out.

'Swallow it,' Daffy ordered, and so she did.

The strange liquid went down her throat and into her stomach. In the meantime, Daffy took small sips of it as if it were lemonade and he was a pro lemonade vendor.

The song was in full swing and it was finally time for Daffy's favourite part—his big entrance during which he shook like a maraca on Red Bull. He looked happy—drunk on life and whatever was in that bottle.

Daffy grabbed Lily's hand boldly, like a lion tamer, putting the bottle to her lips. A flood of goodness came rushing out. Lily wasn't ready for round two, but it was as if her mouth was glued to a faucet turned all the way up. Overflow followed by sputtering and choking. That was way more than a sip—it was enough to get her absolutely sloshed in seconds.

But hey, wasn't that what parties were for?

Down her throat went the drink again, but now, Lily took charge—a proud sipper on a mission. Daffy beamed like a proud bartender admiring his star customer. She met his grin with her own.

Then, like a tornado in tap shoes, Daffy went right back to dancing. And Lily? Well, she was now a dancing dynamo herself. The music spiralled into a madness of beats, and her body obeyed its each and every command. Her joints felt like they had been lubricated with funky oil, her limbs flying like there was disco in her bones. Was this just some wacky effect of the drink?

*Who cares—bottoms up!*

Down went another gulp, and just like that, the invisible chains shackling her body vanished. The world was her dance floor, and she moved like a puppet freed from its strings. No inhibitions, just a dance-induced fever dream. Even the butterflies and bees seemed to cheer them on—the self-crowned king and queen of the dance floor, the daffodil and the lily.

As she got closer to her favourite flower, a secret was whispered by their petals. Their faces drew close together, eyes in a magnetic hold. In those golden lips, she saw peaks waiting to be summited, vistas to be enjoyed, an invitation to a lip-hiking adventure.

And then her lips met his. The verdict was in: soft, sweet, and alcoholic.

Ah, Lily had been waiting for this moment. It was the moment she had circled on her emotional calendar, complete with flashing lights and confetti cannons.

Daffy, that lovely rascal, was into it too. She could sense it.

It was like she had unleashed a stealthy cupid's arrow straight at his lips with hers. And it sent both their bodies tumbling to the ground. But Lily, being the fearless heroine of her own little rom-com, embraced the opportunity. Sure, Daffy's weight had landed on her like an unruly sack of potatoes, but she had been living for that very moment.

The song wrapped up its final chord. Daffy gracefully rolled onto his side, giving up. Lily won. The after-effect was a well of emotions; a little bit of intoxication blended with a dash of 'What the heck just happened?'

Lily tilted her head toward Daffy, spying him in his half-drunk, goofy-grinning glory. He was practically oozing chuckles from every pore. She knew he loved it. Oh, he loved it like a kid loves ice cream on a hot summer day.

So did she. She was swept up in a tornado of love, tipsiness, and inexplicable joy. Ah yes, this was the cocktail of emotions she didn't know she needed. Was this happiness? Was this the secret formula they all talked about—the one with a sprinkle of spontaneity, a twist of heart-pounding kisses, and a generous pour of daffodil-induced bliss?

Lily's grin widened. Daffy's nectar was her happy pill, the ultimate mood-enhancer, her personal cheer squad. And she was addicted to it.

As her euphoria painted Technicolor rainbows in her thoughts, she longed to stretch this moment to last forever. But tipsy elation was a one-way street, and she was now barrelling towards the exit. Her eyelids grew heavier and heavier, until the whole world darkened. Desperation kicked in and even as she tried hard to cling to consciousness, it proved to be a losing battle. And then, with the most dramatic flutter, her eyes shut.

\* \* \*

Lily came hurtling back to reality, as if after a thousand-year sleep. The drowsiness she felt, it's one of the unwritten rules of getting drunk. Her thoughts were moving slowly through her head, and she found it hard to see clearly.

Her mind felt as if it were wrapped in a soft, fluffy haze. Her body felt the strain of having partied like crazy. Her eyelids were still fighting to stay open in her half-awake state. Once again, they shut and she couldn't see anything. She opened them again, but she still couldn't see anything.

Turns out it wasn't drunkenness that was obscuring her vision—the entire world had blacked out.

Everything looked dim and gloomy. The only thing she could make out was the darkness.

Was it late?

One by one, glimmers of memories began to resurface, tapping at her dizzy, furrowed forehead. She remembered, and it shocked her. Hadn't everything looked colourful before?

She now saw a mysterious figure standing straight and motionless right in front of her, staring directly at her. Its body was strong and tall, so tall that Lily had to lift her head. The figure remained still, branching out. Was that a tree?

The horror didn't stop there. Some things were moving on the ground. Lily thought they were glaring at her. Their gazes were sharp and frightening. Could they be the heads of wild animals? The heads looked hungry.

'Who's there?' She bravely asked at full volume. But the only response she got was the wind howling like a wolf and echoing her confusion back at her.

The gust was loud, piercing her like icy needles, blowing until it cut off those creepy heads one by one as easily as pulling flower petals from their stems. Fortunately, they were just flowers.

Flowers? Gladiolus flowers!

Her mind slowly began to churn again, though it still felt like it was struggling. Her thoughts moved slowly like they were trying to find their way through a fog. But a small voice inside her encouraged her to hold on to what she could remember.

Camp. An abandoned Dutch nobility housing complex. Dread slithered down her spine like a spider, leaving icy trails in its wake.

A History lesson. A beautiful garden. A dance to '80s music. And Daffy.

*Wait, Daffy?*

'Daffy!' she screamed, but her voice was swallowed by the silence. Not a whisper returned, not even an echo in this spectral realm. The silence was unnerving, growing heavier with each passing moment. Lily felt weighed down, her body heavy and unresponsive to her thoughts. This was strange because she remembered falling to the ground, but here she was now, sitting in an unknown chair. It felt almost like it was part of her, as if it had sprouted from her own body. She felt trapped, as if held by invisible restraints.

Questions surged inside her and fuelled her growing sense of panic. She wondered desperately, *why was she tied up?* Was this a kidnapping? She spurred herself into action and she managed to move the chair slightly, but it was hardly enough.

She went white with fear. She was desperate to understand what had even happened.

'Daffy!' she called out, but no reply came from the void—just the haunting wail of the wind.

This only deepened her confusion and panic. Her heart raced, and goosebumps erupted all over her flesh. This was madness, utter chaos. Her mouth was parched, a bitter taste lingering on its palate. 'Daffy?' she croaked, her voice a weak shadow of what it used to be. She needed answers from someone, anyone; just something to pierce through the thick darkness.

*WHOOSH* went the wind again, a relentless spectre.

But this time, it carried a faint murmur. It sounded like the hushed sounds coming from a classroom as one passed it by the hallway.

The murmurs were getting close, and it became evident that it was the sound of people chit-chatting.

From behind the tall trees, like the bars of a jail for the forgotten, a blinding light burst out. It got brighter and brighter as it got closer; Lily felt like prey caught in a trap as the hunter approached her. It was impossible to keep looking because the brightness was too much for her eyes to handle.

'My, my! What do we have here? Looks like dinner's served!' The words pierced through the blackness. Each syllable felt like a knife digging into her being.

Foolish Lily. She had been blind to the truth, hadn't she? The lily, naive and pure, never thrived in the presence of pests. This had clearly been orchestrated by them— Derby and his gang of planthoppers.

That pest, that schemer, he exhausted her. Those dazzling lights had been a carefully laid trap, a calculated strategy to fatigue her senses. They closed in on her like a pack of hungry wolves: Derby, Missy and—was that Timmy or Billy? Where was the other one?

But it was the last person whose appearance completely unravelled Lily. The daffodil—no way, it couldn't be. Not Daffy. And clinging to him was ... Rosy? Her red dress, a striking reminder of her name, shone as the situation revealed itself. What a mockery of intimacy!

'Hey there, midnight wanderer! Couldn't sleep either?' Rosy's words, dripping with cruelty, sealed her fate.

The flashlights were turned off and her eyes felt too fatigued to stay open. The scene was hellish and spooky because of the eerie radiance of the night.

Lily didn't notice that a quiet figure was coming closer to her from behind and was caught off-guard. Jerking her head upwards by her hair, his fingers were tangled in her messy mop.

'Check out my hand! I got these callouses from doing thirty push-ups 'cause Mr Verwey punished me for being the first one to laugh at your pool stupidity,' Derby told Lily. 'He whined until he got his fill of payback.'

Lily's entire attention, though, was still focused on the last person who had emerged on the scene. She felt like she recognized the boy, but deep down, she really hoped that it was someone else.

*Daffy . . .*

Her head spun as she tried to make sense of the situation. There wasn't much light, but that face was too familiar, even in the darkness. Besides, it was his cold silence and distant manner that served as a disheartening confirmation of the truth.

'Why the heck are you hanging out with these guys?!' she screamed. His presence irritated her, and she felt betrayed.

'COME ON, DAFFY! What's the deal with all of this?! Are you in on their schemes?!' Her words were filled with hopelessness and her screams pierced through the trees. 'DAF—'

A sudden downpour of cold liquid soaked her, drowning out her yelling and plunging the forest into a fearful silence.

'This wench needs a lesson in silence.' Lily surmised it was Rosy who had silenced her. But it was Missy who emerged as the psychopathic orchestrator this time—the true architect of this new torment.

The liquid had a strong, unpleasant smell that mixed with the flowery, enticing fragrance of the forest. It attacked her senses and made her feel dizzy.

'Yes, I invited them,' Daffy's voice cut through the night. The shocking revelation broke her heart. 'The party was for everyone.'

The venom in his words was unforeseen, a poisoned dagger plunged straight into her heart.

And before his lips could seal again, a girl lunged forth and pressed her lips onto his—Rosy, the lucky one. Her kiss was a fervent claim, as if she was marking her territory. No part of him was spared. Lily had occupied that spot before—why was he allowing others to share what should have been hers?

'He is mine.' Rosy's declaration rang out, gripping Lily's mind with an unyielding force. Frustration swelled within her, manifesting in her clenched fists and the involuntary biting of her lips, which were now chapped due to the harsh wind.

Her heart shattered into a million pieces. She didn't know why Daffy would betray her like this. And in her mind, she felt like a child who had lost a beloved toy.

Rosy got closer to her, and her steps were deliberate. She boldly grabbed Lily's chin, who shrank from Rosy's glare.

'Look at this cowardly face, frozen in terror! Disgusting!' Rosy smirked and spat at her, making her words even meaner. 'You're so uptight, Lily! It's a simple matter, really. Just chill out.'

'Why do you enjoy messing with me?'

'Ever heard the saying that snakes only strike when provoked? User @HornyThornyRose?' Rosy retorted; she knew Lily was behind her hate account. 'Anyways, I know your little secret. You've always wanted to be part of our team, right? Well, guess what—we're inviting you to join in a little game, if you're up for it. Want to play?' Lily felt manipulated like a chess piece in a cruel game.

Lily noticed a clear plastic bag tucked in Rosy's left hand. As she moved away, Lily realized too late that she had been showered with flower petals. She noticed the shape that was surrounding her—a half-circle with Rosy, Daffy, Derby, Missy, and another boy. Who was he? Billy or Timmy? Why weren't there two of them?

She couldn't ignore a thought that kept pushing its way into her mind. Floral fragrance? Sprinkling of petals? A human circle?

'YOU SERIOUSLY BUY THAT STORY?!' she demanded, her question hung in the air and was met with silence from the group. So it was up to Lily to provide her own answer, a laugh bubbling out of her. 'I knew it. You idiots are dumber than a box of rocks!'

No one responded, it was like they didn't even care that she was there. They were all focused on their little ceremony. The strange atmosphere was made even stranger when flower petals fell like fairy dust on her. Daffy started singing the chant; the game was set to begin.

'Garden breeze, blow it all . . .'

The shadow of death grew heavier. The leaves and grass were brushed aside by the whimpering wind.

'Who's the fairest flower of them all?'

Lily felt the stormy wind slam against her face, but it was not good enough to wash off the shimmering droplets of sweat on it. Her forehead looked as though she had showered in heavy rain. The air was flooding her nose, but she was still gasping for breath.

She kept struggling in her chair like a chick trying to break out of its eggshell. The ropes around her tightened, digging into her skin and leaving stinging red marks with every stressful minute.

'What a total waste of time! Aren't you guys embarrassed to be eating up this garbage?'

'In a garden so chic . . .'

'Please, untie me or stop the game!' She changed her tone when she realized that harsh words weren't working. 'No matter what you say, I'll do it. Rosy, I know you're better than me. I agree with that. From now, I'll even try to learn to get used to your pranks, Derby. I swear. Please let me go, stop it, please!'

Lily was beginning to give up; the flood of her words fell silent. Each gulp was met with fiery resistance, as her throat had started burning.

'Which flower to pick?' Daffy's singing stopped, surrendering the stage to the wind's lullaby again.

'CHECK IT OUT!' Lily shouted, back in her mean mode. 'Think some Prince Charming is gonna come swooping in, get down on one knee, and be like, "Hey, Lily, will you marry me?" OH MY GOD! You guys are a riot!' But her words vanished into thin air, lost before she could even savour her sarcasm. 'We're all just having a good time here, right?'

The cruel winds hurled her deeper into the maze of fear; worry filled her whole body.

Meanwhile, an entity appeared . . . for the love of all that's holy! Someone, please tell Lily that her senses are betraying her!

But no, a sinister silhouette draped in a black cloak loomed beside a tree, just behind that mysterious boy, who Lily finally recognized, was Billy. Lily prayed that the mirage would turn out to be just a tree bark or gladiolus buds.

'Guys . . .' she begged. A desperate plea for someone to confirm that she was still just in a drunken haze. Or some sign that it was all just a big joke. 'HE'S REAL!' she screamed.

The figure shrouded in a black cloak defied definition in Lily's frantic mind. Since the void blocked it out, it blended into the darkness without any trouble. The silhouette started to edge towards her deliberately, one step at a time.

'WHERE IS MY BOO?!' the figure said.

Hold on, ghosts levitate, don't they? But this ghost was dressed in a gown so long, it covered his whole body—was he walking or floating? Did he even have legs? The hood of the robe covered his face, too, making him look even more mysterious.

'WHERE IS MY BOO?!'

'Please, answer me!' Lily struggled against the chair, but she couldn't get out of its hold.

'WHERE IS MY BOO?!'

'I beg you, won't you respond?'

The figure broke through the circle, stumbling forward, and lunged at Lily.

'WHERE IS MY BOO?!'

'I beg you! Please, pretty please!'

'BOOOOO!'

Lily's eyes clamped shut.

She felt wet. Drenched. Water cascaded all the way down to the soles of her feet. She was swept away by a flood of worry. Then, a distinct, chilling sound broke through the tense atmosphere.

Was this the time for laughter?

It was very loud and not in tune, completely out of place in the woods' symphony.

Lily didn't know when her eyes flew open. She saw that the 'ghost' had joined in the noise and was doubling over. *What is happening?*

Right after that, the veil fell away. The ghost wore the face of a boy . . .

*Timmy?!*

So it was! He was no ghost. Just a boy with a dirty mop of hair and an insolent grin. He was wearing a mask—from the costume he had donned last Halloween. How could Lily have forgotten about that terrible costume?

'Wait!' Timmy yelled, cutting through the laughter. 'LILY, HAVE YOU PEED YOUR PANTS?'

An icy breeze nibbled around the top of her thighs.

A flood of shame engulfed her, but her inner demons were far louder, numbing the pain of her disgrace. She felt a rush of self-loathing course through her body.

The prank was recorded, framed forever in a digital format so that everyone could enjoy it. A shameful painting of a dirty girl grieving her own filth—what a sad fate.

'Look at her, she's crying so much!'

'Wow, she's really upset, isn't she?'

'Think we went too far? She's really taking this hard.'

The shutters fired, chronicling this grotesque spectacle.

Suddenly, just as the laughter began to slowly die down, Missy screamed. This creepy vibe swept through the crowd, making everyone jump, including the ones behind the whole setup. Missy's phone slipped from her hand, breaking into pieces as it hit the ground. 'HE'S FREAKING HERE!'

'He, who?'

'Come clean, dude!'

'HE'S HERE!' Missy's words rang out, filled with pure fear. There was then a desperate scramble to bring her dead phone back to life. 'He's here, for real! One of the pics I took—it actually showed *him*, right freaking here!'

Who was this mysterious 'he'? What entity had descended upon them?

'Th—that ghost . . .' Missy gulped, clearly trying hard to swallow her fear. 'THE HEARTBREAKER! HE'S HERE!'

There was complete silence, a still air of scepticism. Her friends didn't believe what Missy was saying because they knew she was obsessed with scary movies.

'Ugh, it's driving me nuts!' Missy blurted out, pure desperation in her voice now. 'Okay, fine, I'll come clean. All those spooky stories I shared in class? Yeah, I made them up—totally exaggerated, pure wild imaginings. Agreed. And just maybe . . .' she hesitated, her unforeseen humility cresting like a wave. 'Perhaps, I'm just getting a taste of my own medicine. But seriously, I'm not lying this time. I swear on my life, I *saw* him!' The tension grew thicker. 'C'mon, guys, you have to believe me! Believe! Believe! Believe!'

The forest seemed to exhale forcefully before falling back into its deep slumber; the darkness seemed to be thickening. The clouds above them grew heavier; it looked like this gaggle of teenagers was going to break under their weight. Strong gusts of cold wind sent leaves and petals swirling in a sorrowful ballet around them.

Daffy's conviction was waning; his eyes betrayed how alarmed he was. He hurriedly started making his way out of the clearing, his steps urgent. 'Don't space out, you idiots! We need to bail, like right now! Can't you see the signs? There are like, all the red flags before the big show around us.'

'Oh God, come on!' Derby's words were rushed and unclear. Time seemed to shrink, speeding up and becoming erratic. The flashlights came on again. The bright lights once again cast their blinding spell for the benefit of the witnesses. Amid the commotion, Lily's voice struggled to find purchase. A gust of wind swept her words into oblivion.

Against the backdrop of the howling wind, louder than a wounded beast, they hastily fled from the chaotic situation, leaving Lily behind.

'Wait! Let me go! You can't leave me like this!' Lily hurled her curses into the wind, but her desperate calls were little more than empty echoes, disappearing into the shadows. The glow of flashlights slowly faded from view, behind the trees. From amid the leaves, a figure emerged.

HE WAS DARK. HE WAS REAL. HE WAS HERE.

He began to move towards Lily.

'HELP!'

Lily's screams for help filled the air, but the hungry wind ate up her words.

'HELP!'

Her voice quivered, her breath grating against her throat. Tears coursed down her cheeks.

'HELP!' she cried.

She waged war against the chair that clung to her like an overgrown barnacle, but no matter how hard she struggled, she could only make small movements. Her stamina drained, but her defiance pressed on. She refused to back down.

Sapping her of all her strength, the ropes proved too stubborn, refusing to yield. But pushed to the edge of the chair, Lily fell off, hitting the hard ground, hands and feet still bound.

When there was so much space around her, why did she choose a rock as a pillow? She now had to grapple with the overwhelming agony surging through her head. Couldn't bad luck ever wait? It always picked the worst time to show off, evil disguised as twisted comedy. But it felt like a short break from the chaos of the moment.

Just when Lily felt she was losing her grip on sanity, the figure appeared in front of her. Lily was ready for a wave of displeasure to hit her, but his presence made her feel strangely at ease. Loosened ropes discarded, she exhaled, feeling light, and allowed herself to float.

She was in the air, flying away.

She found herself landing gently in someone's embrace. Before her stood a man. Even in the dark, his pale skin seemed to glow brighter the fading moonlight. His blue eyes were like stars or diamonds and captivated her. Lily was charmed and felt as if she was falling in love. Reality became clearer—he was no myth. He was real and he was here.

Unlike the ghostly tales, the Heartbreaker had no scars, no twisted face, no bleeding wounds. No. In fact, he had an otherworldly charm, like a prince from another era. A classic; an embodiment of the literary archetype—Romeo in search of his Juliet. In his embrace, she felt secure, as if wrapped in a cocoon of warmth.

A calm radiance enveloped her, sweeping her away on a soothing current.

Fear released its hold over her.

A peaceful slumber beckoned, and Lily embraced it.

Like the gladioli beneath her, she fell asleep, in love and at peace.

# Chapter 4

## September

'Summer has come and passed
The innocent can never last
Wake me up when September ends.'

—Green Day, 'Wake Me Up When
September Ends'

She walked down the hallway, her eyes darkened by deep despair. Her heart was heavy. Her thoughts were clouded with scenes from a cheap movie she had seen the previous night, *Pity Party: Part Two.*

The sun had just barely made it over the horizon that morning, but the hallway, painted an uninviting shade of leprechaun green, was already a carnival of chaos. The scene was like a post-concert crowd trying to funnel its way through a narrow exit door, except that these were teenagers with more restless energy than the average adult after a triple espresso shot.

The clock had not even chimed eight and a half yet, but bodies still collided, trying to squeeze past each other. The scene was hell for claustrophobic souls.

Her mind was racing, desperately searching for a strategy to successfully navigate the dense sea of energetic teenagers, when her eyes caught sight of a poster on the wall. It was complete with a fairy tale design that had probably been commissioned by the Grim Reaper's more whimsical sibling.

It announced the rolling out of the prestigious theatre production auditions—not just any auditions, mind you, but a showdown akin to *The Hunger Games*—for the school's annual arts gala.

It wasn't about the play, no seriously. It also was not about the arts. It was about the stupid crown of school celebrity, the coveted 'Drama Queen' title that glittered like fool's gold. Rumours of fame and notoriety spread through the corridors faster than those about surprise math pop quizzes. But for Lily, this was a warpath paved with the promise of redemption; a one-way ticket to ridding herself of the infamous 'loser' label that had stuck for far too long.

You might think she should've rid herself of her audacity instead, right? Like her relentless hunger for the spotlight all this time should've left her? Didn't the gazes she chased to have fixed upon her feel disdainful? Didn't the accolades she collected sting as much as the insults that accompanied them?

You're right, but don't bring it up with her. You just don't understand what she was going through. The scars were nasty, but not as hurtful as being left in the dark, where no one could see her at all. It didn't hurt as badly as throwing a party and nobody showing up. You just don't understand the feeling. So don't blame her—she was still determined to be in the limelight on her own show's stage. It was not her fault that she was yet to fill her audience seats. You might think persistence was hard for her, but you simply don't get that she was sick of living as a nobody.

But those girls hanging out by that wall poster were saying in their own way that they were going to make things not-so-easy for Lily. They looked at her with doubt; their sharp tongues could win against sushi knives in a contest. One would think that with Lily looking so obviously sad, they'd be too busy to scorn her.

Oh, but that look in their eyes was like a recipe for revenge cake. A mash-up they'd been stirring since Lily inadvertently ruined last month's camping adventure.

The details of that fateful night were still shrouded in mystery. Mr Verwey recounted the tale for everyone's benefit as follows: Lily had disappeared from her tent, and the camp's joy transformed into a chorus of chaos. It was as if they were cheering for her disappearance. They seemed to be popping champagne bottles in the depths of their twisted hearts, as if secretly wishing Lily left their lives forever or somehow became permanently invisible.

The dramatic end to Lily's mysterious disappearance had come with her being discovered sprawled on the main road, miles away from the campsite. When she finally woke up, it was as if she'd stumbled into a room full of interrogators who were way too sceptical to accept her confession. Afraid that no one would take her seriously, she kept everything to herself, only letting her heart find solace in her suffering.

And so, her tragic tale was transformed into a comedy once more. The audience rewrote the tale as 'a fucked-in-the-head camper strayed in the forest and got lost'. Meanwhile, gazes sharp enough to cut paper shot at her from every direction, with Rosy, Derby, and the rest of their gang at the forefront of the hate parade. They had had ringside seats to the spectacle but chose to play possum. They acted like they'd sooner believe in dragons and dwarves than admit to knowing what actually went down that night. Each of their faces displayed a mix of coldness and complete bewilderment. Behind their façades, they quietly wondered: 'How did Lily survive?'

Then, there was more. As if the night of that horrifying proposal hadn't already brought enough misfortune upon Lily, she had acquired a new stalker since then. A mysterious pair of eyes that gazed at her as if she was as mystifying as a fortune-telling crystal ball. Those eyes were the bluest she'd ever seen, like polished jewels. They brimmed with an allure more magnetic than any magical enchantment. Yet, the moment Lily dared to return the look, *POOF!* The eyes disappeared faster than a scream in a haunted mansion. It was like being stared at by a pair of neon lights that cast an afterglow. Even as Lily jostled her way out of the crowd, she felt the intense blue eyes set firmly on her. And only she could sense them.

They gleamed like royal blue sapphires adorning a championship trophy behind display glass, beckoning attention with all the subtlety of a siren's song. And those eyes decided to play hide-and-seek again. They employed their see-through edge that always outplayed Lily, again and again.

And that's how the blue eyes became a persistent ghost in her life. Meanwhile, their spying schedule got darker during their night shift. As Lily drifted off to sleep, an abstract presence lingered, preventing her from resting fully, and leaving her suspended between sleep and wakefulness. In that semi-aware state, Lily found herself trapped in a state of inertia—though it was a feeling she was familiar with. But this time, its grip was too tight, like it was more than mere sleep paralysis.

Her mind was so clouded that she couldn't think logically how these inconspicuous, imperceptible terrors relentlessly annoyed her—flowers mysteriously appeared in her locked locker, her hair was played with, lifted, and frozen in the air despite there being no wind, objects were flying paranormally around her just to grab her attention, and someone was intruding in her private dreams. She was unaccustomed to the shivering, terrifying sensations of transcendental whispers, metaphysical touches, and supernatural embraces.

September decided to turn chaotic. The air seemed to encourage rusting. Surfaces that had seen better days were now adorned with layers of dust.

As if that wasn't enough, just when Lily thought life couldn't get any harder, logarithms decided to make an entrance. They threw everyone's head into a tizzy.

The class of innocent minds struggled to grasp these numerical rebels. Their eyes wide with wonder. Inside their brains, chaos reigned supreme.

Among this chaos, poor Lily had to deal with a bout of nausea as well. She gazed at the dull blackboard where the numbers seemed to blur together. Seeking a diversion, she turned towards the window, hoping for a glimpse of freedom. However, the view of the sky through the small pane only intensified her feelings of being trapped.

Her face turned back to the blackboard. She noticed the numbers had changed into something altogether new, leaving her even further behind in understanding. As she struggled to keep up, her attention was involuntarily drawn to a boy at the table to her left, who kept watching her. She initially ignored him, but his gaze became distracting. She gave in to her curiosity and looked his way again, recognizing him. It was Saam, a tall, ginger boy. She recalled being in the same group as him during a frog dissection in biology class.

She turned away from him again, but his peculiar gaze lingered in her mind. Overcome with a need to reassure herself that everything was normal, she looked back at him. His expression was unsettling. He was smiling unnaturally, his face contorting in a way that reminded Lily of a sinister clown, the edge of his lips drawn up sharply. His skin was unusually pale, and his hair was eerily still. He seemed frozen with that strange smile on his face.

Lily tried to elicit a reaction from him. She made various facial expressions, careful not to make any odd noises or look too bizarre for other people around to notice. But despite her efforts, Saam remained unresponsive, as if he were a statue. He didn't even react when a mosquito landed on his nose.

'Saam, are you listening?' The math teacher called out to him, finally, and tried to wake him up from his unresponsive state. 'Saam?'

The sound of a teacher calling you by your name when your mind wanders away from class is the strongest shockwave that can bring your soul back into your body. But Saam still wasn't aware, and Lily didn't remember him being a disobedient student.

All the other kids turned to see Saam staring at Lily. They turned their attention to Lily too.

This inevitably made Lily shift positions. Her hunched spine straightened, and her languid facial expression stiffened with panic at suddenly being the centre of attention. It was like people were accusing her of something; like she was the one who had disrupted the class.

While this was going on, Lily kept shooting looks at Saam's face. And the more she observed it, the more she began to unravel other oddities, and the more it made her shudder.

She shrank at the unfamiliar look in his eyes, as if she was looking at a stranger. She had felt that same intense stare on her before; a gaze that always sparked her curiosity. Whenever she looked back, it vanished. Previously, she had only conceived of that gaze in abstract terms, but here it was now, in a tangible form—and it was horrifying. Her heart raced, yet she couldn't tear her eyes away from his, as if they were locked in a magnetic pull.

What struck her as even more peculiar was the colour of Saam's eyes. She remembered them being green, but they were now an unnatural shade of blue, shining in the classroom's low light. This eerie glow seemed to captivate her in an unusual way.

Then, breaking the bizarre silence, Saam's expression finally shifted. He opened his mouth to declare, 'I love you, Lily!'

Deep down, Lily sensed that these words hadn't truly come from Saam. But she doubted her classmates were aware of that deeper truth. They were initially shocked and speechless, but their surprise quickly turned into laughter— big, big laughter.

The teacher walked over to Saam, to offer him a comforting pat on the shoulder. This contact seemed to break Saam out of his strange trance, returning him to his usual awkward teenager demeanour. He blinked his eyes and, astonishingly, they changed colour from blue to their natural green, like a traffic light.

Saam seemed confused, as if he couldn't remember what had just happened. Or was he just pretending to not be responsible for the commotion? Their classmates continued to laugh, but the teacher quickly restored order.

And then there was Lily, sitting in her chair, feeling overwhelmed. Her mind was filled with questions more complex than any math problem on the board. The 'how' and 'what' of the situation multiplied into many unsolvable queries. But she realized the 'why'. This madness was part of something much more sinister, a creeping terror that was growing in ways her logic couldn't comprehend. And it was threatening to quietly unravel her sanity.

Lily's frown was deep—a reflection of the turmoil inside her. Her temples throbbed from the intense confusion she felt, as if sending out an urgent signal for help. Her heart raced from the uncertainty, and her mind, desperate for a truce, silently screamed for clarity. She yearned for answers, her soul was as chaotic as a storm.

In an attempt to quell the madness, Lily tried to push the thoughts away, but they clung to her mind, unyielding. They tapped her forehead to let them in. So, to distract herself, Lily planned a series of tasks for after school in her mind, each meticulously thought out. Her first mission was to navigate the bustling afternoon market. She envisioned weaving through the crowds, her senses bombarded by the sights and sounds while gathering ingredients for dinner and probably other necessities.

She planned that as evening fell and once the market's chaos faded, she would transform into a chef, cooking and studying simultaneously, in a rhythm of efficiency. Her plan was carefully orchestrated to occupy every moment, ensuring no empty space for the haunting thoughts to return.

* * *

Time hurried by. The monotonous school hours finally ended, giving way to the solitude of nighttime at the Lonely House. Lily couldn't decide which was worse. The floating items in her mind had assembled into a material checklist. By the time she got into bed—the last item on that list—her body was aching with exhaustion.

Despite her intense tiredness, sleep was a stranger. Her bed felt like a small, unstable boat floating in a vast ocean of wakefulness. Her restless tossing and turning caused her sheets to become drenched in sweat. Her body was a dead weight, but her mind was a whirlwind, flitting from thought to thought. Or maybe it was the bright moon outside that disturbed her sleep schedule, its glow flooding her entire room.

She felt as if she was sleeping with her eyes open. And in her half-asleep state, her dream became a confusing blend of reality and fantasy. Her lucid dreams were like a party where nobody got an invite. But the madness she confronted eluded logic, even if she strategized with the most reasonable to-do list to get away from it. It managed to infiltrate her dreams like seeping water.

She dreamed of the strangest things. She dreamed of those blue eyes, their owner strangely shrouded in darkness.

The eyes glared! It was a death stare! Like vigilant sentinels, they seemed to monitor Lily's every move. Like a temptress from a retro romance novel who could spellbind and infatuate anyone who laid eyes on him, he enraptured her so she couldn't move. She felt as if she had been inducted into a mystical circle, filled with a romantic intensity that bound her to this surreal experience. It was as if she had been served a cocktail of sedatives infused with the essence of starlight that made her feel impossibly light.

Liberated from the physical constraints of her body, she took off! Soaring in a universe of her own imagination, she found herself in a place where all the worries of the world couldn't reach her. She found serenity, freedom, bliss, and wonder. But just as she began to get used to this universe, she was pulled back into the real world with a cymbal crash.

She woke up slowly, and her blurred vision made her ceiling look like a canvas stained with a coffee splash.

Her dull old room's ceiling was now hanging over her with a familiarity that felt oddly intimate. But wait, it wasn't the roof that was getting close—it was Lily who was moving towards it! And while she was still somewhat fuzzy every time she woke up this way, she was sure that her cozy snooze had been rudely interrupted.

This flying sensation, however, she wasn't dreaming up—she was actually floating in her room, resisting gravity like a helium balloon!

But wait, she wasn't really feeling like a free bird when she said she felt like she was flying. It was more like she was frozen in midair, an icy hand gripping her, wrapping around her, and squeezing her as if it sought a twisted form of cuddle. Her room, usually a spacious sanctuary, felt suffocatingly small under this pressure, with panic running rampant in her.

Her body was fighting against being held back, turning what was initially light into a crushing burden. Every bone and joint felt like it was made of rock and the thought of lifting her thumb felt like trying to bench press a mountain. Her voice was completely uncooperative, refusing to make any sound, and she was unable to move at all. She was breathless, soaked in sweat, and enveloped in intense anxiety. Her eyelids struggled to open, and her gaze painted a sense of her helplessness.

Her soul was torn between anger and defiance, and her body felt like it had tried jumping without a parachute. Her veins pulsed intensely, her blood was agitated. Her throat felt like she had been breathing fire, but its fiery energy was stuck behind an invisible wall.

Then, in a sudden release of tension, Lily screamed. The sound was explosive, like an unexpected burst of energy. This seemed to jumpstart her body's functions, which had felt frozen in time. Suddenly, she fell back down onto the bed, as gravity reasserted its pull, grounding her once again in the physical world.

Lily sat up straight as if she had been punched in the head. Her sudden wakefulness dispelled all the thoughts from her head. She sprang into action. Leaping out of bed, her muscles reacted with surprising agility as she dashed towards the door to her room and darted for the main door. Her footsteps echoed loudly in a tumultuous rhythm on the floor. She breathed heavily, still breaking in a cold sweat. *Run, run, and then run some more*, she kept repeating to herself. There was no time to think—the urge to run away was far too strong.

As soon as she stepped outside the house, the soft touch of the night breeze was a welcome change from the fever that was making her shiver. She huffed and puffed; puffed and huffed. Her throat was dry and strained from her scream of distress.

In the moonlight, Lily's face was a creased canvas of worry and fatigue. The dark circles under her eyes accentuated her exhausted appearance. She felt as if her soul had been left behind in bed, and her body was now trying to navigate the real world alone and directionless.

But reality had yet another twist in store for her. It was a curveball that not even the best baseball player could have seen coming—a sprained ankle. While suddenly changing direction during her escape plan, Lily's right leg, still weak, hadn't withstood the sharp turn.

The grass was cold below her feet, she didn't even seem to feel that. She didn't feel any pain at all. This gripping fear had numbed her senses.

Then came the second sharp turn, and this time, she couldn't dodge it. Her feet still weren't strong enough, so every step was a huge challenge for her to suddenly escape once more.

*Tap! Tap! Tap!* Footsteps approached, breaking the eerie silence. The distant bushes rustled restlessly, and the trees seemed disturbed as if they longed to flee from their rooted positions. Interestingly, this creepy sound matched the heartbeat of the wind that made her nightgown flutter. And in a moment of desperation, Lily screamed.

'WHO'S THERE!?'

It was as a way to show she didn't fear what the unknown meant. She let out a wild scream that was more like a yell than a question. However, the wind chose to follow her lead and quickly stop, taking a beat with her.

Silence ensued, and she remembered that nothing unsettled her more than the oppressive quiet.

'Reveal yourself, you spineless wretch!'

And there he stood before her, the owner of those blue eyes, supernatural touches, and paranormal embraces. His physicality, which used to be ethereal, finally solidified before her. It was like watching a faded hologram gradually thicken into a tangible sculpture.

There he stood like a prince waiting for his princess. He was like a groom standing at the end of the aisle, waiting for his bride at the altar in a fairy tale wedding.

He was clutching a bunch of red tulips, a bouquet for his bride. This language of love needed no translation. His face was devilishly handsome, like it belonged on a poster for the 'Top 10 Heartbreakers of the Century'.

For a fleeting moment, she even contemplated the idea that he might moonlight as a handsome serial killer, the kind that only killed his victims in the most fashionable and aesthetic ways. Soon, reality struck—here was the hero of the local legend that plagued the entire town. The local. The legend. The Heartbreaker.

Lily's fascination did a quick 180. Her initial star-struck vibe turned into holy terror. It felt like bumping into a guy whose love you rejected, who was already dead in your eyes and was now being . . . hauntingly awkward.

But Lily's realization had come too late—the night had deepened into darker hues, and her way home was obscured by sinister shadows. The wind grew restless. Trees roared and swayed wildly, as if terrorized. Daffy's words echoed in Lily's mind: 'The red flags before the big show!'

The Heartbreaker started moving, wearing the same, unsettling grin Saam had on his face earlier.

The distance between them shrank. Lily strained her legs to move, but it only caused more sweat to trickle down her forehead. She limped along, barely making any progress, and the pain in her sprained leg was excruciating. She glanced back at the Heartbreaker several times, but each look seemed to bring him closer. When she could no longer sustain her futile escape, she collapsed.

Her world fell into a black hole. A place where there was no reason. No self-respect. Thoughts fled, leaving her blank. But it didn't take long for all her senses to return to their posts. And when she woke up, it was as if she was waking from a nightmare.

Because . . .

Because, that drop-dead gorgeous face, it was all a ruse. Once the magic wore off, the horror unveiled, the torn wounds, a gruesome mix of blood and pus.

The *Swan Lake* ballet turned into a macabre dance.

The 'Heartbreaker' had traded his title for one far less glamorous: just 'heartbreaking'.

That face, which had once been kissed by moonlight, was eclipsed. Hidden beneath the shroud of timeless scars, it forged a painting of decay and devastation.

Those eyes, which had once been as deep-blue as the ocean, sank into an abyss of emptiness, all the while murmuring tales of anguish and revenge.

That figure, which had once sparked rage in an entire town, now just sparked life in a ghost town. A walking graveyard of meatless bones and ripped skin, thick blood oozing from its fissures, mingling with the repugnant black liquid of decomposed corpses, exuding an aura of the dead and undead.

And the most terrifying thing about it all was the gaping hole in his chest, right where his heart was. You could see his heart, exposed, throbbing, and bleeding.

Its pulse resonated deeply, evoking both a heartwarming and heartbreaking aura.

Balancing herself was like walking a cursed path, where the ground itself seemed hungry for a misstep. Attempting to stand and sprint ahead was like a desperate dash through a nightmarish labyrinth, the walls closing in with every stride. But surrendering was not an option, it was like allowing the horrors to converge and consume all her hope.

Her vocal cords strained with relentless effort. Her jugular vein throbbed in rhythm with her rising fear. Her muscles clenched and spasmed, betraying her anxiety. Her sweat carved winding paths across her forehead, mirroring her distress. Her bones quivered and rattled like old skeletons in a closet. Meanwhile, her teeth chattered uncontrollably. Just as her body teetered on the brink of rebellion, a shock surged through her soul like a defibrillator, yanking her back to consciousness.

It was as if someone had slapped her with a dream-shattering wake-up call. Now, she stood at the crossroads between dreams and reality, uncertain of her whereabouts.

*Tick-tock! Tick-tock!*

The clock was cross-dimensionally ticking away. Her sudden jolt caused her bed springs to react in surprise. Or so she believed. Her vision wavered unsteadily. Sweat drenched her body, and she felt like a washing machine stuck in an endless spin cycle. The morning sunlight filtered through the window, enveloping her in a hazy glow.

*Tick-tock! Tick-tock!*

The clock was unsympathetically ticking away. It revealed that school had begun its daily grind without her in tow. Entangled in her crumpled blanket, she felt eyeballs-deep in confusion. She wondered if she had managed to skip dimensions or just overslept. She pondered if she was the spectator or the performer in the nightmarish circus of the previous night.

*Tick-tock! Tick-tock!*

The clock kept ticking away. On her dressing table, a single red tulip stood in a flower vase, which had been empty when she had gone to sleep—how had this object from her nightmares crossed over into reality? Lily looked at the flower for a long time. The tulip stared back at her with enduring love.

# Chapter 5

## October

"'Gardeners are never wicked are they?" said Ruth. "Obstinate and grumpy and wanting to be alone, but not wicked. Oh, look at that creeper! I've always loved October so much, haven't you? I can see why it's called the Month of the Angels.'"

—Eva Ibbotson, *The Morning Gift*

'Lily!'

In the depths of her disbelief, Lily stood frozen even as her name resonated through the air.

In fact, nobody in the room had anticipated that. She wasn't everyone's prediction and her name wasn't what everyone had been waiting for. The room was filled with denial, and disappointed and disgusted faces. The collective gasp at the mention of her name lingered like a heavy fog. Some voices demanded clarification, while others pleaded for a rematch.

But Lily had been waiting for this moment. The looks directed at her were no longer condescending. Finally, they looked at her with a bitter taste in their mouths, defying the fate of the world, which seemed to be on her side at this point. She felt like she was being treated like a controversial pop star; like the main character she knew she was.

The role of a lifetime awaited her. She had cleared the auditions and been selected to embody the heroine who every girl in school had wanted to play in the school theatre production.

The school hallways had been rife with whispers that the jackpot of landing this role would be a game-changer that would etch the winner's name indelibly in the annals of the school's history. And the girls were willing to pay the stupid price for that. They endured brutal regimens, pushing their stomachs in with strict diets.

But more than the allure of fame and the excitement of recognition, Lily relished the sweet taste of victory over her arch-nemeses; they'd said she didn't stand a chance. When the perennial favourite Rosy left the room with a crestfallen face and shattered dreams, sympathetic glances followed her. But in Lily's mind, it was a gratifying moment she prayed would never end. A cynical curve was etched on her lips as she revelled in the thought of inciting Rosy's envy.

Anticipation grew within her. Days stretched into eternity as she counted down to that fateful night. The night that was not just a showtime. It was her coronation night when the Drama Queen's crown would be rightfully bestowed upon her.

'You will play Snow White,' it was declared. The play that year was going to be *Snow White and the Seven Dwarfs*. Lily knew, with every fibre of her being, that no other flower was more suited to don the iconic Snow White gown besides her. Her snow whiteness as a lily was the embodiment of purity, grace, and resilience.

The show was next month, but Lily's mind buzzed with anticipation. She was imagining the moment the curtain would rise, unveiling a stage adorned with an enchanting set and the auditorium filled with a hushed audience awaiting her presence. Their faces would display their awe, but the first face she would look for would be the red, flushed, jealous face of Rose who craved the standing ovation and the flattery that were now going to be Lily's.

She couldn't wait; her impatient soul prayed for October to pass quickly.

\* \* \*

October had just arrived, yet the rain came and went and now decided to forsake everyone a little longer. The sky was a monotonous expanse of greyish blue. This dimmed everything colourful into something lonely.

And the most troubling part was that it was now the middle of the semester. This once vibrant school, celebrated as a blooming garden, now stood as a stark symbol of desolation. The garden with a magnificent display of nature's art now resembled a graveyard of wilted dreams. The beetles sang 'Strawberry Fields Forever'. The caterpillars still groomed themselves in their cosy cocoon shells.

The flowers that had once been the pride of this hallowed ground now lay withered under the weight of relentless drought. Look at those hydrangeas! They used to be bright and refreshing shades of blue, but look at them now, they looked like dead husks. The sunflowers—where was their warm and cheerful demeanour? Their golden faces were now bereft of hope. Even the daisies could no longer maintain their brightness. Their petals, once glowing with innocence, paled. And the tulips, which had once painted the gardens with a vibrant rainbow, now hung their heads low, as if mourning the loss of the rain's caress.

The arid thirst also choked Lily's throat and seeped into her very being, consuming her from within. Her petals started drooping and withering too, and her once strong stem now trembled with frailty. The whiteness that defined her faded into a haunting pallor, and she felt so exhausted that it made her head spin.

Lily realized she'd rather be in Mr Verwey's high-intensity interval training than endure the relentless onslaught of theatre rehearsals. They had become unbearably torturous. The theatre buzzed with frenetic energy as everyone prepared for the forthcoming performance. At the centre of it all was Lily. She rehearsed for her role as if it could grant her the stardom of Hollywood's finest. Her determination knew no bounds when seeking perfection on that dimly lit stage. She pushed herself to the brink, determined to nail the performance. Because for her, this wasn't just about applause—it was a chance to avoid the humiliation of her 'Least Likely to Succeed' label in the yearbook. Failure was not an option; the spectre of embarrassment hovered over her like a vulture, ready to swoop down at the slightest misstep.

It's as if the Grim Reaper himself was moonlighting as her personal life coach, demanding she endure trials like surviving a school of piranhas or seriously contemplating a transfer to a school on a deserted island.

As time unfurled, days turned into weeks and the mercilessness of her schedule began to gnaw at her. Her body became like an anchor, settling deeper and deeper into a sea of fatigue. All the while, her mind remained foggy and she felt nauseous. Yet, she masked her weariness with a smile like she always did. She was such a good actress; she was determined not to let anyone see her vulnerability and acted as if everything was okay, knowing that, otherwise, they would find someone to replace her.

On the calendar, date after date was crossed out, counting down the days to the star-marked date. Meanwhile, deadlines compelled compliance like death contracts, pressuring minds with vice-like grips. Nobody had any idea how much crazier things could get. But even before the many possibilities could cross their minds, the actor portraying the prince gave up his role, abandoning the battlefield before the war had even started. He was more concerned with preparing and practising for the end-of-semester Biology Olympiad, as it would look better on his university applications than having starred in a low-budget high school play production.

And so Miss Van der Mey, the director, found herself with no other choice but to hold re-auditions for the role of the prince. The list grew: Noah, Lucas, Levi . . . in voiceless prayers, Lily fervently wished for her prince.

Saam, Jayden, Max . . . None of them could quite fulfil the role of her prince; they lacked the type of princely appeal she preferred.

Thomas, Olivier, Jesse . . . No.

None other than Daffy.

Was she—yes, she was sober. And yes, she remembered his betrayal at camp. Had the wound in her heart healed so quickly? Was it that easy for her to just delete that embarrassing memory from her mind? Or had her mind been poisoned by that narcissistic flower such that she now had a blooming obsession?

Perhaps Daffy's self-centred soul wondered why he should audition for roles in mere high-school-level plays when he could land roles in Hollywood movies.

And the boy who won the position turned out to be a nightmare for Lily. How could she possibly do a romantic scene while staring at the face she avoided and despised the most? But then her mind abruptly smacked her in the face with the unforgiving truth that nightmares had lately become her loyal, bedtime besties.

In that frustrating moment, she had crossed Daffy off the list, and she desperately wished for anyone but Billy to be cast.

*What?! Why?! How?!*

Oh! Maybe this was another one of Derby and Rosy's intricate schemes? Sending Billy to sabotage her shot at shining bright? Everything seemed so obviously calculated, as Lily had long grasped the formula behind the way their brains worked. She knew better than to let her happy ending fall into their nasty hands this time around.

As the rehearsals resumed, the initial excitement that had once danced in Lily's heart seemed to fade, leaving behind a lacklustre triumph. The atmosphere in the theatre grew tense as D-day approached, and Lily's disdain for Billy only intensified.

However, there was an enigmatic quality to him that left Lily pondering, and she decided to investigate it. It was about how he took his role very seriously and showed no signs of malicious intent. It was as if he knew how to handle her hatred with a gentle touch, much like a caring boyfriend calming his upset girlfriend.

Lily sensed that Billy was trying to smooth things over with her. She then remembered a rumour from first grade, which had become well-known in her class. It involved an unsent love letter from him to her, which Derby had intercepted and made fun of before it could be delivered.

As time had gone by, Lily wondered what kind of love story Billy had intended to write. Was it a tale of forbidden love, restricted by his allegiance to Derby as his right-hand man? Or perhaps Billy envisioned a tale of 'enemies to lovers', where a bully harbours affection for his target, mistaking intimidation for intimacy. Or was it a story of heroic love he aspired to, outing Derby's plan to her at camp?

Lily wasn't sure about his perspective, but to her, it was a story of unrequited love where she saw herself both as the object of affection and the antagonist who obstructed that love.

In subsequent rehearsal sessions, Billy embraced his role with a seriousness that appeared more genuine.

When Miss Van der Mey urged him to allow his Prince Charming persona to come out, he became undeniably professional. And in the romantic scenes, he embodied the essence of a lover very well. Lily wouldn't admit it directly, but he was nailing his performance. She remained on high alert; wary and maintaining her distance from him.

They were meant to practise a tender kissing scene— one that had the whole school excited. The school had stringent rules forbidding any physical contact between the students. Lily wasn't particularly invested in a kissing scene with the lipless Billy. She just couldn't imagine living with the aftertaste; she'd go on a hunger strike for a few days after it.

In view of the school's disciplinary constraints, Miss Van der Mey made the decision to replace the romantic kiss with a gentle kiss on the forehead.

'ACTION!'

Lily assumed Billy understood what they had to do, so she didn't ask just to make sure. Playing Snow White slumbering in the glass coffin, Lily tried to ease her nerves despite the unsettling discomfort gnawing at her soul, knowing that Billy's face was hovering just inches from hers. She attempted to soothe her racing heart, trying to mimic the calmness of a corpse. She convinced herself that a simple kiss on the forehead could do no harm.

But Billy was a notorious rebel. In a rash decision, he leaned in and pressed his lips against hers, totally ignoring the boundary set by the director and the school.

A few tense and nauseating seconds ensued, as Lily was left shocked and disgusted. She pushed him away, her cheeks flushed with anger and embarrassment. Her screams and curses echoed throughout the theatre.

'So . . . so sorry,' Billy stammered, appearing sheepish, but his apology gave no comfort to Lily.

'Did you even read the assignment?!' She felt violated and humiliated, her rage bubbling like a nuclear reaction.

'I—I just thought it might be cooler if—if I kissed you on the lips, just like in the original story,' Billy stuttered, attempting to justify his actions. 'I did it for the show, you know? For a better scene.'

'Better scene? Your stupid idea doesn't fix anything about the scene, you dumbass!' Lily's fury erupted like a splitting nucleus. 'Geez, I hate you so much!'

Unable to restrain her emotions any longer, Lily fled to the nearest restroom. Tears streamed down her face as she emptied the contents of her stomach into the toilet bowl. The water splashed, soaking her shirt; the taste of that unexpected and repulsive kiss clung to her mouth, haunting her.

There was a knock on the bathroom door, Miss Van der Mey's concerned voice was on the other side. 'Everything okay?'

'I think I'm done with today's rehearsal. I need time to collect myself,' Lily replied.

'No probs. We can continue in the next session,' the teacher responded, oblivious to the turmoil and how it had shattered Lily's world. Her steps receded before approaching once more. 'Lily . . . I'm not sure what happened, but if it was Billy, I'll make sure to tell him off, all right? I'll ensure he's fully grasped the script. If you need anything, I'm always here.'

Even Lily was unsure of her capacity to rebuild her broken world. It was as if she wasn't sure there existed a strong enough force to enable her to keep her commitment to finish the rehearsals and deliver on the performance.

A glimmer of hope emerged, a notion that changing her shabby, water-soaked clothes might help. So Lily made her way to the locker room. As she stepped inside, silence enveloped her like a comforting cocoon. No ear-piercing screams from the girls. No gut-wrenching gossip. She felt at peace in her solitude and allowed her mind to unwind after the storm.

In the dimly lit locker room, she carefully removed her clothes, placing them neatly in her designated cubicle. She traded them for a soft, pastel polo shirt that smelled like a fresh tangerine, feeling the cool fabric against her skin. The room seemed undisturbed by her presence, and she reminded herself that there was no need to hurry. But she noticed a growing restlessness in her body, which urged her to leave the room immediately, forgetting to button her collar.

She usually arranged her things as neatly as possible in her locker, but this time she let them fall hither and thither. A peculiar sensation crept over her.

*Those blue peepers again!*

She was struck with panic and terror once more. Glowing like ethereal orbs, the pair of eyes seemed to watch her from somewhere off her radar. Her instincts kicked in, and she glanced around; there was no one in sight. The eyes were nowhere to be seen, but the gaze lingered like an unsettling memory.

A sudden noise echoed through the room, resembling the rusty squeak of an old iron gate. It hadn't come from her locker; she was certain of that. It was coming from a far-off corner, where the old and unused lockers resided. They lay there almost forgotten, hidden away in the shadows.

The door to one of them was slightly ajar, like an invitation to peek into the darkness within.

Curiosity mingled with unease. Part of Lily wanted to ignore the strange sound and move on, but an inexplicable pull drew her closer to the enigmatic locker. So, she approached it slowly; with each step, the squeaking sound grew louder, seemingly coaxing her to unveil the mystery within. Hesitantly, she reached out for the locker door, her fingers brushing against the cold metal. She contemplated leaving, but it was too late.

Gently pushing the door, she peered inside only to find forgotten baseball gear. The musty smell inside made her nose scrunch.

Another squeaking sound! It was even louder this time, almost like a growl. It jolted her awake as if she was falling asleep and dreaming about falling. This time, it wasn't coming from the locker Lily was examining, or even from that room; it was coming from outside.

Driven by her curiosity, she left the room to investigate the mysterious sound. The hallway was disturbingly quiet, its stark white walls made almost blindingly bright by the dazzling lights. Across from the girls' locker room, where the boys' locker room had once stood before being relocated to another building, there was now empty space. So the hallway comprised the doors to the girls' locker room, toilets, a physics lab, the empty room, and a large room serving as the school's auditorium.

The sound echoed again, and the lights flickered in response. Lily walked cautiously down the hallway, each step deliberate. As she approached the auditorium, the sound grew louder. She paused momentarily before slowly pushing the door open.

What greeted her on the other side was a scene that far surpassed anything she could have anticipated: a dynamic 3D action display, except the holograms were material beings and the unfolding scenario was unscripted and real. As if she had arrived right at the story's climax, she watched a boy being violently hurled backwards, as if in a car crash. He flew for three metres before collapsing onto the stage. Lily could hear his bones crack. He tried to get up, but everything was a blur, and she could see he was struggling to breathe.

Lily approached the boy to help, suddenly realizing the figure was Billy.

'I'm sorry, Lily! I'm sorry! I won't mess with you again, I promise! Please, just let me go!' His body lacked the strength to stand, and he was crawling on the floor.

Lily remained silent, perplexed. She had only just arrived, her hands still unstained by involvement in the altercation. She couldn't grasp the situation that was unfolding before her. She could neither grasp why Billy had remained in the room nor could she identify who he was fighting with.

But before she could process her predicament further, Billy was suddenly propelled and slammed again. The force behind it was invisible and illogical; seemingly the workings of clandestine, evil, paranormal hands. This time, he'd been hurled with even greater force, his back banging hard into the wall. Lily knew that pain was something else.

For a moment, Billy's limp body seemed lifeless, lying on the floor. His body contorted with pain as if every fibre and cavity in him had been engulfed in agony. He took

a deep breath, then exhaled with a loud, anguished moan
that changed the air of the theatre to resemble a torture
chamber. Demonic coughing choked up his throat.

But before Lily could fully grasp the situation, she
noticed that it wasn't just Billy's bones that had suffered the
brunt of this unknown force. The entire room appeared as
though it had just seen a historic battle unfold. Everything
was in complete disarray like after an earthquake. Costumes
were strewn across the floor, tangled with fallen props
and scripts, while chairs and set pieces lay toppled in
haphazard piles.

Drawn back to Billy instinctively like a dog retrieving
a stick to return to its master, Lily came and sat at his side.
Billy wriggled away from her.

'Let me help you,' Lily offered, extending her arm
towards him.

'Don't come near me, you witch, you bitch! Don't you
dare hurt me with your damn spells!' Billy swore, his words
filled with fear and anger.

*WHAT!?* 'I don't know anything about this! I swear
I didn't do this to you. Something's not right, but I don't
know what's happening!' Lily's response was innocent.

She had a hunch; a feeling that something beyond their
understanding was at play. And it turned out, she was right.

Just a few steps away behind Billy, stood the
Heartbreaker, an entity that had claimed ownership over
her as part of some metaphysical romance. His presence
stirred up the air in the room—made it heavier, charged
with an eerie energy.

The ghost dressed as a gentleman glanced at Billy with
his haunting blue eyes—and as crazy as it sounds—his body
rose, defying gravity, hovering mid-air as if hanging by an

invisible noose around his neck. Lily convinced herself that she wasn't dreaming this up; she could do nothing but watch as Billy's face grew deathly pale and the rest of his body turned as red as a rotten tomato. He started convulsing, struggling to form words, sounding like a broken radio.

Sweat glistened on his face as his breath got stuck in his throat. His eyes locked with Lily's, silently begging for mercy she couldn't provide.

'PLEASE! STOP IT!' Billy pleaded.

Lily, totally clueless, started screaming too. 'PLEASE!' she begged the Heartbreaker to put an end to the chaos, but all he did was smile smugly, like a cynical beast that had cornered its prey.

'STOP IT!' Billy repeated.

Someone outside the room knocked on the theatre room door.

'HELP!' Lily screamed.

Whether scared or only just realizing that they needed a rescue scheme, whoever was at the door, left hastily, leaving Lily and Billy inside. She thought about rushing to the door, but as soon as she took a few steps away from Billy, it felt as if the grip around him got tighter as he groaned even louder in pain. Out of options, she stayed close to Billy, making sure he stayed alive.

'HELP!' Lily shouted to anyone on the outside. 'PLEASE!' she begged the ghost. 'STOP IT!'

She was starting to give up when the door slammed open with a big bang. It made Lily's flesh crawl. But it also distracted the evil force long enough for Billy to escape from its clutches and return to the realm of normalcy, where Newton's laws governed. He dragged his body across the floor like a fallen apple.

'What in the world just happened?!' Miss Van der Mey asked as she burst into the room, her voice full of concern and confusion. In her mind, she was more worried about the mess and how she was going to explain it to the headmaster.

Billy groaned, drawing attention to his deplorable condition that needed immediate attention. His limp body and slow breath twisted the truth in a way that he appeared to be the victim and Lily, the assailant. But instead of trying to defend herself, Lily was at a loss for words. Her eyes remained wide and empty while accusatory questions were fired at her. But she knew who should be the one to explain the situation. However, as soon as she turned her attention to the man responsible, he melted into thin air without a trace.

Nobody would believe her.

She didn't want to be accused of being superstitious, but she couldn't find a rational explanation for those phantasmic blue eyes. She decided to adopt a more traumatized stance instead, because it was the only way for her to be treated as a victim in the incriminating situation.

And with that, she put away another tale of her haunting somewhere in the library of her mind, which was already full of untold sad stories.

\* \* \*

'Oh boy, what a hot mess!' Mr Verwey came upon the scene, sitting down in a chair across from Miss Van der Mey, who was typing away on her laptop. He grabbed her coffee and took a sip. 'So the kids caught wind of the drama? I bet they're going all-out for next month's big show, huh?'

'Yup,' Miss Van der Mey replied, not looking up. 'Thankfully, the props are just in disarray, not pieces.'

Mr Verwey, knitting his brows, whipped out a sheet of paper. It was filled with numbers—an estimate of the damages to the auditorium. He was supposed to show it to the headmaster. 'Let's break it down, starting with the chairs—'

'And don't forget the stage floor. Billy put a hole in it. Our carpentry whizzes made those. It's not just about the money, but the sweat and tears too,' she chimed in.

'Yes, and the ceiling too. Fixing it won't be cheap. Oh, and the curtains!' he gasped. 'Those are no ordinary curtains. Fireproof stuff. Those'll cost an arm and a leg to replace.'

Miss Van der Mey had stopped paying attention a while ago. She felt bad for Mr Verwey; he looked so stressed out. She sighed, 'Insurance might help, but it won't cover everything. We gotta get creative, like maybe organize a fundraiser or something.'

'That has been considered,' he finally put the paper down and rubbed his face. 'I can't believe Lily and Billy turned the place upside down. How did that even happen?'

'Are you saying they're to blame?' she paused, her fingers hovering over her keyboard as she turned to look at him with a mix of curiosity and concern.

'Well, I'm on the fence,' he scratched his head, looking genuinely perplexed. 'That level of chaos? It's like an earthquake hit, but that's no excuse here. If you ask me, I'd bet one or both of them played a part. But honestly, it's hard to believe they could wreak such havoc, like a mini natural disaster.'

Miss Van der Mey nodded thoughtfully, absorbing his words. 'This is a tricky one, for sure. But remember, finding the truth isn't just about pointing fingers. It's more about understanding the whole picture.' She leaned back in her chair, recalling a favourite quote of hers. 'Like Stephen R. Covey said, "Seek first to understand, then to be understood."'

'So what's your take?' Mr Verwey's expression softened as he considered her words.

'Well, we need to approach this with empathy, looking at the whole situation. It's not about blame but about understanding and learning from what happened.'

'But if there was no one at fault, how do we explain all this mess?'

'I'm still on the fence too.' Miss Van der Mey sighed, her gaze drifting off as she recounted the scene. 'When I first found out what had happened, there was this loud bang from Corridor B followed by screaming. Then, when I went to check, the place was already a wreck. Lily looked terrified, and Billy . . . the poor kid had fainted.'

'And?' Mr Verwey urged, his eyes eager for more information.

'So, I need to dig deeper. Hear their sides of the story from Lily and Billy.' She looked down, frowning slightly. 'But it's turning out to be more complex than I thought.'

'So what have you found out so far?'

'Still a big mystery right now. Billy's been out cold for three days,' she shared, her voice tinged with worry. She looked down, recalling the unsettling details. 'He was freaking out in his sleep, yelling, "I'm sorry Lily! Stop, Lily!

Don't kill me, Lily!" Then, this morning, his mom called me, saying he woke up last night. But he was even more of a mess than before, rambling on about how she's a witch and she's put some evil spell on him for kissing her, making her mad and now she's out to get him.'

'Wait . . . They kissed?' his eyes widened in surprise.

'In the play, Snow White and Prince Charming kissed. I'd changed it to a forehead kiss, but Billy went for her lips instead. Said he forgot, had only skimmed through the script.' She sighed.

'So what about his parents?' he asked, his concern evident.

'His mom's got a cool head, so she's handling it better. But his dad's all worked up, insistent on seeing Lily. I'm doing everything I can to avoid that. Lily's been through a lot lately. And things only seem to be getting tougher for her, I'm afraid.'

'So what did you get from Lily's side?'

She sighed, frustration creeping into her voice. 'Well, what else? She's been totally silent, won't say a word.'

'Ah, that kid is quiet, right?' Mr Verwey nodded, a slight smirk appearing despite the gravity of the situation. 'One won't shut up, the other won't open up.'

'Exactly, that's how it is.'

'I tried reaching out to Lily's mom. Like you mentioned, she's super busy, didn't even answer my text. So, I called this Toby guy, her relative, right?' He leaned back in his chair, 'But instead, he started giving me this lecture about how it's all because of some evil spirit in the school, blaming it on us for not teaching kids enough about spiritual stuff.'

'He's not very helpful. I have learned that from Lily,' she said, leaning forward, wearing a frown. 'By the way, have you checked the CCTV footage of the incident?'

'That's also damaged. But there's a bit, like three seconds, where Billy gets shoved hard, yet no one's visible. I'm thinking it's Lily . . . isn't it?' he scratched his head.

'You really think Lily could shove Billy that hard? The same girl who struggles with twenty push-ups in your class?' she said, raising an eyebrow in disbelief.

'Well, I mean, I did wonder that,' he admitted, shrugging slightly.

'Like I said, think about other perspectives,' she shook her head. 'There wasn't an earthquake, but remember the last time they checked and fixed up the auditorium? It was . . . oh man, last year!'

'So a technical glitch, maybe?'

'Possibly,' she nodded, her eyes narrowing in thought. 'Something could've fallen. Maybe that freaked Billy out too much and made him jump and crash like he did in the video because . . .'

She stopped suddenly. Mr Verwey was about to interrupt her, but he shut his mouth immediately. They each got lost in their own deductions.

'Because think about it—in the last hour of rehearsal, Lily had already left for the locker room. It was just Billy in the auditorium, all by himself. I'd asked him to stay back to really get into the script,' her voice finally cut through the silence, steady and certain.

'Then?'

'So here's my guess. At the time of the incident, Billy was alone in the room. Then, Lily, hearing the noise, headed to the auditorium and found it all chaotic, and Billy hurt. Maybe Billy, being half out of it, didn't even realize Lily had just come in. He pointed the finger at her, claiming she's got supernatural powers and was punishing him for the kiss. I say this because Billy's always been jittery about mystical stuff—he once wrote a poem about a ghost lady living in a tree at his grandma's house. And Lily, she's so tender-hearted, she must've been really hurt by his accusation.' Her expression grew more intense, as if she was visualizing the scene in her mind.

'Sounds pretty plausible,' he nodded thoughtfully.

'I thought so too, but this morning, something made me rethink everything,' she said, her voice trailing off a bit.

Curiosity flickered in his eyes as he leaned forward. 'Why? What changed your mind?'

Miss Van der Mey looked thoughtful. 'My theory is missing one thing: Lily's perspective.'

'You mentioned she's hard to talk to, right?' Mr Verwey enquired.

'I did. But then it hit me. She might not open up face-to-face, but her poetry—it's deep and full of her innermost thoughts and feelings. That's how we can understand her.'

'That's kind of unusual. But I've come across cases similar to Lily's. Trauma can silence people, yet they express so much through their art, like paintings or sculptures.'

'Exactly. I think that's how Lily works. And here's my approach, don't laugh. I assigned her a "punishment". Told her to write a poem about the incident. It's not really a burden for her,' she said, a hint of a smile on her lips.

He chuckled softly. 'And? Did it work?'

'It did, surprisingly. She accepted the punishment. It's been five days since her leave. I spoke with her yesterday and she emailed me the poem. It's untitled,' she continued.

'Can I see it? It won't go over my head, will it?' he asked, half joking.

'The poem's long but straightforward; no complex metaphors or anything,' Miss Van der Mey reassured.

'That's good to hear.'

'But I haven't had enough time to fully digest it—she just sent it this morning. There's a part I can't quite grasp,' she frowned slightly.

'What's that?'

'It's about someone she mentions in the poem. Seems like this person was there at the time.'

'But you said it was just Lily and Billy, right?'

'I thought so too. Everything was falling apart, and I swear it was only them. But the poem even says Billy didn't see this person,' she replied, her tone laced with confusion.

'That's . . . so odd. I'd like to see the poem for myself.'

'I've sent it to you already.'

### (no title)

In the quiet of Toby's car ride, through streets full of hidden stories,
it was eerily calm, like a half-forgotten dream at night.
They told him about my dance with mischievous shadows at school,
but his holy verses couldn't reach me anymore.
He gave me a prayer note, his last piece of advice, his final try.
He dropped me, then, his car quickly disappeared at the crossroads.

Silence came back, an old friend, and his prayer note quickly left my mind.

It talked about changing, a heartfelt request, 'Open your heart,' but to whom?

I was deep in thought, trying to figure out why I needed to change.

I'm sure I'm not at fault, I don't see any problems in me.

Just blame those annoying kids, their tricks, their mess, their loud games.

Also the school, the rules, they're all in my thoughts.

Toby, always praying, and even Mom, with her digital love.

I keep thinking hard, trying to find the real reason, a hard truth to face.

I end up thinking it's the world's fault, with all its issues. Why should I bother trying?

In this big web of blame, it's always someone else, never me!


But when I'm in my deepest loneliness,

my problems point their finger at me, declaring I'm the problem.


I always sought peace when I was under the big oak tree, the one near the Lonely House.

Its branches spreading wide. There, one branch held a rope, tied to a tire.

In the quiet of a forest somewhere in Western Europe, I found a swing.

This swing moved gently with the wind, like a calming lullaby, matching the beat of my heart, stuck between past memories and future hopes.

I should have been in my classroom, not alone on this swing.

But fate, in a weird way, put me in this spot, hanging mid-air.

My story, hidden in the dark, was twisted by others.

They made me out to be the bad guy in a story where I had no fair chance.

Wrongly blamed for causing trouble, an easy target for others.

The real trouble came from Billy, lost in his own world, saying harmful things.

He spread rumours about me being a witch, a bitch in the night,

using dark magic, hurting others without even touching them.

His crazy stories painted me in a really bad light.


But in the end, Billy was the one called crazy,
not me.

I heard Billy was thought to be crazy for his strange stories, but if you listen to me, I can tell you the real story behind his confusing tales.

'He says it's madness,' I'll tell you, 'but Billy never saw *him*, it's true,'

I saw what Billy couldn't—a face moon-bright, eyes deep blue.

Billy, in a dance of horror, floated and then was slammed, his neck in a ghostly grip; I stood back, my hands unclamped.

I'm not strong, don't look at me, I'm not the one to blame,
I saw the real culprit's hand, around Billy's neck, a wicked game.

That hand, oh, it was a sight, black magic coursing through its veins,

but the horror peaked when *he* smiled at me, a memory that forever remains.

Billy's screams echoed mine, in a duet of terror and despair,

both of us helpless, yet only he was seen, it seemed so unfair.

And when the world saw Billy as a victim, a question burned within me,

should I bear the cross of guilt, let myself be the scapegoat, set him free?

Then, a sudden explosion, a door blasted open, I was left alone with doubt,

questions stormed in me, but I couldn't bring myself to talk about that eerie smile.


Yet . . . in that haunting smile, there lies another angle, a twist,

a secret that changes everything for me, a mystery hidden in the fog.


It all started in a place that felt unreal and scary,
on the edge of a cliff, where it's hard to tell life from death.
There, I met *him*.
But my own life, as dark as it may seem, was just as close to the edge.

People call me the 'look-at-me girl', so go ahead and stare into my eyes.

I've always wanted attention, love, something I never got from my distant mom,

so, they call me 'look-at-me girl', and I find myself under *his* watchful eyes.

Then the days turned to surveillance, eyes on me, like a wizard watching keenly.

*He* watched me in ways I never realized, *his* gaze subtle, *his* eyes the deepest blue, holding stories untold.

But it was during that scary moment, in the middle of the school auditorium falling apart,

I noticed those magical eyes, so deep and mysterious.

In *his* ghostly look, I found a tenderness I didn't expect, a rare kind of safety, making what was once spooky feel comforting.

What used to scare me, now feels like a sign of deep care, *his* ghostly presence fills the emptiness in a world where I often feel ignored.

*His* strange but meaningful gaze made me feel truly seen, not as a scary flower but as a lily, beautiful and holy.

So let's talk about what went down in the school auditorium.

It's just *him* and me, in our own world, invisible to everyone else.

The way *he* dealt with Billy, with a ghostly hand, majestic and unseen,

a strength offered to me, no need for words, just to be accepted.

*He* showed me that true bravery often comes in the most unexpected, transparent forms.

Billy got what he deserved, something I always thought those troublemakers needed.

*He* taught Billy how sorry he'd be, from beyond the realm of the living,

a deeper lesson in respect, more meaningful than anything classrooms can teach.

*He* made it clear to Billy that every bad thing you do comes back to haunt you.

*He* showed Billy that even if teachers don't always fix things,

there's always a way for karma to find the bad kids.

So, Billy decided to back off and promised to stay away from me.

Billy now gets it, justice has many forms, some ghostly, some holy,

leastwise one parasite has been insecticided, and the rest are on the loose.

They should understand this lesson too; one for everyone to learn.


Today, my mom finally gave me a call,

she usually does that when I mess up at school.


So, should I keep messing up just to get her attention?

To make her show she cares about me?

But our phone calls are always the same,

she asks how I am,

I say I'm not doing great.

Then, she says things will get back to normal.

She thinks I'm strong enough to handle it.
Then, to check on me, she asks for a picture of me.
I fake a smile for her.
And somehow, I pull it off really well.
But this time, Mom noticed something was off.
Not with my smile but with someone else's smile in the picture.
That can't be right, I thought!
My pictures always make me look lonely and by myself.

In the photo, there's me standing,
standing behind me, there's a man.

*He*'s tall,
*he*'s warm,
gentlemanly in *his* looks,
bold in manner.
The photo's inviting, the setting cozy with natural light,
and the man is shining and fitting in perfectly.
*He*'s almost see-through; like you can see the background through *him*,
hardly noticeable at first, kind of blending into it.
It is as if *he* isn't a solid object,
 translucent figure, *his* existence is an apparition!
I look at myself a little longer, and she looks back at me.
I find a calmness in those eyes that I have never found,
In *his* ghostly embrace, my heart learns a new rhythm,
one where fear dances away and love takes its place.

*He* is standing behind me, and it made me understand,
that the *deepest love stories* are often the ones that most people can't see.

# Chapter 6

## November

"'... I know," said November. He was pale and thin
lipped. He helped October out of the wooden chair.
"I like your stories. Mine are always too dark."
"I don't think so," said October. "It's just that your
nights are longer and you aren't as warm."'

—Neil Gaiman, *M Is for Magic*

The violet-coloured stage curtain hung flawlessly from the
ceiling to the floor, concealing everything, offering nothing.

Its cryptic hue exuded a nerve-racking aura, sending
those who dared to gaze upon it into a delirium. The theatre's
atmosphere felt frenzied. The dim light casting a silhouette
of Lily who stood frozen behind it; nervousness gripped
her in its icy hand. She felt butterflies in her stomach.
The minutes before the show began felt like an eternity.
Anticipation weighed on her like a dark, suffocating cloud.
She fought to maintain the fortress of her bladder while
her brow turned into a waterfall of sweat.

Lily peered through the partially open curtains. The audience appeared as a sea of murky figures taking their seats, which were lined up like rows of tombstones in an old cemetery; they were indistinguishable and faceless. Each person, each face, seemed ready to judge, silently waiting to react to any mistake she might make.

But this time, she would get the last laugh and, you best believe, it would be vindictive and pleased. She was there to claim victory. She could feel it. So, before those cynical faces could drag her down to the hell of losers and clowns, Lily's determination burned brighter, dispelling all doubts and scorn aimed at her.

Tonight, she was the star. She was the new queen of the garden. And she was ready to rightfully claim her crown and throne, ending the previous era of tyranny and dishonesty. She was so ready that she, strangely enough, easily spotted something 'Rosy' among this grey and hazy audience. The queen bee had arrived.

Lily's lips should've curled into a victorious smile, right? But she noticed how, seconds before her downfall, Rosy still had the audacity to don that mask of condescension and contempt she always wore. It was as if she was certain that the curtain concealed nothing more than a pitiful girl with crumbling confidence. Rosy was pretending like she didn't wish she had been the one to play Lily's part. It didn't exactly discourage Lily. She took the pain to cheer herself on. It merely enraged Lily to see Rosy's pretence.

It was almost like Lily's hatred for Rosy was consuming her, shutting out the world around her. Her pupils, laser-focused, were aimed at Rosy like dots on a dartboard. She analysed every move, every behaviour of her bully, vowing never to fall for her tricks again.

Clutched tightly in Rosy's hand was a red apple, its skin marked with a violent bite. With curved lips, she chewed on it. Her smile oozed mercilessness. Lily couldn't decipher the implication. But the sight of that same guise on her face, the one she had worn when scheming a nasty, bloody plot against her, sent shivers down her spine.

It was an omen, a sign that this day would bring nothing but misfortune. A thousand questions raced through Lily's mind in mere seconds, but answers eluded her.

However, locked within her mind, where forced idealism clashed with haunting doubt, she thought it was probably safe to say there was no room for Rosy to ruin her moment this time. The mounting pressure forced her to direct her gaze towards an empty seat in the front row to regain focus.

At least for most people, it appeared to be an empty seat. But Lily's keen eyes caught a glimmer; a translucent figure sitting there. The Heartbreaker. He was dressed so fancy, he was right out of fantasy. Among the sea of uncivilized spectators, it was him and him alone who sat in waiting to watch the play like a Victorian English gentleman. A smile adorned his face: his gentle allure had now melted her heart, and she adored his romantic mystique.

His warm gaze served as a legendary sword, piercing through her anxiety. As Lily's eyes met his, it was like words of encouragement resonated from deep within her soul. It was as if his spirit reached out, intertwining with hers, steadying her trembling hands and calming her frantic heartbeat. It infused her spirit with a confidence she had never known—a sweet consolation she had never found in the physical world.

His transcendental presence smoothed her movements and loosened her tongue. Her newfound confidence became a shield against the piercing barbs of criticism that the audience would direct towards her at the smallest slip-up. The confidence made the fear of being perceived and judged as a failure vanish like fog under the morning sun. She no longer felt like a lamb to the slaughter for the audience's pleasure but rather, she felt the stage was like an altar for a ritual in honour of her superlunary lover.

Miss Van der Mey's voice called Lily back from her daydreams to give her a few last words of encouragement. The stage manager's bell rang; this meant that the door to the new world was about to swing open.

With a few tweaks to her posture, Lily looked like every young girl's dream in her Snow White dress. She took a deep breath to calm herself. Her nerves were making her hands sweat. She felt a mix of joy and fear as the curtain was raised. The lights illuminated a bright path for her to walk along. She stepped into the spotlight and the loud cheers made her feel better. She began to sing Adriana Caselotti and Harry Stockwell's 'I'm Wishing / One Song'—the signature soundtrack of Disney's *Snow White and the Seven Dwarfs*.

Snow White sang, 'Wishing for the one she loved to find her.'

Lily's heart swelled with emotion. Her voice carried the weight of a thousand dreams; her forlorn longing on display for everyone to finally see. With each tender note of the song, she poured her hope and ambition into the melody. It soared like a songbird in flight. She was most delightfully surprised when the audience broke into the song; she'd never dared to hope the crowd would sing along with her.

She twirled gracefully in her dress. It stirred up a whirlpool that overturned the world that used to hate her, and they gave into the clutches of her awesome spell. Envious whispers turned to euphony, while scepticism morphed into praise. Tomorrow, Lily's name would ring as an upbeat echo through the school hallways, mending her reputation and fuelling many a conversation.

But she no longer felt sick about pursuing their approval. All she did now, she did for *his* pleasure. Amid the rapt onlookers, her focus was solely on the one person who blurred the world around her. She sang exclusively for him.

Living in a world of restraint and repression, she found solace in the song's verses. They reflected her longing for liberation from the bonds of her mundane existence. She envisioned a prince from a faraway realm who could break the barrier spells and rescue her. She felt the promise of a magical union with the man who fixed his stare upon her in that empty seat with every heartfelt note.

Snow White finished the song, 'Wishing someday, my prince will come.'

In her reverie, she yearned for him to be the one, the Heartbreaker, the prince who would lift the veil of her enchantment, freeing her spirit to soar across the realms of fantasy.

The Evil Queen entered. Pretending to be a common old woman, she sweetly extended a special apple towards Snow White, who curiously reached out to accept it with gratitude.

Lily took the apple. A ripple of unease gnawed at her gut. The fruit's surface glistened, but beneath the vibrant hue, there seemed to be lurking an uncanny pallor that pulsed with an unnatural energy. The atmosphere changed, and goosebumps erupted along her spine as she held the apple in her palm. Its presence felt off. At this point, Lily desperately wanted to stop the pretence, run away, but the show must go on or the audience would never forgive her. They were thoughtlessly unaware of the real-life wicked undercurrents. Lily's fingers brushed against the fruit's spookily cool skin—its hidden venom  making a shiver run down Lily's spine.

The Evil Queen slyly proclaimed, 'It is a magical apple that can make dreams come true.' Snow White, intrigued by the promise, marvelled at the prospect.

She was expected to bite into the apple soon after, and everybody knew that; everybody was waiting for it. But Lily hesitated, deliberating her next move. She felt a raw, natural, and unscripted confusion for which she undoubtedly deserved an award. Just in that one scene, she was the best Snow White.

The audience grew restless. Snow White was such a predictable tale, it was cliché, and everyone already knew how the story ends. But they expected her to conclude the scene quickly, creating loads of pressure. She raised the fruit to her lips. She held her breath and took a bite.

*For real?* It turned out that Lily should've just gone with the flow of the scene. She had clearly been overthinking. But her hesitation had come across as her mastery in acting that near-death scenario.

Suddenly, Lily was anguished and tormented; she could smell the dreadful, sulphurous odour of hell. Her body convulsed, and she began to writhe on the floor.

When Lily had been six years old, she had a strange interest in watching worms wriggle when salt was sprinkled on them. And here she was, dancing the same dance of suffering, oscillating between unbearable agony and fierce resistance. It left the audience stunned, how Lily was capable of making their blood run cold.

Every inhale seemed to sap the life out of her for real. But with each exhale, she breathed new life into her character, mirroring Snow White's harrowing realization of doom, as if Lily herself was doomed. The stage beneath her was as icy as a frozen lake's surface yet her blood was boiling with such rage that she didn't shiver.

Her right to form coherent words was seemingly gone. They came out twisted like the words of some terrible spell ensnaring the audience, compelling them to recognize and empathize with her character's desperate fight—or maybe Lily's own misfortune, she was not sure. She puffed and panted. The audience's awestruck silence only intensified her agony.

Her once luminous look now dulled. Even the stage lights couldn't illuminate it well enough. As the poison's grip tightened, it caused her body to convulse in unusual synchronization with her fading heartbeat.

Her performance flowed seamlessly. Lily herself didn't know which world she was in right now. Uncertain whether she had immersed herself too deeply in her role or if the spirit of Snow White herself had taken hold of her, but the pain she was facing, SHE WAS NOT FAKING.

The poisoned apple had been no stage prop. It really was pushing her to the edge.

An overwhelming sense of disgust kicked her in the stomach. She threw up the pieces of the apple in a nauseating rush. As if this wasn't enough, the rotten pieces of fruit were covered in blood!

The people watching stayed stock-still, not out of empathy or concern but sheer astonishment as Lily seemed to put her *soul* into this play.

But soon, they erupted into synchronized applause; they viewed her tragedy merely as entertainment. Unhelpful homage drifted through the air. Howling ovations ensued:

'What an absolutely breathtaking performance!'

'You left us speechless, Lily!'

'I didn't know Lily was so talented. She is the star of tonight's show.'

'What an extraordinary performance, Lily!'

'Staggering! You truly embodied the character with brilliance.'

Fate's clockwork had finally brought about Lily's long-awaited moment. The shower of compliments that she had craved with bated breath for years came down on her like rain on a parched, drought-struck earth. Her soul soaked in the long-awaited validation. She was finally the star of the show—the main character everyone would talk about at school.

However, no one had warned her about the hidden cost of this sought-after fame, a secret hidden among the congratulatory whispers. Lily had turned into a victim to her own monstrous ambition. It found her triumph to be fleeting, with no time left to contemplate celebrations. The very validation she had craved had become an unattainable burden, demanding a toll she wasn't prepared to pay.

'Well, look at that, isn't anyone shocked how well Lily actually managed to do the scene so perfectly? A true miracle, isn't it?' Praise from a voice that usually pierced her heart, pierced the air now. Her hope for this moment to arrive had been a flickering candle in a dark room, casting a glimmer of anticipation despite the long years of yearning and waiting for it. But when the moment finally arrived, it didn't make sense at all!

Or did it? The disturbing smile, the late arrival, the venomous apple, the real-life poisoning, bittersweet acknowledgement—the mastermind behind it all was, of course, Rosy—THIS WAS SABOTAGE!

Oh wow, look how stupid Lily was! She shouldn't have acted in this drama. Her life was already dramatic. She had been living in a manipulated show. Now, she found herself back in the role, trapped in a conspiracy crafted by her real-life antagonists.

This time, however, Lily was left grappling with the notion that Rosy had gone too far. Did she intend for this to be Lily's last time onstage? It's quite possible Rosy had grown accustomed to the brutality of plucking Lily's petals or humiliating her for her pistil. But Lily found it hard to believe that Rosy was now after cruelly uprooting her altogether.

Lily vividly imagined how Rosy and her accomplice, Missy, might have stealthily entered the prop storage room and swapped the prop poisoned apple with a real one! The scene played out in her head with the clarity of CCTV footage revealing the truth. It resembled a scene from a murder mystery where the culprit is exposed, and now Lily felt like she was watching her own dramatic biopic.

'Oh, bravo, Lily, bravo! Your parents must be so proud of you!' Derby celebrated. Every good gardener knows that, in the presence of beetles, the safety of the lily remains compromised.

As the poisoning scene played out, a spooky and intense melody started to fill the air: a ghostly orchestra. The mournful build-up and violent violin strains reflected the sad endings of both Lily and Snow White.

Then, the creepy music met its end in a heart-stopping way, leaving behind a deep, chilling quiet. The spotlight that had lit up the stage started to fade, throwing the murder scene into a deep darkness.

The music stopping so suddenly made it feel like even the air had stopped moving. The dark shadows in the corners started to creep out, feeling more and more solid and large every second. It made everything feel even more unsettling. The audience was stuck in a deep pit of not knowing what was coming next, every sense on high alert.

But through all this change, Lily continued to lie on the stage, which also appeared to be a crime scene. She didn't move, but something suddenly shifted, throwing a soft shadow over her.

From the unseen depths backstage, disjointed whispers echoed, calling for her return to the stage of the living scene. People watching didn't know what to make of it, seeing Lily so still or hearing these strange voices. It was creepy, they couldn't tell what was real and what was part of the play anymore.

Then, out of the dim light, Miss Van der Mey appeared. She looked worried as she walked carefully towards Lily's still form, sprawled on the stage. Miss Van der Mey suddenly gasped as she touched Lily, who was barely moving and really cold, almost like she was dead. Miss Van der Mey got so scared that she screamed and it sent chills through everyone watching. It was so sudden and so intense, it just hung in the air and freaked everyone out.

With no light to soften the scene, some people stayed in their seats, curious and trying to guess what would happen next in the play. Others got up and left, upset at how scary it was. It seemed too real.

Miss Van der Mey's cries for medical aid reverberated through the auditorium, but they didn't have medical staff on hand. So, for a while, they let Lily's frail body lie on the stage, bathed in dim light.

In her last moments, Lily finally accepted it was really the end of her. So, she promised herself; she wouldn't let her spirit rest and would haunt them all. She promised to repay this cruel treatment by turning their nights into endless, sleepless torments—each and every one of them, one after another.

But seeking revenge upon such an extensive set of people would be a tremendous effort, even for a restless ghost. So, before she edged closer to eternal sleep, Lily wished a dark, dark wish: a massacre to take them all down.

A disaster that would go down in history as a gruesome theatrical tragedy—a 'bloody Snow White play', or 'The outrage of the bleeding Lily'.

Poised on the threshold of her semi-conscious state, Lily envisioned witnessing the total destruction of the theatre. She imagined a terrifying scene, a raging inferno, a mass murder. Should her vengeance remain unresolved, she feared her soul would be doomed to wander forever as a restless ghost.

Lily fantasized about the theatre crumbling like a fragile, paper-thin façade. She imagined objects flying through the air, as if in a mad dance, juggled, bumped, while others tumbled uproariously to the ground. She wanted to breathe in that air full of aggression. She wished to witness the theatre directing its own downfall, its every groan and crash sounding like a desperate cry for freedom. She fancied hearing their screams as if they were singing her a funeral song.

A terrifying, terrified scream. In her daydream, Lily directed a death stare towards her floral rival, the mastermind behind her death—Rosy. She deserved to die screaming.

When Lily's eyes found Rosy at her seat, she pictured Rosy experiencing the same ordeal Billy had on that rehearsal day—floating and choking to death, hanging in the air, throat constricted, breath caught, body rigid. But Lily was terrified, too terrified, to say that this bloody curse was not yet complete. The final damage should be a grim fate that almost took Billy's life.

Now, Lily's curiosity was piqued, like Pandora's, eager to unravel the mystery of how the curse ended. She had selected Rosy as the key to unlocking the misery.

Rosy suddenly coughed up blood, which splashed out with an aching squeak. The pitch of the squeak gradually mellowed, tempo slowing, yet still harrowing. There was a softer gasp as Rosy struggled for air. It took a toll on her.

In a nightmarish struggle, she fought to spit out something from within, only to be horrified as a devil plant emerged, growing uncontrollably out of her . . . throat.

The plant, defying all logic, grew at a relentless pace—its leaves unfurling, budding, then blossoming. Blossoming into, into beautiful, beautiful lilies. A bloody blossom!

Each petal opened with a sensuous allure. Their fragrance masked the tense horrors of mere seconds ago. Rosy's wide-eyed, lifeless stare spoke of her horrifying fate—transformed into a creepy pot for lilies, forever trapped in a cursed existence.

Lily flashed a deadly grin. But then, she remembered a dark, cold saying: 'If your enemy is a hive of hornets, you must kill them all. Leave even one alive, and the swarm will return with a vengeance.'

So, Lily shifted her unforgiving glare to Derby. He was sitting right where the large auditorium light was above him, and something astonishing happened! Derby seemed to float up and then suddenly crash into the lights. The blinding light reflected in his eyes before a surge of electricity coursed through his body, jolting him into a twisted, contorted deathly figure. The extermination was complete for the time being. Shadows cast by the dying light danced bizarrely. Derby's final, pitiful screams merged with the sinister crackling of his trap, creating a haunting soundscape.

Now, Lily's eyesight was growing hazy, too hazy. She hoped the mass annihilation would happen in a flash before her eyes surrendered to eternal sleep. Or it might happen right after Lily closed her eyes, so she wouldn't have to wait long for them in hell.

One last glance she reserved specifically for that empty seat. But now, she literally just saw an empty seat.

The Heartbreaker, the prince who would rescue her from the turmoil of the world whom Lily had sung about in her song, was nowhere to be found. Or had he ever really been there?

Lily was uncertain. But before Lily could ascertain the truth, absolute darkness crept around her. She was now in the grip of death.

* * *

She awoke in a dizzying haze of maelstrom, her mind mistaking reality for a dream. She didn't know if she woke up as Snow White or Lily, but the show must go on. Her cheek bore a splotch of dried blood. Her gaze was as hazy as the forest's midnight fog. Her skin was as pale as a thousand-year-old corpse. Her lips were cold. She played everything well, perfectly sincere.

Then, entered the prince. The prince planted a magical kiss upon the dying princess. It was the peak of fantasy.

A kiss that radiated warmth and life. A true love's kiss.

A fairy tale moment unfolded. The spell of her slumber was broken, awakening her from a deep sleep like Snow White. A fusion of electric energy and soothing comfort surged through her veins.

A rush of vitality crept up within her. Breath returned to her lungs and colour to her cheeks. Her eyes fluttered open, and she found herself alive once more. A soul returned to her body. Not as Snow White, but as Lily.

Fairy tales had come to life. A cheap high school play production had shifted into unscripted destiny. And the prince was neither a mere fictional character nor was he played by an actor. The prince she had always dreamed of had come to save her from a colourless forest. The prince with his horse had vanquished the Red Queen in her classroom. Her Prince Charming was the one who she had chosen. The Heartbreaker, dark fate brought them together.

Meanwhile, what she had dreamed of, he turned it into a living nightmare. It was like waking up in hell, although her world was already more torturous. The school theater had morphed into a chamber of torment. A graveyard of skeletal frames of furniture torn by hungry fire. The air was thick with acrid smoke. Walls wept soot, they turned to ashen abstract paintings. Scorched earth carpeted the floor, a wasteland of debris. Blackened beams sagged like the limbs of the damned. Heat-warped metal twisted into grotesque sculptures. Echoes of crackling flames haunted the silence.

The prince carried his princess from the ruins. Every step he took led her out of darkness. Each step he took, chrysanthemums grew.

The stage curtain fell, the end.

# Part II

## Second Semester

# Chapter 7

## December

December is the best month for romance!
Romeo and Juliet, Prince Harry and Meghan Markle,
Frank Sinatra and Barbara Marx, Pierre Curie and
Marie Skłodowska, Oscar Wilde and Constance Lloyd,
and many, many couples choose this festive
month to celebrate their love and start a new
chapter in their lives.

'I said I don't know anything! Can you please back off for now?'

'I understand this must be incredibly difficult for you. We're just trying to piece together what happened. Can you describe the sequence of events as you remember them? Anything at all could be helpful.'

'I really don't know. It's all a blur. When I woke up, everything was just ... destroyed.'

'I see. It's completely understandable, given the situation. Before the chaos, did you notice anything unusual or suspicious, even something small? Sometimes the smallest detail can lead to important insights.'

'No, nothing. I was focused on my performance. I didn't notice anything odd.'

'Okay, let's move on. Were you with anyone at the time? Any fellow actors or crew members? We're trying to account for everyone's whereabouts.'

'Yes, my fellow actors and the crew, most of them backstage waiting their turn, but I don't remember where exactly everyone was.'

'That's all right. About the incident itself, did you hear or see anything that might help identify the cause of the disaster? Any unusual sounds or disruptions?'

'I didn't hear anything unusual. Just the play, the audience . . . Then it was chaos.'

'Understood. Your reaction during such a situation is also crucial. How did you react? Did you help others or were you seeking help yourself?'

'I was also a victim. I don't know. When I realized what was happening, I was already injured.'

'I'm sorry to hear that. Thanks for letting us know about your condition. It's an important part of this interview. Have you spoken to anyone else about the incident? Any friends or family? They might remember something you shared.'

'No, I haven't talked to anyone. I don't know what to say.'

'That's perfectly fine. In your opinion, do you know of anyone who might have been involved or responsible for the disaster?'

'I really don't know. I can't imagine who would do such a thing.'

'All right. Regarding the theatre's security measures, were they in place; how did they function during the incident? Your experience might add to a critical aspect of our investigation.'

'I guess, but I don't know how effective they were.'

'That's good to know. It helps to rule out a pattern. Lastly, is there anything else, even a minor detail that you think we should know about the incident? Anything you remember could be significant.'

'Got it. No. Can I go back to sleep now?'

'Yes, you're free to go for now. Please remember, if you remember anything or if you think of something that might be relevant, let us know. We're open 24/7.'

'Yeah.'

Detective Lars discussed with his colleague the oddities he had discovered from that morning's report of the incident.

'You won't even believe it. Lily bushes growing out of the mouth of one of the victims; a teenage girl, one of the high school kids. And weirdly, the theatre caught fire right in the middle of the show, and when the fire guys showed up, the girl was in a super bad state. And get this—this morning when they did another inspection, they found a boy hanging on a large light from the theatre ceiling; he got zapped or something.' Detective Lars's phone lit up with a message revealing the identities of the two victims. The girl was Rosy, seventeen years old, and the boy was Derby, sixteen years old. They were from the same class.

\* \* \*

Chills,
      Thrills,
            Amaryllis.
December's wintry chills,
and the thrills of the foggy forest,
amaryllis unfurled when everything else was hibernating.


There, I saw him,
the lone star when everything else was fading.
Still with the serial terror of those blue eyes,
which should have made me
cower,
      shiver,
            lose my mind.
But now I dared to meet his gaze for longer.
This wasn't mere bravery, I supposed.
This was now
      obsession,
            adoration,
                  possession.
That pair of eyes was a sincere witness,
the supernatural spy was a secret admirer,
now I knew the feeling of my essence,
once always shunned, now finally seen.


That silent gaze told me like a revelation,
'Fear not the light that blinds your reason!'
And that's how I found my courage.

He was the light,
a beacon that dissolved
    the shadows of solitude,
            the oppressive twilight,
that once eclipsed my life.

He stood there,
    he stood before me.
            He stood as if he was the proud gardener,
who banished the pests from my domain,
the vicious cycle of predation,
the rivalry that plagued my garden.

In his oasis,
my floral soul found solace and calm,
an environment where
I,
    a budding lily,


                        I
could flourish in unbridled beauty.

Now shall we talk about his touch?
It was paranormal.
    It was chilling.
            It was mischievous.
But that night, as I performed a death-defying act,
risking my life just to play the role of a sacrificial lamb,
I believed I had fallen into the clutches of a soul reaper,
instead, I was cradled by his arms, rescuing me from a
tragic fate.

That fateful night changed the course of my thoughts.
His touch, a cold gale through my veins, once I thought,
was a fresh breeze that breathed life into my being, I was
wrong all along.
Even now, I still remember how enlivening it was to
be reborn.
A gentle zephyr whispering freedom,
    liberating me from the rose's thorns of my past,
        mending my crown, once marred by the
        bug's bites.


He came suddenly, but always at the perfect moment.
His sudden apparition should have sparked electric chills,
yet I had grown familiar with his spectral jests.
He came in with the rain that quenched the parched
earth of my heart,
nurturing my growth with each droplet of
attention,
    affection,
        acceptance.


In this forest,
carpeted with amaryllis,
blooming in undisturbed harmony,
I found my place as a white lily,
pure and holy,
among the resplendent flora.

The
    Heart
        breaker,
the misunderstood phantom of lore.
Local tales painted him a demon,
but in my book, he was written as 'angel',
his affection deep and earnest.
His gaze, a soft persuasion caressed my fears into oblivion.

Tick,
    tick,
        in a whisper of mystery, I watched his
           form fade.
Tock,
    tock,
        but I knew, this was but a prelude to our ritual
game
    of
        tag.

So, I rushed,
    buzzed,
        dashed,
each step I took drew me deeper into this enchanting forest,
leaving behind the shattered remnants of my past.
I roamed not merely the woodland paths,
but it was the rediscovery of the iron in my veins,
the compass in my heart.

These tall and proud amaryllis flowers, in their company,
I learned the importance of standing tall,
  like an oak in a storm,
    like a cedar braving the tempest.
Above, birds soared, sang, and spun,
I absorbed the essence of
a phoenix's rise,
  a released dove,
    a metamorphosed swan.
In this ethereal play of chase with him through the veils
of existence,
I discovered a world where my heart could rest from
chasing acquiescence.


Amaryllis petals, they brushed against me.
One by one, they fell out and down.
Then, they took flight,
  they floated,
    they stayed afloat.
I watched as the petals continued their gothic ballet
in the air,
they defied gravity's order!


It was a moment of intuition.
It was not a whimsical wind's prank.
Something was at play!
  Something . . .
    OTHERWORLDLY!

There, I saw him.
It was he,
    indeed he,
        who else?
He orchestrated this
illogical,
    irrational,
        unscientific deed.
But it was still unreasonable, the way my heart leaped,
like I've seen this magic trick before.
They say you shouldn't be fooled twice,
but what if I say the second time was a delightful surprise.
    No longer was I haunted,
        I was enchanted.
    No longer was I possessed,
        I was blessed.
    No longer was I damned,
        I was coaxed into paradise.

Cat and mouse had switched roles.
I chased him, he should have been wary as I had
once been.
Yet, this game without arbiters was never just.
I caught him.
I should have claimed victory.
But on the brink of a tumble as I reached for his body.
I slipped,
    I fell,
        I was deceived.

I found his entity was but
a translucent shadow,
    a phantasmal glimmer,
      a misty relic.
This game was rigged, a battle I could never win.

I fell into his arms, or so I thought,
but no plunge into warmth did I take.
Instead, I went through him,
    I pierced his very core,
      I delved into his hidden heart.
Like dawn's first light, it enfolded me,
weaving through the epochs like a traveller adrift in
time's grand loom.

Then, I landed on the bed of amaryllis.
    Lying there,
      almost fell asleep,
        I felt as if I had become one with
        the forest.

He leaned over my lying body,
body on body.
His blue eyes looked down at me,
eye to eye.
Then, everything fell,
lips on lips.
The kiss,
it felt like
    my spirit
      leaving
        my body.

It felt like I was floating on a calm sea,
>   where all my worries were just distant ripples,
>>      soothing and freeing my soul from my
>>      broken bones.
I felt like I was flying,
>   and flying,
>>      and flying,
lifted by a magic force.
The same magic that had made the petals dance
was now lifting me up!
In a whirlwind of love.

I was in the air.
>   I was in the air.
>>      I was in the air.

I had endured this witchcraft before,
and I was more like a cat flung into water.
Flailing,
>   gaping,
>>      eye-widening.
But this time, someone showed me how to do it,
like an occultist, he was,
like Jack taught Rose to 'fly' on the bow of the Titanic.
So, I closed my eyes,
and extended my arms wide.
He held me firmly around my waist
and let those extramundane energies possess me,
exorcising the burdens from my body; I felt weightless.
The wind rushed through my hair harder,
>   even harder,
>>      and harder.

And that's how I knew
my feet getting further away from land.

So, I opened my eyes.
Below me, the world was a tapestry of
red,
    green,
        and less grey.
The ship swayed, but my captain was steadfast and true.

I couldn't fathom that now, I believed in phantomic magic.
I guess renouncing the worldly and the rational was
not defiance,
but an escape, a little escape never hurt anybody.
Given the choice, I'd embrace the forbidden
paradise with him,
over returning to the inferno with them.
My mind now awakened to how sweet his love
haunted me,
    the supernatural intrusion from those blue eyes
        filled my empty jar of affection and attention,
          the spell that always numbed me,
            it felt like a warm hug.

Bit by bit, I got used to feeling weightless,
    like the lightest paper, I was
gliding through the forest,
    like Peter Pan, I was.
My arms outstretched,
    like a shark's fin cutting through the ocean's
    embrace, they were.

He followed me like a gentle breeze,
    like lovebirds chasing each other in the
      sky, we were.


Each movement was a gentle push against the air,
carrying me in a dance of freedom.
A poltergeist's dance.
A heavenly dance floor.
A divine disco ball.
I played 'Art Deco' by Lana Del Rey in my head.
Swaying,
    swinging,
      grooving.
I couldn't help but put my hands up.
Then he grabbed them and put them down.
He wouldn't let me dance alone, no.
We'd conquer the unpredictable beats together, if I just
said yes.
Spinning,
    twirling,
      whirling.


Here,
in the embrace
of his metaphysical romance,
    of his supernatural kisses,
    of his transcendental defense,
I found
    my release,
      my power,
        my grace,

an escape,
    a cure,
        a haven
            from
life's tumult,
    past's chains,
        where all my scars ceased.
In this dance above the world,
    where only spirits roam,
        the secret song sung by the living and
        the dead,
I rediscovered my truest self,
    my lost star,
        my lily's essence.

I commanded him to kiss me once more,
a kiss 10,000 feet above the ground,
the kiss that tore my very soul from my body.
He bade the wind to be still,
only leaves' whispers and birds' distant melodies.
Eyes closed, I felt his energy merge with mine,
    a fusion of new life
        and ancient scars.

This kiss was superpower,
    an interdimensional experience,
        shattering the veil of space and time.
This kiss was a clairvoyance.

I was shown a storm of emotions—
    anger,
        vengeance,
            a history of disasters.

These feelings, the familiar shadows under my bed,
whispered of a past heavy with hurt,
        a love forbidden,
                a curse borne from deep wounds.
I hovered in his arms,
        felt the weight of his pain,
                as light as a feather,
                        as sharp as a blade,
                                as bitter as mine.


He's tortured like me.
We are but mythical beings,
        This is a ghost story shrouded in a dark past,
                too fearsome for readers to grasp.
We are haunting spirits,
        injustice wouldn't let us rest in peace.
We are two vengeful ghosts,
        refusing to be dragged to our graves,
                we bring the graves to our killers.


So, I whispered promises into the wind, vows to heal.
So, I whispered promises to him,
let
        me
                love
        you
till
        all
                the
pains
        in
                your
        soul
mend.

# Chapter 8

## January

'Feeling a little blue in January is normal.'

—Marilu Henner

'Ah, here we go again . . . another semester begins.'

Time to face reality. Holiday season ending left people with many stories to be shared.

'Welcome back, everyone! I see we've all collectively decided to ignore our haircuts having gone wrong.'

'Have you met Peter? I think he grew over the break or is he just wearing taller shoes to impress us?'

'Honestly, I don't think I'm ready to handle another semester right now. I think I forgot how to write with a pen.'

'Nobody's ready, Ashley.'

'Oh hey, Susan! How was your family holiday?'

'Oh, I tried to bake a cake. It was supposed to rise . . . it didn't. Now we have a new family frisbee!'

'Well, did anyone actually try to eat it, or was it straight to the frisbee field?'

'My dad took a bite, then claimed he needed to "check his dental insurance". So, frisbee it was!'

'You think that's bad? My family went to the beach, and my brother buried himself in the sand. We forgot where he was and had to follow the sound of his snoring.'

'Oh, I got one, too! I accidentally sent a "Happy New Year!" text to Mr Bakker, our new math teacher, instead of my friend. He replied with, "New Year, new equations to solve!"'

'Has anyone seen the locker room? The lockers are painted aquamarine now. I miss when they were pink.'

'Not yet, but I've seen our principal's poster five times already, and it's still only 8 a.m.'

'I passed by the teacher's room, and most of the desks were still empty. Even Mr Verwey, the disciplinarian, hasn't arrived yet.'

'I think this semester was postponed, and they forgot to tell us.'

'Maybe we're too early. It feels like half of us have already graduated.'

'Usually this corridor is already crowded. The first day of the new semester at Bloementuin High School used to be so hectic.'

'Yeah, is it just me or is the school unusually quiet today?'

The hallways should have been echoing with the freshest rumours. But the children, this semester, wore a creepy blankness like they had learned a thing or two about stoicism over the break. Devoid of greetings or smiles, they moved with heads bowed, quickening their pace as they hurried to claim their designated seats. Meanwhile, unsolved math problems sat still on the chalkboard from last semester; there were no paper planes flying around.

That night's ill-fated theatrical performance, its horror seemed to still have a bearing on the whole school. It was like its very essence had been altered by that tragic event. A flower garden had turned into a cemetery.

'It's so weird being here. It doesn't feel right.'

'Yeah, I noticed that too. I tried to start a conversation, and everyone looked at me like I'd broken some sacred rule.'

'I walked into class, and for a second, I thought I was early. No one was talking—just eerie silence. Even Catherine the Chatty Cathy is too quiet today.'

'It's weird, right? I barely slept last night thinking about coming back to school.'

'I'm not gonna lie, it's kind of freaking me out. I keep expecting something to jump out at me. It's like I'm walking on eggshells everywhere I go.'

'Wish we had more time to process everything before starting again. I don't know how I'm supposed to concentrate on classes with all this hanging over us.'

'My boyfriend overheard someone whispering in the corridor . . . They say our school's cursed now.'

'Shhh . . . Don't talk about that!'

That night of calamity retained an iron grip on the headlines of the local news for weeks on end. Newspapers said that the school wasn't taking care of its building properly, and word on the street was that there was a ghost living inside its walls. At school, the tale became a subject shrouded in secrecy, a taboo.

'Have you noticed? No one even dares to mention that night. It's like speaking of it might bring the calamity back.'

'Yeah, ever since that night, it's like the school's lost its soul. Even the cleaning staff look afraid.'

'Remember, we're not discussing the incident in class, okay? It's best if we focus on moving forward.'

'You know what? Every time I pass the auditorium, I get chills. It's like the tragedy is still lingering there.'

'Really can't believe we have to come back here after everything that happened. Seeing everyone trying to act normal is just . . . unsettling.'

'Yeah, I hate how everyone just acts like everything is fine when it's not.'

'I heard that Timmy changed schools because he believes he's going to be the next victim.'

'Yeah, I asked my dad to transfer me too, but he said it's too late, since we're already in our second year.'

'I tried to ask my parents about it, but even they were evasive. They just said, "Focus on your studies."'

'I don't know what's going on, but do you guys feel like we're living in a horror movie where no one acknowledges the monster?'

'I guess so. I wonder if they're hiding something bigger about what happened.'

'It feels like there's this big secret they know but won't discuss.'

'Who are they?'

'Teachers.'

'I overheard some teachers saying they were instructed not to discuss it with us. It's like the whole school is under some unspoken rule not to mention it.'

'Oh, it's so frustrating! I don't know how this school is going to fix its reputation after this.'

'Do you think the school will ever be able to shake off what happened? I mean how do you repair trust after something so tragic?'

'And the worst part is the media won't let this go. It's like they want to keep the story alive. Everyone in town is talking about what happened here. It's all over the news. It's not just us who are affected; the whole community is looking at the school differently now.'

'How can they expect new students to enroll here after this? Even colleges might look at us differently now because of all the bad press.'

'I feel bad for the incoming freshmen. They didn't sign up for this.'

'Even this morning, my parents were actually hesitant to send me back because of all the negative publicity.'

'Do you think the principal has a plan to address all this bad publicity?'

'He has. Did you hear the principal is calling an exorcist? It can't be real.'

'WHAT!? No way. Does that mean the ghost rumours are actually true?'

'I thought all those ghost stories were just to scare us. This is insane.'

'If they're bringing in an exorcist, things must be worse than we thought.'

'I can't believe the principal actually believes in ghosts. This is wild.'

'What if the ghosts are real? How are we supposed to feel safe here?'

'An exorcist, though? That's like something out of a horror movie.'

'Oh God, what are our parents going to say when they hear about this?'

'I can't decide if this is terrifying or just ridiculous.'

'I've heard about haunted schools, but I never thought ours would be one of them.'

'This is going to be all over the news. Our school's reputation is doomed.'

'How can we concentrate in class knowing there might be ghosts around?'

'What if the exorcism doesn't work? What do we do then?'

'Do you think they'll let us watch the exorcism? Not that I want to see it.'

'Ah, enough with these ghost stories!'

'Yeah, I'm so tired of it. My distant cousin keeps asking me about what happened. I had to tell him I wasn't there that night because I had a fever.'

'Oh, I still remember how everything collapsed and fell apart during that performance. Believe it or not, I get goosebumps every time I think about it.'

'Everything happened so quickly, like in no more than five minutes.'

'I was sitting next to Tina. We had the best seats in the newly renovated theatre auditorium.'

'Yeah, I remember admiring how the place looked. It was so pristine and modern.'

'It all started when the scene changed, didn't it? The lights dimmed, making the whole theatre pitch dark.'

'Yeah. At that time, I was holding back from going to the toilet because I didn't want to miss the next scene.'

'Not gonna lie, the show was pretty good. I saw the curious expressions on everyone's faces. We were all waiting eagerly.'

'Agree. But then, out of nowhere, Miss Van der Mey went up on stage and suddenly shouted. It shocked everyone.'

'I remember that! But I couldn't hear what she said, but I knew something was not right on stage. It was like a chain reaction.'

'Some people got scared and immediately ran away, but others stayed, frozen in their seats.'

'Everything was happening in the dark. I remember the tension, the fear in the air.'

'I was about to leave the theatre when I heard a loud roar. The sound made glass shatter.'

'Yes, I'll never forget the roar. It was so loud, like the whole building was growling at us.'

'Suddenly, fire appeared.'

'That fire, oh my God, it spread so fast, it was terrifying. One moment everything was fine, the next it was chaos.'

'I can still see the terrifying flames in my mind. It was like a nightmare.'

'The heat of the fire and the smoke made it hard to breathe.'

'And do you remember how objects were flying everywhere afterward? I saw chairs, pieces of the ceiling, even stage props just hurtling through the air.'

'I tripped over a chair and nearly got trampled. It was so scary.'

'Eric tried to record the incident on his phone, but an object flew and hit his device.'

'I don't know about that. I just tried to escape, but people were pushing each other. It was chaos.'

'Yeah, someone fell and got stepped on in the rush. Horrible.'

'Something hit me on the shoulder. I don't even know what it was, but it hurt so much.'

'Mr Verwey was like a superhero at that time, trying to direct people out. He was so brave, but it was utter chaos.'

'And don't forget about how the ceiling collapsed several times, hitting people and causing even more panic. It felt like the walls were closing in. Everything was falling apart around us.'

'Yeah, yeah, I saw one of my friends get hit by a falling piece of the ceiling. It was terrible.'

'Yeah, people were screaming, crying, trying to find their friends and get out. Someone grabbed my hand and pulled me up. I don't even know who it was.'

'Bella told me someone handed her a wet cloth to cover her face. It helped a little.'

'The darkness made everything worse. You couldn't see where you were going or what was happening.'

'I was so scared. I could hear things crashing down all around me, but I couldn't see anything. And the smoke was getting thicker. I could barely breathe.'

'No, the worst thing is that there was debris everywhere. I saw fragments of the ceiling falling all around us.'

'Oh, I remember now! I saw one of the spotlights fall and smash into the stage. Dude! It sent shards of glass flying everywhere.'

'Yeah, that was the messiest thing, like making everything chaotic even more chaotic. But then, right at that moment, I remember the sound of sirens getting closer, but it felt like forever.'

'And when we finally got out, the fresh air felt like a miracle. Everyone was in shock. Some people were crying, others were just silent, staring. I looked around for my friends, hoping they had made it out too.'

The day after, news of the disaster had been everywhere. Headlines screamed 'tragic', 'calamitous', and 'bizarre'. Reports detailed the chaos, the panic, and the bravery. Eyewitnesses recounted the horrific scenes of fire, falling debris, and thunderous screams. Authorities confirmed the scale of the devastation, and rescue efforts continued well into the morning. Hot off the press: Two found dead.

'Have any of you heard the tragic news about Rosy and Derby?'

'Yeah, may they rest in peace. One of our best students gone. Rosy was so talented and beautiful. Her parents must be so devastated.'

'No, I mean, do you know what actually happened to them?'

'Perhaps getting hit by thrown or falling objects. It was tragic, no?'

'Rumours say it was worse than that.'

'The rumours are true. People are trying to cover up what happened to Rosy, because it's . . . terrible. You won't believe it.'

'What happened?'

'She died with her mouth wide open, and if you think that's weird, get this—flowers grew from her stomach and out of her mouth.'

'Oh my God, that's so sick.'

'We're truly doomed.'

'What about Derby?'

'The police found him hanging from a spotlight on the auditorium ceiling.'

'You know, it sounds crazy, but I saw weird things happening that night to him. Umm ... Derby was flying!'

'What do you mean?'

'It doesn't make sense to me either. I panicked and tried to run off too, but I saw Derby get thrown up, as if he was being abducted by UFO. He hit the spotlight, then got electrocuted and caught on fire.'

'That's terrifying. I think we've talked enough about this.'

'Clearly, this is all the work of something supernatural.'

'Have any of you actually seen the ghost?'

'Nope?'

'Actually ...'

'What? Go on, don't leave us hanging!'

'I didn't see the ghost, but there's something even scarier.'

'What's that?'

'Remember how Lily was the main character?'

'Yes?'

'Do any of you remember what happened to Lily?'

Lily strolled through the school hallways. It was much easier now than in the last semester. It was less clamorous and more spacious. Gone were the days that had been more energetic and enthusiastic than a catfight. The groups of students who used to block her way, just for chatting about their favourite artists, had finally learned to steer clear of her path. She used to take notice of the posters on the information wall and always wanted to read them, but they were empty now.

As usual, she felt entirely detached from everything. Her classmates frequently shifted their gazes, quickly looking away before any meaningful eye contact could be established between her and them. She felt isolated in that room full of people who seemed disinterested in her. She felt out of place once again.

While this was Lily's standard experience at school, they'd usually show disregard toward her, making her feel diminished or intimidated. However, this time, there was a scared and awkward quality in the way they avoided her gaze and looked away. To her classmates, she seemed like a ghostly character from a horror novel that no one wanted to read. Her return from the tumultuous time had lent her an almost zombie-like aura.

'Did you see Lily today?'

'I can't believe Lily's walking around like nothing happened. It's like she's come back from the dead . . .'

'I overheard someone saying Lily's a ghost now. That's why she's so quiet and keeps to herself . . .'

'I think it's fair to say that she's to blame for this havoc. Remember the last summer camp? She literally brings bad luck everywhere she goes.'

As Lily was about to turn into her classroom, she was stopped unexpectedly—that same old, familiar tune. Surprisingly, the person who stopped her wasn't one of the usuals. In the past, she had wished for this encounter many times, but in this moment, she thought it too odd.

Daffy stood in front of her, his face still carrying the warmth and charm of the daffodils he was named after. But his enchantment no longer affected Lily. To her, he was as ordinary as a wildflower in a vast meadow. He was about to say something, but other students began pouring into the classroom, signalling that the class was about to start. 'Meet me at the cafeteria at lunch,' Daffy commanded.

Lily didn't quite grasp his intention, but she didn't care. She had run out of time for contemplation as the Physics teacher appeared at the end of the hallway. Entering the classroom, she left her curiosity at the door.

But one thing that hadn't changed about school was the boredom. In fact, this semester was even duller than the last. It felt foggy and grey, Lily mused, wishing it was as bloody and chaotic as the red days of the previous semester.

It might sound crazy, but Lily started to think she was missing the verminous drama and rivalry that used to leave her in tears. Those enemies, the masters of mischief and the absence of their pranks left a silence that was more piercing than the loudest she ever screamed because of them. Lily hated to admit, but it was like they had been the seasoning, the spice, that had added flavour to her boring school life and her otherwise bland existence.

The interplay of silence and monotony caused time to feel as if it was stretching out. The air that filled the room was full of peace, not a calming serenity but more like the stillness of a graveyard. However, it didn't last long. The tranquillity was abruptly shattered. A thunderous scream from outside pierced through the stillness, a piercing cry for help.

The suddenness of the sound jolted people out of their reveries. It sent their hearts racing. Panic swept through the room like wildfire, fuelled by the terror that they still felt from their last such encounter. Everyone was in a frenzy. Everyone scrambled to their feet, their chairs scraping against the floor in a cacophony, screeching, shattering the eerie silence.

Fear was etched on every face as they desperately sought to escape the room, driven by the haunting memory of the horrific scene that had played out on that fateful night, not long ago. The trauma from that experience seemed to have resurfaced, sending shockwaves through their minds and bodies.

Amid the chaos and disarray, rumours began to run amok. Hushed whispers passed from person to person, narrowing the indoor swimming pool into the epicentre of the disturbance.

Fear and anticipation hung in the air; everyone felt both anxiety as well as curiosity. The swimming pool area—the crime scene—quickly became a hive of activity as a crowd of people thronged around it. Lily's gaze flickered with a mix of emotions as she tried to find a vantage point amid the crowd, desperate to catch a glimpse of whatever had elicited such varied reactions from people. The bloody blossom curse had struck again.

This time, lilies had sprouted out of a young boy's body. Lily didn't seem to know him—so why had the seeds of her revenge taken root in a complete stranger?

Perhaps she did not recognize the boy because his visage had been brutally disfigured, rendering it unidentifiable. His face was contorted in a desperate struggle, his eyes were wide with fear as the water's relentless grasp tightened its hold around him. His lips parted, releasing silent bubbles that rose to the surface. His cheeks flushed from the strain of the battle, his wild gaze searched for a lifeline amid the waves.

A murmur passed through the onlookers. Doubt clouded the minds of some while others were filled with sympathy and sorrow. Once more, the school found itself bereft of a shining luminary—a daffodil torn from the lively garden. The young lad was floating lifelessly in the middle of the swimming pool.

The fallen figure was Daffy.

Mr Verwey burst through the crowd, dove into the pool, and retrieved Daffy's swollen body. Sprawled along the poolside, Daffy's body looked stiff, wet, and cold. His eyes wide, his mouth wide open, lily shrubs sprouting out. The scene was frightening particularly for those under eighteen. Some left the pool room spontaneously while others were forced to leave after Mr Verwey intervened.

It had been over an hour since the cops had arrived at the scene of the crime. They couldn't move forward with their investigations until they had taken several permissions from Daffy's parents, who were still in a hurry to get to school. But they hadn't said anything about what they had found as yet. The fact that they didn't want to label the event for what it was, only made the rumours more rampant.

The curse remained a mystery wrapped in enigma—questions arose: Was this truly an accidental tragedy or was something more ominous at play? But who was the sinister culprit behind this? All the students and their mothers asked, but no fathers could figure out the answers.

Meanwhile Lily had a front-row seat to the show, she knew exactly what was happening. And guess what? The very culprit who had orchestrated the drowning was chilling in the corner of the room.

The Heartbreaker, he flashed his mesmerizing blue eyes, created a vision only Lily could decipher, a tale spun like a fairy story. Daffy had stood at the pool's edge, entranced by his own reflection, teetering on the brink of a love affair with himself, until he slipped into the depths of a drowning romance. What followed was a fate as tragic as Narcissus's.

CCTV might label it a mere accident, blaming a slippery floor, but Lily knew the truth. The pool's water, enchanted by the Heartbreaker, had cast a spell on Daffy, pulling him into a hypnotic embrace.

* * *

Lily's return from school was usually uneventful. Textbook-induced exhaustion and a solid dose of teenage angst, each shouldered a backpack full of trouble. And let's not forget the occasional jeers and jabs she got from her bullies. It made her backpack feel like a punching bag in training.

But today, her backpack felt empty. Today's class learning was not that meaningful. Meanwhile, she had graduated from the lessons taught by her bullies. She was sure she had learned something more profound than any textbook could teach.

So, as she walked home, the familiar path felt unchanged, but everything felt different. She felt lighter.

She felt weightless, as if the burdens she had carried for so long had finally been lifted.

Peace.

No, no, it wasn't just the absence of conflict. It was something deeper. It was confidence.

A sense of self forged in the fires of adversity. Lily had come to understand that the cruelty of others was a reflection of their own struggles, not a measure of her worth. Their harm had taught her more than they intended. She had learned empathy, understanding, and, most importantly, how to stand tall in the face of adversity. She had learned her lessons, and now, it was time for her bullies to learn theirs too.

She remembered the days when she would come home with tears hidden behind forced smiles. Her heart was always heavy with unspoken pain. And, at night, when she went to sleep, she'd lay in bed, staring at the ceiling, hoping she would never wake up tomorrow, only to return to the dungeon called school.

But now, she could confidently wave goodbye to those memories. The foggy days were gone. She could now see the world with clear eyes, unclouded by fear or doubt. The lessons of the past might've shaped her, but they did not define her. She was free. She was at peace, at last.

The fresh breeze hit her face, washing away the wrinkles etched by sadness. The rustling of tree branches played a song of victory, and warm air kissed her forehead in congratulations.

The warmth, Lily was sure, was not from sunlight. It was mystical, but she had grown familiar with the spine-chilling sensation it caused.

Then, that invisible warmth kissed her lips. A warm kiss, a lover's kiss. Her breath hitched, and her heart began to race.

Lily couldn't do anything; it always paralyzed her like that. So, she closed her eyes, surrendering momentarily to the surreal experience.

She reached out, her fingers brushing through the cold air, trying to grasp the kisser. But her hands met nothing but emptiness.

When she opened her eyes, she was greeted by a hiker with his husky, looking at her with raised eyebrows. The hiker's face seemed to suggest she might be crazy. Yes, she had a crazy obsession for these non-physical things that ordinary people, like that hiker, couldn't see. But dogs are sensitive to the supernatural. His husky could probably see that metaphysical love.

It wasn't the first time this astral kiss attack from another dimension had terrorized Lily. Once, when she was trying to focus on class, these invisible kisses had played across her cheek, shoulder, and neck, breaking down the fortress of her mind. No one in the class had noticed; they probably just thought she was swatting away flying insects.

Now, as the hiker moved on, this ghostly disturber was about to launch his attack again, like a blind shot. But this time, Lily decided to make it a game.

Run and hide was the game. Moving from tree to tree, she sought the strongest defense. Under the shade of an old sycamore tree, she thought she was safe. But then her neck felt warm, the baby hairs around her nape stood on end. It was alarming. She was under threat.

So, in a rush, she left that haunted wooden fort, thinking the black alder tree, with its branches almost touching the ground, would be a safer hiding place. She leaned her back against the trunk, regulating her breath and calming her racing heart. Oddly, sweat hadn't yet dripped from her forehead, but her mouth was starting to feel dry.

She tried not to move. She still wasn't moving. She couldn't move!

She was frozen in place. She thought the black alder branches were wrapping around her, but her sweater was still clean, free from wood splinters or dust. The embrace wasn't really like a snake's coil. It felt more like a hug from strong arms.

The naughty spirit framing these spooky pranks hadn't revealed himself yet. It should have spooked Lily like a ghost story and made her lose her mind, but instead, a childlike smile curved across her lips. Her flushed cheeks translated this as the most romantic story, complete with roses and guitars.

Lily mustered all her strength to break free from the mystical grasp, and for the first time, she was strong enough to unchain the spell. Her smile slid into a playful one, gesturing that she hadn't given up, that she hadn't been defeated. It was a taunt, daring him to come and get her again.

Again? Yup. These ghostly moments had slowly become the happiest seconds of her life. She ran with her heart pounding, not in fear, but in a whirlwind of excitement. She giggled.

This time, she hid behind a slender silver birch. It was her most foolish and useless defense yet. Half of her body was uncovered, and the surrounding trees were too sparse.

The wind stopped whistling.

The leaves stopped raining.

There were no signs of squirrel communities or other rodents around this silver birch grove.

The shadows returned to peace, and her breath and heartbeat flowed steadily.

Total silence.

It lasted for a fraction of a second.

The quiet unsettled her.

She might need to wait a few more seconds. But time's heartbeat had lost its tempo, and seconds felt like forever.

The last leaf fell to the ground.

Why hadn't he come and got her?

She was overwrought.

So, she stepped out of her hiding place, ready to surrender like a fatigued fugitive. She handed over her wrists to be handcuffed, turning herself in to be his hostage.

She was on edge, thinking what if he no longer wanted to play the con artist in her show?

She overthought.

What if this fantasy paradise was only temporary, and hell was eternal for her?

What if the gates between life and death had closed tight, and they were never meant to be together?

Her lips grew cold; she needed him to plant that warmth in her again.

Her sweater was no longer enough to keep her body from shivering. She needed him, just him.

She returned to that sloping black alder then that old sycamore tree, hoping he would still be there.

The sunlight fractured into delicate beams, swallowed by the gaps between the trees. Lily retraced her steps, one by one, leading her back to the path home, back to the real world.

The game was over. She had won, successfully evading the pursuit. But she would have preferred to lose if his jailhouse was her punishment; it would have been the best trophy.

* * *

Lily walked the final stretch of the trail back to the Lonely House.

Upon arrival, her curiosity was piqued when she saw a car parked there. She walked over quickly, her heart a mix of excitement and slight worry. The car was out of place in this familiar setting; it shouldn't have been there, not at this moment.

As she got closer, she became more alert. Her footsteps imitated her fast heartbeat. The car's dark windows hid its secrets. Lily looked through them, ready to discover what was inside.

But the car was empty. A familiar voice came from inside the house, solving the puzzle for her. It was her mom.

'Mom, you have no idea how long I've been waiting for this day!' Lily said as her mom ushered her into the house.

'Me too,' her mom replied, unpacking her suitcase. 'So how have things been for you, how's life been?'

Lily hesitated for a while before responding, as her mom should have already known the answer. Part of her wanted to tell her everything—all the hard stuff that had happened while she was gone. But then, she couldn't shake off the feeling that maybe her mom didn't want to talk about it, or maybe was even pretending not to know anything about it.

So, Lily painted everything her heart wanted to express on her face—frustration, sadness, and longing blending together. Her mother spoke many languages; Lily just hoped she could read this one.

'Lily, I understand that it's quite complicated, but, hey, how about we focus on the here and now? Let's talk about something a bit lighter, shall we?'

Her words hurt, feeling like she might be ignoring all Lily had been through. There was this weird mix of being happy to see her but also feeling let down. Every time they skirted around those tough topics, Lily felt more distant, wondering if things between them had changed too much.

'I'm just curious, did Toby keep his promise to look after you? Sorry for asking this question right now, I should have asked at the very beginning.' Her mom's concern was evident in her voice.

'Toby? He rarely came home after he decided to move to the rectory,' Lily replied.

'Seriously?' Her mom's voice sharpened, becoming serious all of a sudden. She stopped tidying her things, 'He wasn't chilling with you at home? So you've been doing this alone this whole time?'

'Yeah, he just came home once to check on his cat and pick up some of his stuff that he had left behind.'

'Well, I'll be darned! That must've sucked for you. Well, he's a bit strange. But I'm grateful you're strong,' her mother sighed, shaking her head.

'Yeah, I'm calmer when he isn't here, actually.'

Her mom nodded in understanding. 'I know that, I also can't stand being in the same room as him. We'd definitely argue.'

She paused, placing her empty suitcase on the cupboard with a soft thud.

'But Lily, we had no choice but to stay at his house for a bit.'

'Yes, I understand, Mom,' Lily replied, her voice expressing her acceptance of that fact.

The second wave of long pauses came and went.

'Anyways, I've been thinking about something. I think it might be a good idea if we moved.'

'Move? But Mom, I really love living here. It's familiar and comfortable for me.' Two months ago, Lily wouldn't ever have thought she'd utter those words, but now she said them with complete confidence.

'What?' Of course, her mom was surprised too. 'Can't believe you actually enjoy living out here in the middle of nowhere, Lily. Listen, sweetheart, I've been thinking about our future. This house is a bit isolated, and I worry about you being alone here when I'm at work.'

'But I can take care of myself, Mom. I've been doing just fine all this time.'

'I know you can, but I just want what's best for you. Plus, there are some safer neighbourhoods out there, and it might be good to make a fresh start.'

'I appreciate your concern, Mom, but this place means a lot to me. It's where I feel comfortable.'

'I know change can be tough, but sometimes it's necessary. And I'll be honest, I won't feel at ease knowing you're alone in this house.'

'Mom, I promise I'll be okay. I don't want to leave this house. Please understand.'

'Lily, come on! I'm trying to be a good mom here! I just want to make sure you're safe and happy. Let's at least explore our options and see if there's a place that could be just as good for us.'

'Okay, I'll think about it, but I can't make any promises. This place is my home.'

'That's all I'm asking for, sweetie. Let's consider all sides and make the best decision for both of us.'

Her mom enveloped her in a cosy hug. Lily felt the warmth of her embrace and it brought back memories of her childhood. As they stood there, in the middle of the room, the world seemed to pause for a moment. But then, her mother gently let go, stepping back with a puzzled expression.

'Holy smokes! Lily, do you smell that? It's something . . . funky,' her mother exclaimed, wrinkling her nose in apparent disgust.

'What? No, Mom, I don't smell anything weird,' Lily replied, looking around the room, trying to detect any unusual odours.

'Are you sure? Oh my, goodness gracious! It's like . . . a really strange smell,' her mother insisted, sniffing the air dramatically.

'Mom, seriously, I don't smell anything. Maybe it's just your nose playing tricks on you,' Lily suggested, slightly amused at her mother's theatrics.

'It's kind of like . . . I hate to say it, but . . . something . . . corpse-like?' her mother continued, her voice tinged with a mixture of curiosity and revulsion.

'You're not seriously thinking that I've got zombies stashed somewhere, are you, Mom?' Lily joked, trying to lighten the mood.

'Well, not exactly zombies, but you know . . . it's not like a field of roses, either,' her mother replied with a faint smile.

Lily couldn't help but defend herself, 'I promise I never skip spring cleaning.'

Without another word, her mother abruptly left the room. Lily watched as she scanned the surroundings, her gaze finally landing on a pot of tulips near the window. The tulips were a gift from her heartbreak prince. A flower language of love, but Lily had forgotten one crucial detail— her mother's aversion to the smell of tulips. Even from a distance, she could detect their distinct aroma.

In a swift motion, her mother picked up the pot and placed it outside the house. She then returned with a different pot containing carnations. As she set it down, Lily noticed the gentle look in her mother's eyes. The carnations, with their soft, ruffled edges and vibrant hues, were more than just flowers—they were a symbol of a mother's undying love; something she had always longed for.

'Well, just make sure your scent isn't strong enough to attract any zombie admirers, all right?' Mom advised.

# Chapter 9

## February

'February is a suitable month for dying. Everything around is dead, the trees black and frozen so that the appearance of green shoots two months hence seems preposterous, the ground hard and cold, the snow dirty, the winter hateful, hanging on too long.'

—Anna Quindlen, *One True Thing*

Normally, it would be transcendental fingerplay and the consequent hair-raising sensations that gently tickled her awake. Celestial handsomeness used to be her morning coffee. His mystical smile was her morning sun that greeted her each day when she first opened her eyes.

But this morning, she woke up in her usual room, and nothing more. It was unusual, like returning to reality after being lost in a long, pretty dream you never wanted to leave. The dream had been so vivid that she had adapted to the surreal, accepting it as her new normal. Now, it was strange for her to readjust to the mundane, which had once bored her. It felt more disorienting than adapting to something new, even if it was beyond normal.

She even forgot about how she had once described her room as a set piece from an old black-and-white movie, and now it felt like she had awakened in a silent film. There were everyday items everywhere, each coated with a thin layer of dust. The wallpaper sagged from the weight of nostalgia. It whispered tales of yesterdays that weren't very bright. Her bed was the sole witness to her countless dreams. It appeared worn and tired now, as if it had borne too many nightmares. The cabinet's peeled paint and dusty window frame was a silent observer. They were The Great Library of Alexandria for her sad stories

The sun was too bright, the air too humid. The light had invaded her eyes, abrupt and uninviting, jolting her awake. It clung to her skin, exposing a sheen of sweat. She blinked rapidly, her eyes adjusting with difficulty as she lay in bed, disoriented. It didn't take long for Lily to awaken fully, and when she did, a harsh reality settled over her— gone were her paranormal days, she was back to reality.

Lily had been thrust back into the very reality she had managed to escape painstakingly; a world she had feared and disliked, an old world before she came to know of magic. She replayed an old version of herself that she hated, restarting the gloomiest days of her life. She now woke up in the same room, with the same feeling—a frustrating self-hatred about why she had to wake up again, the same fatigue of having to go back to school, and the same anxiety of waiting for her mom to come.

Her heart raced as she looked around. She looked for someone to save her like her old-self used to do. Back then, she didn't know who she was crying out to, but this time she knew it was that person—it was him.

She desperately searched for that comforting, cryptic gaze that soothed her. She stooped to look under the bed, half-expecting to see those blue eyes looking back at her from amid the dust. Then, she looked into the mirror across the room. She hoped to see his ghostly body materialize, as it often did, in its ethereal form. She closed her eyes, letting her guard down, hoping his blood-curdling touch would play on her body, inducing that flying sensation, and she would be in the air when she opened them.

However, it was the darkness of her lonely past that said hello to her. It led her to believe that everything might have been just a dream and that she had been asleep much longer than she realized. She couldn't help but wonder if the Heartbreaker had just been a creation of her own twisted mind. Was he a mere figment of her imagination, conjured by her brain to make her world more interesting? Or was all this the result of her heart being too ill, creating a fake scenario of a knight who would save her life?

Her thoughts were suffocating and she needed to immediately restore the oxygen supply in her lungs. She looked out of her bedroom window. The glass surface seemed to paint the strange atmosphere outside more intensely. It added to the feeling that something unusual was happening.

Outside, the world seemed more mysterious and creepier than any ghost story Lily had ever heard. Shadows moved between the trees and the sun rays seemed to flicker. But what truly sent shivers down her spine were the figures surrounding her house. Their silhouettes appeared ghostly in the foggy morning light. They seemed like they had come from different periods in history, more precisely from the Medieval era. They were all dressed in ancient robes and moved in an eerie synchronicity, as if they were part of . . . a ritual of some sort.

*The Ghostbuster Gramps!*

The Heartbreaker wasn't just a figment of her imagination—he was real. But his absence now took on a new, more ominous meaning. The realization hit Lily harder than before—the bridge connecting her world to his was under threat of demolition. The mysterious figures outside were working to sever the connections between their two dimensions.

Lily gasped in astonishment. The sleepiness that had been clouding her mind cleared away quickly. She jumped out of bed. Her feet hit the cool floor, ready to find out what was happening and put a stop to it. Filled with a mix of curiosity and determination, Lily left her room. The doorway seemed like a gateway to the answers she was seeking, and she went through it, ready to face whatever was waiting.

Outside her room, in the early morning chill, she saw that the Ghostbuster Gramps had left behind some of their strange tools and gadgets, arranged in strange patterns, as if they were trying to set up a barrier of some sort.

Lily apparently wasn't the only one disturbed by their purification ritual. Her mother also struggled to come to terms with it. She took on the task of follow-up purification; meticulously deep-cleaning and removing the odd objects they had left in their yard. Lily went to her. 'Mom, who were they?'

'I don't really know much about them, hon. They're kind of like those annoying phone salespeople, but for ghost hunting, and the church has actually given them a legit stamp of approval,' her mom answered. 'I told them to go away, but they've made our yard into a weird ghostly playground or something. I don't even know what these things are called. It's all just so odd.'

Lily mulled over her mom's words, her silence pregnant with contemplation.

'Gosh, can you imagine?' her mom went on. 'It's strange, isn't it? Nowadays, who's really worried about ghosts playing tricks on them? We already have people who fool others without being seen—identity thieves and hackers and the like. I bet the ghosts are out of a job because of all the tricks people have been pulling with technology lately.'

A mischievous glint flashed in Lily's eyes, and she dropped a bombshell. 'Actually, I do believe in some of it.'

Her mom's eyebrows arched sharply. 'You? Believe in what?'

Lily leaned in, conspiratorially. 'I believe in you, Mom. But the mystical mumbo-jumbo, not so much.'

* * *

Today at school was another boring day, and it seemed everyone in her class agreed.

Lily sat there, waiting for her teacher to show up, looking at the clock, feeling like time was crawling by slower than ever. She looked around at her classmates, noticing how everyone was dealing with the boredom in their own way. Some were daydreaming, lost in their thoughts, while others were doodling on their notebooks.

Someone was throwing paper planes with notes saying, 'If you're reading this, send help or at least some snacks!'

But the boredom of the class seemed unbeatable, leaving Lily to wonder about one of life's great mysteries: if you fall asleep in class and the teacher isn't there, does it even count as a nap?

Just as she was about to give in to the temptation of sneaking a nap, something unusual happened. For the first time in what seemed like forever, someone unexpected walked up to her seat.

'Hey, um, Lily, can we have a moment?' Missy had walked up to Lily, her expression a mix of someone who'd just been caught doing something wrong and someone who'd seen something really scary. She looked like she had just watched a horror movie that genuinely frightened her.

'Whoa, you're talking to me? I'm flattered. I mean, when was the last time someone wanted to chat with me, right?' Lily said.

Missy looked as ordinary as a friendless student in classroom, since her usual partners in crime, Rosy and Derby, had passed away. The only companions she now had were Timmy and Billy. Well, Billy had made a vow to leave Lily's petals in peace after the little incident in the theatre while Timmy, having taken up residence in Rotterdam with his grandparents, had pleaded to switch schools.

And then there was Missy, a weathered branch of mistletoe, which no one wanted to stand under. She was the only one who had a deep understanding of horror films;

she knew these stories were all about cause and effect. She had produced and directed the ghost summoning ritual starring Lily at camp, and now in an unexpected twist, the ghost she had summoned actually reached out to her for advice. It seemed to want her help in figuring out the scariest possible ways to end what she started.

'Yeah, well, damn it . . . I know it's going to be awkward.' She didn't know how to start. 'So . . . all right. Repeat. Hey, Lily! Can I borrow your time machine for a sec?'

'My time machine?'

'Exactly! I've got some past actions I'd like to do over, and I thought a little time travel might do the trick.'

'Ah, the classic "regret rewind". What's on your list of do-overs?'

'Um, remember when I nicknamed you "Queen of Crayons" in front of the whole class?'

'Oh, how can I forget? You forever nipped my artistic talents in the bud.'

'Well, the thing is, I've realized my artistic criticism was slightly misguided. And by slightly, I mean wildly off target. Can I borrow the time machine to fix it?'

'Tempting offer, but my time machine is in the shop for an oil change.'

'Damn it! Okay, Plan B. Please, make this easy, Lily. I'm thinking of going with a good old-fashioned apology.'

'A good ol' apology? Revolutionary!'

'I'm trying to be better. But how do I do this? How do I take back what I said?'

'Step one: admit the wrongdoing. Step two: express remorse. Step three: avoid any further nickname-related incidents.'

'Got it. So, I just walk up to you and say: Hey Lily, sorry about the crayon thing. I was wrong. You're not just good with crayons; you're really great, even as a person.'

'Close, but you might want to tone it down a little. Let's keep it humble, shall we?'

'Right, right. How about: I'm sorry for the whole crayon thing. Turns out, you're a pretty cool human being. And artist.'

'That's better. Just be genuine, and you're good to go.'

'And if that doesn't work, I guess I'll have to actually build a time machine to undo calling you Queen of Crayons.'

'A solid Plan C.'

'So, you forgive me?'

Miss Van der Mey entered the classroom.

'I'll let you know right after class ends.'

The kids were all sitting at their desks. They still looked bored and uninterested. Miss Van der Mey decided to change things up. 'Ladies and gentlemen, it's time to bring out your inner poets!' she announced.

The students didn't expect what was coming next. They had to read out their poems before the class. This made everyone very nervous. Some students turned pale, and others started to sweat from the anxiety. One student tightly held onto their poem, clearly not looking forward to reading it aloud. Another seemed as if they wanted to hide, feeling very self-conscious about sharing their work.

Miss Van der Mey stood at the front of the class. She seemed completely oblivious to the students' growing reluctance. She started calling out their names and the tension rose. But Lily, sitting in her seat, was unaware that she was going to be the last student to be called upon. She had no idea that she was the closing act of this unexpected line-up.

'My poem is entitled "Did You Know That Lily Is a Poisonous Flower Too?"'

Lily stood up straight, holding onto her poem firmly. With wide eyes and raised eyebrows, some of her peers were clearly underestimating her, while others just seemed bored, still trying to look like they were paying attention. Some of the faces looked very disturbed, like they didn't know what to do or were too overwhelmed by the situation for some reason.

> In a realm where blossoms tell tales untold,
> Lily's presence shimmered, a story to behold.
> Did you know, amid the petals' soft embrace,
> her beauty hid a secret, a venomous trace?

As Lily prepared to recite the second stanza of her poem, she took a deep breath, ready to impress the class with her words but an unexpected interruption stopped her dead in her tracks. A girl sitting in the third row, wearing a cozy, oversized sweater, suddenly choked on something. The quiet attention of the classroom quickly diverted from Lily to the girl. Everyone's reaction, including Miss Van der Mey's, was that of surprise. Lily continued, hoping the girl would stop coughing soon.

> A canvas of colours, delicate and rare,
> Lily's allure, a dance of light and air.

> But beneath that façade of fragile guise,
> a paradox of poison, a hidden surprise.

The ambience in the classroom suddenly turned foreboding. The girl's choking had now turned into agonizing coughing. Her coughing, at first a mere annoyance, grew into a jarring noise that reverberated through the room. Out of nowhere, things took a turn for the worse when she started throwing up. It was quite disturbing and unsettling. The classroom swiftly transformed into a realm of pandemonium and disbelief. Students quickly moved their chairs away, trying to create some distance from the horrifying sight of the victim in front of them. Whispers of dread and confusion passed through the room.

The girl caught in the middle of all this commotion was Missy. Lily continued:

> Did you know, within her petals' grace,
> Lily wove a symphony, a dual-faced embrace.
> Her fragrance a potion of enchantment and harm,
> a melody playing both charm and alarm?

Missy's raspy spectacle transitioned into a suffocating symphony of shortness of breath. She huffed. She puffed. Lily felt a creeping sensation crawling up her spine, knowing that the next act in this bizarre production would be a grim encore of what had happened to poor Rosy.

Missy was suddenly suspended in midair, as if held in the grasp of invisible tendrils by the neck. The scene unleashed a cacophony of hysteria and frantic efforts—some students were desperately trying to break the invisible ropes that were holding Missy hostage, while others were running out of the room in fear. Amid the surreal chaos, there was Lily, continuing to recite her poetry with determination. It wasn't just about the applause anymore; it was about avoiding that dreaded F grade.

> In gardens of intrigue, she stood with pride,
> a riddle unspooling, secrets to confide.
> Did you know, beneath her floral canopy,
> Lily whispered stories, beguiling yet free?

The air grew thick with a sense of torment. And then came the grand finale. The room bore witness to the creepy bloody blossom curse again. Lilies sprouted from Missy's mouth with supernatural urgency, their stalks curving like serpentine dancers. The lily buds—an emblem of innocent beauty—erupted and bloomed with petals that cried crimson tears.

And our Lily? She continued reading her poetry. Each stanza was read out in defiance of the surreal turn of events unfolding before her—a testament to her determination to not let the final stanza slip into oblivion:

> A puzzle of petals, both tender and fierce,
> did you know her beauty held a universe?
> For Lily's tale is more than meets the eye . . .

The chaos in the classroom grew. More students rushed out, deciding it was better to leave to avoid the dangerous situation. But then, a new set of people walked in. They carried different kinds of odd tools. They made their way straight to Missy, who was still suspended in mid-air; they looked puzzled, trying to figure out how to help her down. They somehow succeeded and carried her body out of the room.

A poisonous flower, both truth and a lie . . .

The final syllables of Lily's poem floated in the air, and the room fell quiet. It was like her poem had made everything stop. She was the only one left in the classroom. The silence felt heavy around her. Her poem echoed in the empty room, but there was no one there to clap or say anything nice about it. Her performance ended without anyone to see it.

No applause. No ovation. It was the same old song.

* * *

Lily strolled along her usual route home as the sun hung lazily in the sky, as if taking a long afternoon nap. School had been a blur, leaving her mind feeling like a chalkboard wiped clean of its contents. The Lonely House seemed to await her arrival, with an aura of quiet melancholy.

As she stepped closer, an unexpected sight greeted her—her belongings, meticulously packed and neatly stacked up, sat outside.

'Mom, why are all my things out here?'

'We're moving, don't bother me with questions. We've made up our minds.'

'Hold on, Mom, I told you I needed time to wrap my head around this. We can't just leave right away.'

'Lily, change can be a good thing. We're doing what's best for the family.'

'But Mom, my friends, my school—' Lily pretended like she cared about all that.

'Cut it out, Lily! We're not discussing this anymore.'

'I can't believe you're not even listening to me!'

'Watch your tone, young lady!' Her mom raised her voice and threatened to slap her.

'Mom, you can't just threaten me like that!'

'Well, maybe if you weren't so caught up with that ghost thing you've got going on, we wouldn't be having these problems!'

Lily froze. *How did Mom find out about that?*

'Oh, you've got to be kidding me, Lily! Shut the front door! I can't believe my own daughter is involved with . . . the phantom flirt, the uh . . . the spooktacular sweetheart, or whatever that is. Oh, the humanity! We're moving, end of discussion.'

'It's the Heartbreaker.'

'So, you admit it? He's your boo? What a shocker! What in the disgusting world is that? Aren't there any human lads in your school whom you like, huh? You go for this . . . uh, Casper the Not-So-Scary instead?'

Tears streamed down Lily's face.

'Can you ever just not be weird? Can we please just be normal? Remember the logical Lily I used to know?'

'You don't understand anything! You never even listen to me.'

'Oh, spare me the details! What's so lovely about this ghost? Did he gift you the ring off of Marilyn Monroe's bones or what? Took you out on a "soul music" date with Marvin Gaye performing live, huh?'

'Nope! But he gave me what I lost from you. He mended what you had broken.' Lily squared her shoulders, a newfound resolve in her eyes. It was like the Heartbreaker's embrace had taught her how to stand up for herself.

Her mother, trying to find a middle ground, said, 'Okay, then moving is the best way. If we move closer, I can handle things easily.'

'It's already too late for that. That's what you should have done in the first place, not now.'

Her mother was silent for a moment, clearly taken aback. She had probably never thought that Lily would say such a thing to her face. 'It's never too late, Lily. We can still fix it.'

Tears brimming in her eyes, Lily's voice broke. 'But I'm too sick, Mom. It's like I don't know how to get better. I don't know what's worse—feeling neglected by you or being rejected by my own peers. I was so broken and I didn't have anyone by my side. I needed you there by my side, but you were always wrapped up in work. I felt like you abandoned me when I needed you the most.'

'Lily, I—' Her mother started, but Lily cut her off, clutching her wrists.

'And that's when he came into my life, Mom. He's been my saviour.' She paused, gathering herself. 'He killed all those bad kids.'

Her mom's expression turned icy as she processed everything her ears had just heard.

'He stood up for me when they tried to hurt me, in ways you can't even imagine. He's my strength, my support . . .'

Lily continued, a fierce determination in her voice, 'Mom, I know it sounds strange, but he was there for me when no one else was. Not even you.'

'But why didn't you tell me any of this before? Did you talk to your teachers about it? They would have helped you, right?' Her mother was struggling to understand.

'They only made things worse. The more they punished those kids, the more I suffered.' Lily sighed, feeling a weight lift as she spoke her truth.

'What about Toby? I'll talk to him about this.'

'There's no point. You don't even trust him, right?' she looked away. 'But the ghost, only he knew how to stop them for good.'

'Lily, you sound scary. We're moving means we're moving.'

'I was supposed to grow into a beautiful lily. But you know what happens if lilies are left uncared for?' She looked directly at her mother, her eyes burning with pain and defiance. 'Mom, YOU made me into a wild and untamed flower.'

'I'm doing all this for us, Lily. You can't blame me for our situation.' Her mother tried to defend herself.

'But this was not what I asked for! Have you ever thought about what I wanted?' She clenched her jaw. 'That ghost, he knows what I want. He's always there for me . . .'

'So you don't want me? Your mom?'

'If you really want to know, I feel like I don't even have a mom. Especially when you're like this!'

Her mom, pierced by reality, tried to hug Lily, but the maternal caress had vanished from her mom's embrace. It didn't feel warm and loving anymore. Lily's heart was pounding as she stepped back to avoid her mother's touch. She could feel the tension in her legs as she made up her mind to run away.

All she could see was the thick forest—her only way out. She sprinted, moving swiftly between the trees, as if she knew the woods like the back of her hand. It was as if she had a map of the forest in her head; she could have navigated through the trees even with her eyes closed.

'LILY!'

As Lily ran ahead, her mom tried hard to follow. But at almost forty-five years old, she found it a lot tougher.

'LILY!'

Her mom's loud screams echoed through the woods; loud enough to wake up all the hibernating animals from their slumber—they cast annoyed glances at each other. Her mom followed her anyway as Lily took her deeper into the recesses of the dark forest with its hidden secrets. The deeper they went, the more it seemed like a place out of a fairy tale, where the sun barely shone through, and the paths were impossible for even satellites to find.

'LILY!'

Suddenly, Lily disappeared as if magically. She blended into the dark shadows of the forest, leaving her mom behind. Propelled by a mother's instinct, she kept moving forward—what kind of a mother would abandon searching for her child, right? Her steps eventually led her to a colossal gate. Towering before her was a portal that held the promise of unveiling secrets.

'LILY!'

As her mom got closer to the gate, her voice echoed off its walls, returning to her as a soft, inviting whisper that seemed to pull her in. No gatekeepers, no hosts waiting to welcome her in, she crossed the threshold like an uninvited guest.

'LILY!'

Before her sprawled an abandoned Dutch aristocratic housing complex, its grandeur now concealed by the passage of time.

'LILY!'

Her voice echoed through every hallway and every corner.

'LILY!'

She persisted in her pursuit.

'LILY!'

But Lily, too, seemed determined to remain elusive.

'LILY!'

'LILY!'

'LILY!'

'LI—'

At long last, she found Lily, but was that the Lily she knew? There she stood, confidently, on a moss-covered path near an old manor house. She wasn't alone; she was in the arms of a handsome man who looked like he belonged in a fancy, old-timey painting—at least in Lily's eyes. She kissed him, like in a scene from a fairy tale.

But her mom saw it completely differently. It made her feel sick; like her breakfast was about to come back up. He who appeared to Lily as beautiful, in her mom's eyes, looked like a beast, a creepy, scarred zombie, rather than a charming prince. She felt like she was about to lose it, like her sanity was a sandcastle getting washed away by the ocean. She had to decide—stay there and feel worse or leave worried, like a mother watching her daughter drive off with her new boyfriend, not sure what to think.

Homecoming wasn't a victory march for Lily's mother—Lily hadn't come back with her. All she could think about was how unbelievable it all was. She felt sad and heavy, realizing that her once sweet daughter had turned into a corpse flower.

# Chapter 10

## March

'Dear Family, I hope you are well. I want to let you
know that the Japanese Imperial Forces have invaded
the Dutch East Indies, and the situation has become
uncertain and challenging . . . Many of us are leaving
our homeland due to the changes and uncertainties
brought by the occupation. Our safety and well-being
are our top priority. I promise to keep you updated as
we navigate these difficult times. Please keep us in your
thoughts and prayers. With love . . .'

—A letter from a Dutch colonial officer,
3 March 1942

### I Dreamed a Dream

I dreamed a dream . . .
of a world inside ancient photos, wandering through
sepia memories;
of a painting of 'Floris de Jong', a figure I knew but
now saw anew;

219

of the Heartbreaker I knew, the man in the painting, his mystery unveiled;
of a piece of furniture whispering its history from an inexistent land named the Dutch East Indies;
of a delicate glass frame, an unfamiliar yet familiar reflection staring back—tan skin, cascading black hair, but not me.

I dreamed a dream . . .
of a man, nicknamed the Heartbreaker in my world, but Floris in this world, now a living soul, his every stride pulsing with life;
of a carpet of flowers in the backyard, he led me there;
of yellow daffodils blooming like miniature suns, filling me with energy;
of a botanist in the Dutch East Indies. It was his past job, he had achieved a miracle, cultivating daffodils in the tropics;
of his beloved Javanese concubine, a role I play now, together they nurtured these blooms.

I dreamed a dream . . .
of a shattered dance, a thunderous roar, a Japanese force's invasion in the 1940s;
of running away with him from guns and cruel soldiers;
of burned gardens, burned daffodils, burned dreams;
of a thrilling escape to the ocean's brink, where we defied fate and set sail.

I dreamed a dream . . .
of a distant realm, of Floris's birthplace, a cold, blue continent, where the love story restarted;

of a Dutch housing complex, a temporal kaleidoscope
where the grimness of my time gave way to opulence and
majesty;
of a gated community of Dutch nobility, magnificent
arches carved in intricate designs, red-bricked pathways
meandering through verdant gardens, fountains
murmuring tunes of bygone centuries, majestic walls
whispering tales of aristocratic splendour;
of scornful glances, silent judgments cast upon the girl
I played, a non-white woman, just like me.

I dreamed a dream . . .
of a beautiful mansion atop a hill, embraced by a sea of
flowers, Floris brought us there;
of a flower dance, a celebration of love transcending time
and societal divides;
of destroyed tranquility as flames crackled to life;
of wildfire ignited by the torches of those who opposed
our love, devoured the mansion from the lower hill,
plunging our haven into chaos;
of an embered hill, of flowers and fire;
of a lily of the valley, standing resolute in the face of the
roaring flames;
of an unfathomable chill seizing my body as the flower
brushed against my lips;
of the flames enveloping me;
of a beauty marred by tears of despair, of Floris, weeping
for me burning alive;
of a wild crowd looming with evil intent, shadows of
torment over this fiery tableau of agony;
of a metaphysical transformation—Floris morphed into
the Heartbreaker I know.

I dreamed a dream . . .

of a cursed neighbourhood, of hands stained with bloody flowers, a beautiful village turning into a ghost town;

of the bloody blossom curse, of a living flowerpot—tulips, daffodils, hyacinths, irises, crocuses, and lilies;

of plant tendrils consuming the neighbourhood with a vengeful wrath, turning what was previously lovely into a nightmarish fantasy, like in my world;

of the tale of the Heartbreaker enduring, its curse not merely an old myth but a living terror;

of a supernatural force, a master of nature—commanding weather, flowers and plants, the pull of gravity, the depths of water, and the rage of fire—continuing to spread its wrath;

of the curse's relentless spread, claiming its victims in modern day: Derby, who flew; Daffy, engulfed by water; an auditorium consumed by fire; and Rosy and Missy, shrouded in lilies;

of how he constructed this deadly rage, the bearer of this cruelty, his expression terrifying, a visage that only haunted but never throbbed the heart.

I dreamed a dream . . .

of the Javanese Lady, whose role I once played, now stood before me as a distinct entity, her scent reminiscent of jasmine, as if it were her very name;

of her speaking to me spiritually, her eyes restless, reflecting how the rage of the curse unfolded, but her words offered a glimmer of hope in a tale darkened by vengeance and sorrow:

'What was wounded in the past must not be avenged in the future. It must be healed. To seek a cure, we cannot return to yesterday, but we can always find a tomorrow.'

\* \* \*

Lily stirred from her nap, her mind still foggy.

The weight of grogginess clung to her, disorienting, confusing. Was it day? Was it night? She couldn't tell, the line between them blurred. Her hands moved automatically, rubbing the sleep from her eyes, trying to clear the haze.

It was there, that strange dream. Too strange, too vivid to be forgotten. A fragment, a whisper in the recesses of her mind. She grasped at it, but it slipped away, elusive. Was it real? Or just a shadow of her thoughts? The questions lingered, persistent, echoing.

Or maybe it wasn't just the post-nightmare haze. Maybe it was the silence of the Lonely House, too silent, too empty. Her mother's absence echoed through the halls, a ghostly reminder of the day she had found out about Lily's hidden relationship. Lily had left, needing to escape. When she had returned, the house had been empty. A note on the table, in her mother's handwriting, shaky and rushed, had read. 'I had to go away for work again. Don't know when I'll be back. Sorry.' Sorry. It sounded hollow, more for her mother's sake than Lily's. An explanation that explained nothing. A nudge to face her demons alone, as always.

Lily wondered, was this it? The final goodbye? Had her mother finally abandoned her for good?

She sat there, alone on the bed, the room around her mundane, suffocating in its normalcy. Feeling a bit stifled, she moved towards the window. She pushed it open. An ambiguous breeze wafted in—it contained a strange mix of winter's lingering chill and the approaching warmth of summer, typical of March. It carried the scent of damp earth.

The clock on the wall showed that it was 3 p.m. She glanced at it, then at the sky. It was dark—unnaturally so, like time had skipped ahead to 3 a.m. Lily's eyes drifted downwards, towards her garden. She remembered planting daffodils there. March was supposed to be their blooming time, as if they were operating on a timer set by nature.

But now, looking at the place, Lily felt a sudden unease. No vibrant daffodils, no sign of life. It's not like the flowers had not yet bloomed—it was as if they had been plucked.

The cuts on the stems didn't look natural, either. Neither were they jagged, as if by an animal's claws nor were they withered by nature's hand. They looked precise—calculated and cold—as if someone had cut them purposefully; but why?

She wasn't sure, but then she remembered. The day the Heartbreaker had given her a sprig of daffodils. A gift that was vibrant and full of life. Suddenly, a knot of regret and disappointment twisted in her stomach. She had promised him she'd take care of those flowers. Now, they were gone.

Bits and pieces of her dream began to resurface, tapping her mind like fingers on a keyboard. But the melodies were not harmonious but messy, untidy. Memories of her dreams flooded her mind, an odd mix of images and sensations. Each one clear, complex, chaotic.

There was a colonial-style botanist, a wise-looking Javanese woman, and, of course, dancing daffodils. It was still a mystery to Lily, though. The Heartbreaker— as his living version, Floris—gave her a daffodil in her dream. When she woke up to reality, there it was, a pot in the window with a plant standing tall—daffodils, still buds. How did these daffodils slip out of her dreams into reality? These daffodils were more than just flowers. The Heartbreaker had put *his heart* in that gift.

Then, there was that impressive residential complex, turning apocalyptic in fleeting seconds. Near that neighbourhood was a garden—the garden of gladioli where Daffy had taken her during summer camp—with a small lake in the middle.

Further south, the forest grew denser, the ground carpeted with amaryllis—the amaryllis forest, a magical place that had made Lily fly.

To the north, a mansion on a flower-covered hill. The Heartbreaker had taken her there in her dreams. A place of beauty, disturbed by sceptics. People didn't believe in the love that seemed to infuse the very walls of the mansion. So that star-crossed love story, haunting the town, had been rewritten as a horror tale whispered among generations.

After more than fifty years, haunting and dead, the fire in that forbidden love had reignited, with Lily playing Juliet. But a dream she had just dreamed during a deep sleep at 3 p.m. forewarned her that history was going to repeat itself. And now, as then, the mansion was circled by cynicism, the same doubt that had destroyed that peaceful place before.

* * *

Lily found herself marching through the dark forest, her bare feet feeling every cold, rough edge of the forest floor. She moved quickly, her pace mirroring the racing thoughts in her head. It was one of those times when fear and curiosity propelled her forward, despite her discomfort and the eerie quiet of the woods under the gloomy sky. As she moved, her mind continued to unravel the many threads of her dream about the mansion on the hill being under attack.

Suddenly, a scream echoed in her brain, a sound so chilling, it seemed to come from the mansion itself. To anyone else, it might have sounded like the wail of a ghost, something out of a spooky tale. But to Lily, it was more than that. She heard layers in that scream—of pain, anger, and even a hint of vengeance, the familiar sounds screaming inside her body. It was as if the mansion itself was crying out, burdened with untold stories.

Then, in her mind's eye, she saw the daffodil, the same one she had lost, now in the grip of a cold, unfamiliar hand. She trekked towards the mansion. It was as if the place was calling out to her, pulling her in with an invisible force. Each step took her deeper into the forest, closer to the source of her unrest, to a place that seemed to hold the key to her strange, unsettling dreams.

As Lily strutted into what was meant to be a lost castle from a wonderland, her heart danced an intricate ballet of anticipation tinged with confusion. Her strange dreams had lied to her. The mansion that now loomed in front of her was anything but grand. It appeared weathered by ages of neglect and buried under the weight of thousands of forgotten dreams. The walls wore a shroud of dust and the shadows whispered tales of secrets held within its cracked façade.

Meanwhile, the sea of flowers turned out to be just a myth. Their hues of reds, oranges, yellows, and the full spectrum of the rainbow were just muted shades of sorrow, a palette of melancholy.

Despite the mansion's dilapidated state, which was unlikely to attract any tenants, it had drawn a gathering of people in white cloaks, which caught Lily's attention.

The Ghostbuster Gramps again! But this time, they looked more like a bunch of yoga enthusiasts assembled in a geometric formation than people conducting a spooky sermon session.

They stood with an aura of grave intent, like guardians braced to battle unseen demons residing within the mansion's walls. The mansion was shackled by a massive chain, and it appeared to be feeling suffocated in its very essence being thus imprisoned. Its windows and doors and every conceivable entrance was sealed with heavy timber. Not even the strongest winds could tear through the bounds.

Along the mansion's edge, a man was dousing it in gasoline. Not in jest but as a grim ritual, as if purging it of some unspoken curse.

From a slender gap in the mansion, barely more than a slit, came a sound that defied the rules of nature. It was

a roar; deep and earth-shattering. It echoed as if it were
the cry of a caged beast, protesting against its inevitable
fate. It was not just a cry; it was a lament—a primal scream
from the depths of the mansion's heart. The Ghostbuster
Gramps, however, had a less-than-enthusiastic response,
treating it like a Gen-Z music playlist that didn't match
their tastes.

There was even more mayhem when a symphony of
shattering and breaking was heard from inside the mansion.
It seemed like the ghosts were having a furniture-tossing
party. It sounded like the mansion was trembling with
violent eruptions, shaking the dust off itself, cracking the
fragile bricks and glass that constituted it.

Upon her arrival, Lily was met with stares hardened
by years of dogmatic scrutiny. They were piercing and
judgmental, as if she was a branded devil's slave. This
intense scrutiny, far more daunting than any taunts she had
faced from peers, was meant to subdue her soul. In that
charged atmosphere, she felt an acute, intense need for his
support. Standing her ground, she countered the disdainful
watcher with a defiant glare of her own.

Yet, amid the tumult, Lily's mind struggled to keep
pace. The revelation dawned on her slowly. Her protector,
the one with the blue peepers, was already there, peeking
out from inside the mansion like a ghostly observer. He
was the source of the unearthly roar, the imprisoned
spirit behind the entire tumult. The magic in his eyes had
dissipated, leaving behind a sorrowful longing, a silent echo
yearning for freedom.

His moonlit charm eclipsed any hopes of a romantic
glow. This shift deeply unsettled Lily. She understood

the critical need to preserve his light, for without it, her days threatened to be engulfed in a suffocating darkness. Shaking off her initial shock, Lily steeled her resolve to infiltrate the mansion and save him. Yet, as she moved forward, her path was abruptly blocked. A firm grip around her wrist anchored her in place.

'Mom! What are you doing here?'

'Lily, I swear it's for your own good!' her mom's voice trembled.

'You believe all this craziness? You swear you're all about the future then why are you stuck here?'

'I know! But . . . this supernatural thing is too wacky, but, umm . . .' Lily's mother looked perplexed. 'But here's the deal, Lily, I hate horror films as well as classic love stories, and you're playing a part in both at the same time. You're the one who got me into this mess, so let's get away from it together! We're here to rescue you!'

Her mother's grip was unyielding, reminiscent of a stubborn lid on a pickle jar, refusing to give way.

'BUT THE ONLY HELP I NEED IS FROM FLORIS!'

'Who the hell is Floris?'

Lily didn't answer the question. That was because her anger had already lowered to a simmer. Her emotions were like a volcano on the brink of eruption. But then, there they were, those determined gramps, they were conducting a supernatural cleanse.

'STOP!'

The Ghostbuster Gramps started chanting. Lily noticed Toby was there too, leading the ritual while others followed him in unison.

'NO!' Lily screamed.

'Let peace return, let this soul rest!' they began.

Of course, it wouldn't be an exorcism without a good old-fashioned eerie ambience, and the sky didn't disappoint. The sun retreated entirely, shrouding everything in a twilight that felt thick with dread. Tension hung heavy in the air.

'Hold the circle firm! We can't let the entity break through!'

'Stop this madness,' Lily cried. 'You just don't understand!'

*Our love's not a ghost story, why can't you see it's a tale of two hearts refusing to part?* Her heart cried poetically.

'Let peace return, let this soul rest!' The Ghostbuster Gramps frantically chanted, their voices laced with fear.

'Light the fire! Light the fire quick, fool!'

Dark clouds loomed above them. Shadows lurked between the trees, as if nature itself was waiting with bated breath. A tense silence enveloped the forest, broken only by the distant rumble of thunder.

'Let peace return, let this soul rest!'

Then, suddenly, piercing the heavy air, a scream erupted. Jarring and discordant. It tore through the silence with the ferocity of an unexpected tempest.

A terrible silence reigned.

'Don't take him from me!' Lily screamed. *I hear our love song die, with every incantation, love's melody begins to fly.*

'He's not a curse!' she insisted. *What went wrong with our love song?*

'Please, he's all I have!' *I, mere blood and flesh; he, spirit and energy, I love him to the moon and the world to come. Is our symphony too dark to play?*

'Lily, we must let go for your own good,' her mother was clutching her too tight. 'He's not meant for this world, and you belong here with us.'

Lily's dress tore while struggling against her mother's firm hold, and it made her cold.

'Let peace return, let this soul rest!'

The impending rain seemed to sympathize, hesitating to fall on this poignant scene. The forest seemed to watch in resignation.

The mansion quivered like a living entity under siege. Its windows rattled as if the ghostly chaos within was trying to escape. The mansion seemed to breathe, exhaling ghostly sighs of despair. The Ghostbuster Gramps exchanged glances. Doubt flickered in their eyes. In the face of mounting terror, their resolve wavered, but they held on.

'Quick, intensify the chant; something's not right here!'

In her mind's eye, Lily envisioned a macabre scene where a bloody blossom curse sprouted from the Ghostbuster Gramps' stomachs.

*Come on, show them how scary it is!*

Sweat glistened on the men's brows, their eyes darted around, their hands trembled as they fought to regain control of the situation.

*Show them that our love is a bond not even the strongest spell can break.*

'The spirit is resisting; maintain the barrier at all costs!'

*He may be a ghost, but our love is more alive than any of you can ever know!*

A spectral scream, mournful and unrelenting, once again struck like a thunderclap, shaking the earth.

A ghostly glow moved behind the curtains of the mansion and the grand entry door quaked. Meanwhile, the wind grew in strength, as if protesting against the ritual.

'Hurry, we need to light the fire!'

'The mansion is our only chance!'

'Get the torches ready!'

'We're running out of time!'

'The spirits are winning!'

'Fire, now!'

Fire was added to the chaos.

'Let peace return, let this soul rest!'

And the fire was raging!

The flames leaped around the mansion with such enthusiasm. They twisted and twirled, pushing back the shadows that clung to the mansion's façade. They leaped and crackled, devouring the end of the day with their fiery tongues.

A scream roared again from within the burning mansion. A tormented cry. A wail of agony.

'Let peace return, let this soul rest!'

'STOP IT!' Lily insisted. 'PLEASE!'

As the anguished cry grew louder, the clouds twisted and churned like a vortex. The heavens themselves seemed to writhe in turmoil. A maelstrom of clouds painted the sky in shades of obsidian.

Then, raindrops began to fall, the sky weeping. They gently brushed away Lily's tears. It was as if nature was crying with her.

The mansion's fury was finally extinguished. Hissing as the rain met the fading embers, the downpour's embrace put the fire's dance to rest.

'The fire's dying! We need more fuel!'

'Don't let the light go out!'

'We won't let the darkness win; not now!'

As they desperately attempted to reignite the fire, the rain beat down harder, making it impossible. Everything was soaked. The roaring fire eating up the mansion had died down completely. All that was left was a smoky, burned ruin that made the already dark atmosphere appear even darker. Panic set among the men as they realized their struggle against the ghost was far from over.

But the fire was out, and so was the nerve-racking scream that had been coming from inside the mansion. The burned mansion, a skeletal relic of its former glory, appeared strangely calm now, like its ashes had been washed away in the rain after its cremation.

'Let peace return, let this soul rest!'

The mansion's once fiery spirit was reduced to an eerie stillness; the sudden silence was deafening after the chaos that had consumed them moments ago. Lily felt a sense of unease creeping in. Her mind overthought the notion that she had truly lost him, even though their love story had been almost unreal.

But mysteries always waited just a few seconds to be revealed. Perhaps that place had crossed too many boundaries between the mundane and the supernatural.

The house was shaking again, and the charcoal ashes from the fire were flying about everywhere. The gathering, already exhausted, was on edge again. The weary lips of the Gramps murmured the chant again, its sound muffled by the violent rain.

The fire had done nothing but burn away the mansion's shackles. That made it easier for the Heartbreaker to escape its grip and further disheartened the exorcists.

Toby, who had given up hope that the light would ever return, extracted something from his robe. He revealed himself as the one who had ruined Lily's daffodils—as he always had. In his palm, shrivelling under the cold rainwater, he held the missing daffodil sprig. It radiated a yellowish glow, the sole source of light in the dimness.

He also pulled out a matchbox. He struggled to light a match in the relentless rain. Although each match stayed lit a bit longer than its predecessor, none survived long enough to ignite the daffodil. Lily's focus was fixed on Toby, who was too absorbed plotting against the daffodil.

There was a sudden explosion in the mansion, now sporting a sizeable hole. Despite its crumbling state, it ominously hinted at the looming evil that was about to emerge. The explosion's aftermath lingered, stretching out long enough for the onlookers to catch their breath, their hearts pounding. The tension was palpable—a silent moment suspended in time; all eyes were fixed on the scene before them.

As the rain began to ease, a startling development took shape: one of the Gramps was suddenly thrown a considerable distance. The sound of the impact echoed like distant thunder.

Before they could fully grasp what had happened, a second, more shocking attack was launched. The youngest member of the Ghostbuster Gramps was lifted in the air. The disturbing sounds from his constricted throat filled the air. This moment marked the beginning of the feared climax: the bloody blossom curse. From the man's mouth emerged plants sprouting white lilies, each petal gruesomely stained with blood.

Meanwhile, the large hole in the mansion revealed a darkness within, surrounded by a blue glow. The tension heightened as the wind grew louder and more turbulent, as if ready to sweep away everything in its path. In the midst of the howling storm, Lily's mother's grip eased into a warm, protective hug. She shielded her child against the biting wind with her body, shivering from the cold gusts striking her back.

Toby suddenly appeared and quickly ushered Lily and her mother away from the chaotic scene at the mansion. They all hurried down the hill to get to the safety of Toby's car parked at its foot.

Once inside the car, the cold and fear began to fade. The windows framed a blurred, grey world outside; there was a distinct smell of old paper in the car. Starting the car took a moment. As the engine came to life, the car radio accidentally turned on, playing a pop song Toby detested. There was no time to change it, though; his focus was solely on getting away from the scene as fast as possible, leaving the chaos behind.

'See what can happen?' Lily's mother's voice shattered the silence in the car. 'This is a total disaster!'

'But Mom, all of this could've been avoided if you hadn't interfered,' Lily retorted. 'He was just trying to protect me.'

'You don't need his protection,' Toby cut in sharply. 'There's only one place where you can find true safety.'

Lily remained silent, her anger boiling up inside her, making it hard for her to speak. Unable to express her fury in words, she lashed out in desperation. In a sudden outburst, she attacked Toby, who was caught unawares. She clawed at his face, and he groaned in pain until her mother pulled her back into her seat.

But the damage was done. The car veered wildly, swerving left and right before crashing into a tree. The impact sent everyone jolting forward: Toby's head slammed against the steering wheel, her mother's forehead hit the rear window, and Lily was thrust into the front seat. The crash resulted in a disorienting quiet, filled only with groans of pain from all of them. Toby appeared to be the most injured, blood trickling from his temple.

As their senses slowly returned, they realized the shocking truth. The object they had hit was not a tree. Standing before them was a figure; it was no ordinary human—they could not have survived the impact of the car. His bright blue eyes pierced through the greyness around them: it was the Heartbreaker.

His look was not charming as usual—something reserved for Lily. Instead, he wore a twisted smile of vengeance, the kind Lily wore during her own moments of unleashed fury.

In a weak attempt to dispel the apparition, Toby honked the horn, but the ghost remained unmoving. 'You won't move, Sir Style? Fine, I'll make you die a second time!' Toby's words reflected his escalating anger.

With a determined expression, he shifted the car into gear. The vehicle's menacing façade confronted the Heartbreaker, as if challenging him to a lethal duel, with the Grim Reaper playing the arbiter. The ghost's sharp eyes remained unflinching, and Lily knew he was preparing a cruel spell. Toby's intent, however, burned unwaveringly. His eyes were determined and he had no second thoughts on executing a deadly hit-and-run.

Time crawled like an endless nightmare in Lily's mind as Toby revved the engine, its roar reminiscent of a lion, and then released the brake.

'NO!' Lily's cry was filled with dread.

In her mind, the car lunged forward, but in reality, the scene before her remained unchanged. The Heartbreaker stood unscathed before the car.

Despite the car's engine groaning at its highest pitch, the vehicle didn't budge. Lily recalled a similar scene from the past—a majestic noble housing complex gripped by magically sprouted plant vines, turning it into the setting of an apocalyptic story. Now, she realized that similar vines were entangling themselves around the car's tyres, and now she knew what to expect.

Suddenly, the car was lifted in the air!

Her mom screamed, bewildered by the bizarre turn of events. Toby, on the other hand, seemed frozen, processing what was happening. His foot remained unknowingly pressed on the accelerator.

But the weight of a car was not something the plant's tendrils could bear, even though they were imbued with supernatural strength. They snapped under the strain, causing the car to plummet back to the ground, obeying gravity's pull. As the wheels hit the ground, the car, propelled by Toby's foot still on the gas pedal, surged forward. Toby, his mind clouded and disoriented, struggled to regain control, causing the car to swerve erratically.

This led to a second collision, this time with a tree directly in their path.

Once again, a dizzying silence enveloped the car's occupants. Lily, her head spinning, saw Toby in pain and her mother lying unconscious beside her. Seizing the opportunity to escape, she flung open the car door and tumbled out.

Her mind still reeling, Lily's movements were unsteady, her steps staggering and dragging as she ran. Her gait resembled that of a zombie.

Believing she had put enough distance between herself and the car, Lily was suddenly enveloped in an unexpected embrace. She initially thought it might be the Heartbreaker coming to her rescue, but the hug lacked any sense of comfort.

'Lily, what are you doing? We need to leave this place!' It was Toby, intent on taking her back home with him.

But before Lily could respond, she noticed a figure standing behind Toby, looking ominous. Her attention was fixed on this new presence, and she disregarded Toby completely. Sensing this, he turned around.

In an instant, his body was pulled into the air as many before him had been, his form convulsed, his breath caught in his throat, signalling impending doom. Yet, unlike previous victims, Toby was still able to utter words. 'It's not with me,' he managed to say.

But as his sentence ended, plants emerged from his mouth, and lilies bloomed. Toby's eyes widened in shock while Lily was captivated by the haunting beauty of the blossoming lilies in the gruesome scene.

A massive explosion blew up Toby's car. A wave of worry crashed over Lily as she feared her mother might still have been inside. But she had somehow managed to exit the car and clutched in her hand, Lily noticed—even before she noticed her mother—a daffodil, still a vibrant yellow. The Heartbreaker's gaze remained intensely focused on that daffodil.

That led Lily to wonder if he was trying to save not just her but also the flower? Or . . . was the flower his sole concern?

Maybe she hadn't realized that the flower held more significance than she had initially thought. It was important to her too, but not as much as it was to him, who was fighting with all his strength to take it back.

Her mother, grasping the daffodil, suddenly threw it into the flames of the burning car. The heavy rain was powerless to douse the gasoline fire.

Lily was at a loss, unsure of what this action meant or what to do next.

The Heartbreaker appeared to ready himself, poised for rapid action. Lily braced herself, expecting him to deliver a fatal blow to her mother. But, to her surprise, he turned towards her instead; in place of an expected attack, he planted a kiss on her lips.

A final kiss. It was the most gentle and ethereal of all his kisses. There was a poignant tenderness, a sad resignation to fate for a connection that could never fully be realized. It tasted like the tears of farewell. But as his lips met hers, it brought a bittersweet solace, like a fleeting calm before the storm. It stemmed her tears—temporary respite from the overwhelming sadness that she didn't know she was likely to feel for an eternity.

He enveloped her in his tender embrace, lighting up her life like he always did. But now, it felt as delicate as a wisp of smoke. With each passing second, she could feel him slipping away. The warmth she had cherished was fading, leaving her alone yet again in a cold and uncertain world.

She tried to hold on to the moment, to etch every sensation into her memory forever—the soft pressure of his lips, the faint chill that emanated from his ghostly form, the way her heart ached with a mixture of joy and despair as he faded away. But it was like trying to grasp water—there was nothing she could do to stop it from slipping away.

Around them, the world was silent, the raindrops fell like tears at the farewell that was as inevitable as it was heartbreaking. She wanted to scream, to beg him to stay, but what good would it do? He was a ghost, a fleeting shadow bound to a world she couldn't follow him into.

As the last traces of him vanished, leaving her alone in the cold, rain-soaked reality, a sob escaped her lips. She stood there, drenched, her face lifted to the sky as if seeking answers. But there were none. Only the rain, the lingering touch of his kiss on her lips, and the hollow emptiness in her chest.

And thus concluded the dark tale of the Heartbreaker. The one that had always begun with the line, 'Beware of falling in love with him.'

His last message would almost have been lost, if not for Lily, who had caught it at the final moment—a haunting promise that beckoned her: 'Meet me in the afterlife.'

* * *

Lily was lying on a huge outdoor bed, covered with a floral blanket. The bed was so large, it seemed like a sprawling field of wildflowers that needed tending—or maybe that's what it actually was.

On this giant bed of flora, Lily found a tiny spot of comfort. Here, she let her imagination roam freely, picturing scenes from a dreamy past. She imagined deer playfully romancing or birds chasing each other around.

In her drowsy state, unable to sleep, she longed for the playful glint of those blue eyes, like blue hydrangeas swaying in the wind, that used to sneak peeks at her constantly. She missed the thrilling touch of those invisible hands that used to send shivers down her spine. She could almost feel it now, the playful tickling.

Nature seemed to play a sad jazz, pulling Lily back into the here and now. It wasn't the sound of actual trumpets but something more mystical; a melody that seemed to emanate from the earth itself. She wandered through the greenery, but she soon realized it wasn't coming from anywhere around her—the sound was in her head, in sync with the trumpet-like flowers swaying in the breeze.

Daffodils, a flower that remains oblivious to the relentless march of time, marked the season for her to become a tiny wonder, with its six petals unfolding in perfect symmetry against the green leaves.

To Lily, these flowers were more than just pretty things to look at. They were a promise, a constant reminder of the bond she shared with her beloved. They felt like keys to another world, the sole path to reunite with him; a mysterious place she'd always been curious about but never fully understood. In that world, it seemed as though the love she shared with her spectral lover thrived and bloomed endlessly. It was the final proof of how much she wanted him—so much that she would go after him even though death was right around the corner.

Yet, her intentions remained veiled. Would she try to bring him back into her world, rekindling the love they had once shared? Or was she going to weave their love into his world, a place where it could grow without the shame of 'forbidden love'?

Truth be told, she hadn't planned that far ahead. The decision was yet to crystallize, but a daffodil twig was already in her palm.

In those fleeting moments, her opportunity to reconsider her choice hung in the balance. A poignant memory from the past briefly flickered through her mind, a recollection of a choice she had once unequivocally declined. However, she skipped those few seconds of contemplation, and instead, ate the daffodil as if it was a soothing sedative.

Her teeth delicately ground down each yellow, shining petal, filling her senses with an aroma as sweet as cotton candy. It felt as though spring had erupted in her mouth, imbued with flavours of purity, rebirth, joy, and affection.

A sinister influence, concealed beneath the radiant façade of the flower, flowed across her tongue, unleashing a discordant revelry that messed up her heart's rhythm. This was promptly followed by the onset of nausea and an expulsion that sent her world spinning.

This vertigo was unlike anything she had experienced before, casting her into a maelstrom of ever-shifting, kaleidoscopic visions. In the middle of this fascinating chaos, a mysterious gate appeared—the threshold between the dead and living realms.

The gate was open, Lily was too young to uncover what lay beyond it; it should have remained shut tight. When it opened, an ethereal mist crept out, carrying the hushed secrets of the dead, an otherworldly ambience shrouded it. Towering obsidian pillars flanked the entrance, adorned with intricate, age-old symbols signifying passage. The gate was made of a bright, mysterious material that gave off a luring but ominous vibe. Its carvings told stories of both reunion and judgment.

As Lily drew nearer, the gateway emitted a gentle, melodic hum that lured souls to cross its threshold. The atmosphere surrounding it had an inexplicable serenity and a refreshing coolness, in stark contrast to the capricious and tumultuous realm of the living.

Stepping through the gates, Lily found herself poised on the edge between life's uncertainties and the enigmas of what lay beyond.

She had never been prepared to see the unseen or reckon with the timeless, yet here she stood.

# Chapter 11

## April

'Do you really want to know where I was April 29th?
Do I really have to tell you how he brought me
back to life?'

—Taylor Swift, 'High Infidelity'

Lily held a bouquet of daisies in her hands, their petals a vivid mix of reds, yellows, and blues. They were a gift from her father, accompanied by a note that read, 'New Beginnings!'

As she gazed at them, she couldn't help but feel a sense of déjà vu. These flowers were not new to her; they were a reminder of her past. She recalled a similar bouquet she had received when she was twelve, a first-period gift from her father; a symbol to mark her transition from girlhood to womanhood. But as she stood there, lost in thought, the bouquet mysteriously disappeared, as if it had never been there. Just poof! Gone!

This kind of thing had been happening a lot lately. At first, it was thrilling, like living in a fairy tale. She'd feel this rush, this incredible joy, as if all her old dreams were coming true. But the magic of it all had worn off. Lily knew now that she wasn't just dealing with some kind of trick. It took some time for her to grasp that she had crossed over into a dimension far from reality—into a realm that defied explanation.

In this otherworldly place, Lily found herself wandering through a Technicolor dream. It mirrored her own world, yet it was distorted, as if being seen through a coloured lens of a fever dream. The colours here were amplified to an extraordinary degree—the reds blazed with the intensity of a raging fire, the blues shimmered like the ocean under a midday sun, and the yellows glowed fiercely like the core of a star. The forests around her were a deep shade of green, reminiscent of a traffic light glowing through an evening fog after rain. The sky above was a rich blue so vivid, it felt like being inside a giant sapphire.

In this vibrant, almost surreal landscape, the natural world was alive in a way Lily had never experienced. She could hear the trees whispering to each other and the flowers chatting away as if they were old friends at a garden party. But the most interesting thing about it was that time seemed irrelevant. Lily could relive her happiest memories instantly, like unwrapping a surprise gift from Santa. The key was to never doubt the reality of it all because the moment you questioned its authenticity, the magic evaporated, leaving you stranded in the strange realm.

The allure of this place was blinding. It was a world of enchantment and illusion, tempting Lily to stay forever,

making her forget why she was there in the first place—
to find her lover. But this world had a drawback. It was
unpredictable, and you couldn't expect to receive anything
specific from it.

The haunting words of the Heartbreaker, 'Meet me in
the afterlife,' reverberated in her mind. But where exactly? It
sent her into a whirlwind of anxiety, weariness, and despair.
Even though they were supposedly in the same realm,
finding him was a daunting task. She had no map; he had no
phone or other mundane stuff we called technology—there
was nothing to guide her on her mission. His instructions
were too vague. If only he had given her a specific street, a
building, a number of some sort—anything to help her find
him in this perplexing world.

Lily meandered through fields of gladioli, where they
had first met, and then through amaryllis fields, where he
had opened her eyes to supernatural marvels. She even
revisited the grand mansion on the flowery hill, their last
meeting place. But nothing came of her search, and she felt
drained. Though she was no longer flesh and bone, merely
soul, she felt exhaustion of an inexplicable kind.

This relentless quest, driven by burning longing, felt
excruciating. It was pain that cut deeper than the loss of
her father and the endless wait for her mother. It even
surpassed the torment of the exorcism she had witnessed
and eclipsed the agony of consuming the daffodil—which
had severed the connection between her body and soul.

The glittering lights of this world, once mesmerizing,
only served to blind her now, and the wonders that had
once enthralled her, seemed mundane. Realizing that this
world had lost its allure, much like her own had done before,

Lily decided to return to the familiar routine of her old life: the daily school grind and the solitude of the Lonely House.

The school in the afterworld mirrored her school in reality—a hub of youthful energy, bustling with children studying, playing sports, and chatting. Lily could see that. But would they notice Lily? Nope. In both realms, they never truly saw her or acknowledged her presence. She was an invisible ghost both in her tangible or immaterial form. So, in a way, nothing had really changed.

She took her usual seat in class, the day unfolding as it always had—no interactions, nothing fun. But navigating the crowded hallways felt different this time; she moved through them effortlessly, as if she were made of air. Even when she brushed past the other students, they remained oblivious to her presence. This invisibility, both here and in her former, real life, confirmed to her that she was a ghost.

Her invisible journey led her to the school's indoor swimming pool, yet she didn't know why was she there. Arriving at its door, Lily heard a distressed scream, like a lament from a troubled spirit. She found the door locked. But then, inspired by her ghostly nature, she attempted to pass through the barrier. To her surprise, she passed right through it, as if it was nothing but air.

At the pool, Lily found the source of the frustrated howl: a boy who had lowered his body, leaning towards the water surface, as if searching for lost fish or bubbles.

'Daffy?' Lily called out, recognizing the boy. To her surprise, he was the first one who looked up in response to her voice.

'Lily!' Daffy exclaimed, a puzzled expression crossing her face as he walked closer to her.

It was then that Lily remembered Daffy was already dead.

'Lily, you have to help me,' Daffy implored, grabbing her arm and pulling her to the pool's edge. 'I can't find my reflection in the water. Is my hair messy? Is there a mark on my forehead? It could ruin my whole look.'

Lily remained silent, observing Daffy's unawareness of their shared predicament. Then, Daffy urged her to look into the water. When Lily peered into the pool, she found that, like Daffy, her reflection was absent too.

'Oh, that's a relief!' Daffy sighed, mistaking the meaning. 'I thought I was the only one with this issue.'

'Daffy,' Lily began gently, 'the reason we can't see our reflections is . . . well . . .' She took a deep breath then continued, 'we're not . . . physical anymore.'

'What?' Daffy asked, confusion written all over his face. 'What do you mean?'

'Well,' Lily explained softly. 'We're like the wind— invisible and intangible. We're just souls now, separated from our bodies. We're ghosts.'

'A ghost? No way! I'm surely still too handsome to be dead,' Daffy protested.

'Believe it or not, Daffy, but you're no longer alive,' Lily stated, a hint of sadness in her voice.

Daffy, in a state of panic, desperately looked at the pool's surface once more, hoping against hope to see his reflection.

'Don't you remember?' Lily asked softly.

'Remember what?' Daffy's confusion was palpable.

'How you died?'

'No, I don't. I just recall waking up here, over and over. Whenever I go home to sleep in my room, I end up back here,' Daffy explained, his voice laced with confusion. 'These past few months have been so weird. I approached some girls swimming here, and they screamed and ran off. It was odd because they used to seek my attention. That's why I kept checking the mirror to see if something was wrong with my face. Is there, Lily?'

'There's nothing wrong with your face,' Lily reassured him. 'It's just that, like I said before, you're no longer in your body. That's why the girls were scared; to them, you appeared as a ghost.'

Daffy sat on the edge of the pool, his face crestfallen, as if his heart had sunk to an unfathomable depth. Lily sat beside him, trying to comfort him. She dipped her feet in the water, but she couldn't feel the chill of the water anymore.

'Tell me how I died!' Daffy asked, his tone showing that he had accepted his condition.

'Your death . . . it was tragic. You drowned in this very pool. That's why I believe you're still here,' Lily revealed gently, sensing his readiness.

Daffy, absorbing this, asked with a trace of his old humour, 'What about my funeral? Did I look handsome in my coffin?'

Lily scoffed, rolling her eyes, 'Handsome? More like you were trying to win a sleeping beauty contest, Daffy.'

His face clouded over, etched with regret and dreams left unfulfilled.

'Before you died, you were about to tell me something, but you never got the chance. What was it?' Lily enquired, steering the conversation to unfinished matters.

'What did I promise?' Daffy's confusion was evident.

'To meet me in the cafeteria,' Lily reminded him.

The pool remained tranquil, undisturbed by their dangling legs. The school seemed deserted, the end of the day marked by an eerie silence. Then, abruptly, Daffy's demeanour changed.

'LILY, YOU HAVE TO STOP ALL THIS!' he burst out.

'Stop what?' Lily asked, startled.

'YOU MUST END YOUR CONNECTION WITH THAT GHOST BEFORE IT'S TOO LATE!' he exclaimed.

Dusk was approaching, and in this realm, it marked the most frightening period. Bizarre beings emerged from dark recesses to partake in a chilling celebration of some sort.

'But it's already too late,' Lily answered.

Following his sudden outburst, Daffy's mood shifted once more. His anger dissipated, giving way to a more subdued and reflective state. He settled back, enveloped in a quietness that was both calm and introspective. The storm of his emotions had passed, leaving behind a tranquil, thoughtful silence.

'Ah, now it hits me. My death, right? It was because of the Heartbreaker. Dude dragged me into the pool. And he ... he just wouldn't let me get back up. Man, the agony of that water in my lungs ... still gets to me.' He let out a shaky breath, his eyes clouded remembering that fateful moment.

'That's rough, sorry to hear that.'

'So who was next on the hitlist after me?' he asked curiously with a bit of unease.

'Only Missy. She's the one who thought up that twisted game, right? Back then, I really wanted her to learn her lesson. To understand that her actions have consequences.'

Her voice still had an edge to it, a remnant of anger not yet quelled.

'Hold on . . . You're a ghost too, aren't you? Does that mean you're, like, dead as well?' His eyes grew wide as the realization slowly sank in.

'I'm not sure, honestly. Am I dead or still halfway there . . . ? Is my body buried somewhere, or just lying around in some field, undiscovered . . . it's kinda weird. Nobody ever really noticed me, you know?' She looked away, her gaze distant, lost in the thoughts of a life that now seemed both far away and painfully present.

'But how did you end up here?' he asked, a spark of curiosity lighting up his face.

'Daffodils. I ate them. Played his little game to track him down here. But for some reason, he hasn't spotted me yet,' she shrugged nonchalantly, her face a blend of annoyance and resolve.

'Lily,' Daffy began, pausing for a moment, 'I've got something to confess.' Another pause followed, stretching the tension in the air. 'I was actually the mastermind behind that game.'

Lily remained silent, her confusion evident.

'The game wasn't just a harmless prank,' he continued, 'I chose you to play the game, and I had no idea it would have such a profound impact.'

'You're telling me I was deliberately picked for this fate?' Lily's voice rose in anger, her eyebrows knitting together in frustration and disbelief.

'Yes,' Daffy confessed, his voice softening. 'I'm sorry, Lily. But please hear me out! I believed the game would work with you, and it turned out to be even more incredible than I had anticipated. It all goes back to . . .'

Daffy took a deep breath and jumped into the story. 'I'm actually the Heartbreaker's kin.'

Lily remained still, absorbing the revelation.

'You wouldn't have guessed that, right? But he brought shame upon my family, a stain so deep that my grandfather and father have been tirelessly working to erase any connection between us and him. They wanted people to forget that he was ever a part of our family, to forget that we were once respected. Those years were tough for my family, and they left behind generational trauma. So, my only goal was to wipe him from existence once and for all; to free my family of that burden.'

'Why did you involve me?' Lily questioned, curiosity and frustration evident in her tone.

'My grandfather, who was his cousin, was always too traumatized to discuss it, and my father also avoided the topic at all costs,' Daffy explained. 'I, on the other hand, have been intrigued by him. Everything I've ever shared with you about him is the result of my own digging around. As for that game, it was a way for me to connect with him, and you're not the first, Lily . . .'

He continued, 'When I was fifteen, I had a girlfriend from The Hague Academy, and we agreed to play that game together. I learned a lot about ghosts from her before she became too stressed and moved to Brussels, just to escape it all. Then there was my neighbour; we played the game, but the ghost inexplicably refused her. I don't know why. I ended things with her after that.'

Lily couldn't help but feel a sense of unease. Daffy's revelation was unsettling.

'After that, I chose you. Yes, even though we'd just met, you were an easy target. But it turns out, you were the most formidable of them all.'

'Daffy, it's cruel to involve those girls in something that I once believed was terrifying and dreadful,' Lily admonished him.

'I know, Lily. I had no other choice. It was the only way to gather information about him.'

'But do you truly grasp how dangerous he is?'

'I understand that. And I know a way to stop him.'

Lily fell silent, unable to comprehend it all.

'When the Heartbreaker succeeds in dragging his lover to the afterworld, where you are now, he plays that song again—the same one I used on you at the camp. And you have to answer. It's a promise that binds you to him here forever.'

Lily furrowed her brow, puzzled. 'Answer what?'

'As I mentioned back then, the song is actually a love song about him and his past lover. But the version we know is incomplete—we only have the ghost's part. The missing piece is the response to the previous lyrics; the part sung by his lover. It's something like "I'm the flower to pick." But . . .'

Daffy paused uncertainly. 'We need to modify the lyrics so that they pertain to his past lover. This will summon her spirit, and they can reunite, allowing him to peacefully depart with her.'

Lily raised an eyebrow, her curiosity piqued. 'If you knew how to do this, why didn't you attempt it earlier?'

'The challenge lies in gathering what kind of flower his past girlfriend was,' Daffy explained. 'Perhaps it was a flower he gave her. That flower must be of special significance in their relationship.'

Lily pondered for a moment before an idea struck her. 'The flower is jasmine.'

'How do you know?' Daffy looked at her, surprised.

'Jasmine, or "Melati" in Indonesian—that's her name,' Lily replied with confidence.

'So, jasmine's the flower to pick. Lily, you're a genius.'

Lily remained silent. She kept her thoughts to herself, a complex mix of emotions swirling within her. Confusion still lingered about the mystifying world of spirits, the game and the chant, and the hidden agendas that were now emerging around her.

Yet, beneath the confusion, a pang of jealousy gnawed at her heart. She couldn't help but envy the idea that the ghost might be reunited with his long-lost love and have a chance at closure that seemed to elude her own grasp.

'We have to reunite him with his past lover,' Daffy began to say, his voice filled with determination. 'That way, his soul will—'

'NO!' Before Daffy could finish his sentence, Lily's sharp and resolute voice cut through the air.

Daffy was taken aback by her fervent objection.

'I'm the one who will be with him,' Lily continued, her tone unwavering. 'I'll be by his side here, where no one can disrupt our love. That's the promise he made.'

Daffy persisted in trying to convey something to Lily, but she remained resolute, her mind made up. She had journeyed this far into this strange and eerie world, and she was now steadfast in her decision to stay with him, whatever the cost.

Then, a sudden realization struck her, and she turned her gaze towards Daffy, her eyes wide with alarm.

'DAFFY, YOU'RE FADING!' she screamed.

Daffy's form began to fade, it was as though he was slowly evaporating, becoming translucent and insubstantial, like mist dissipating in the morning sun. The contours of his form blurred, and his features lost their distinctness.

'That's because I don't have anything else to do. I'm kinda stuck in this world because I have made a vow to you,' Daffy explained, his fading presence imbued with a sense of resignation. 'I'm grateful that you crossed paths with me so I could pay off my vow because, otherwise, I would have undoubtedly become as infamously ominous as the Heartbreaker.

'Listen, Lily, some spirits let go of their problems, others try to solve them. But there are those stubborn ones who can't solve anything and can't let go either. We call them the creepy ghosts, the ones that wreak havoc and incite terror in the living world. They can't save themselves; they need help. The Heartbreaker, he needs your help to confront his troubles, Lily.'

Lily remained silent, her gaze averted from Daffy once more.

'Listen, Lily!' Daffy's voice pleaded desperately. 'That ghost isn't your true love. You deserve authentic love among the living. Return to the human world. He has caused you so much anguish and turmoil. This peace isn't just for the living but for him, too. If you truly care for him then you must help him rest in peace.'

When Lily turned her gaze back to where Daffy had stood, he had vanished completely. His soul had found tranquillity, and he was no longer the guardian ghost of the school's indoor swimming pool building.

Meanwhile, Lily remained an unsettled spirit, trapped there in the eerie silence. The waters offered no answers, and she found herself unable to make a choice.

The weight of her decision pressed upon her, a ghostly burden in this enigmatic afterworld.

# Chapter 12

## May

'A lily of a day
Is fairer far in May,
Although it fall and die that night—
It was the plant and flower of Light.'

—Ben Jonson, 'The Noble Nature'

It took Lily a while to understand that this upside-down world was wrong for her. Everything was reversed, unfamiliar. She felt out of place, yet again a stranger in a world—even in one that defied logic. The colours were too bright, the dark was too dark, the sounds were too muffled.

Gravity seemed to mock her, pulling her in strange directions. She moved cautiously, each step a challenge. The world didn't fit her; like she was wearing a coat several sizes too large. She realized she didn't belong here. But she was too late.

At first, this strange world replayed her happiest memories. It resembled a feast of delightful desserts where various versions of her at different ages gathered, exchanging their joyful experiences—days of laughter, moments of love. She relived her dad's hugs under a starry sky, the warmth of her mother's embrace. But then the sweetness faded. The memories repeated, over and over, until they lost their joy. Like a favourite song played too many times, they turned dull, then bitter. The laughter sounded forced; the present felt empty. The hugs under the stars seemed cold. Her happiest moments were now like traps.

Now, this world was replaying her worst memories—failures, rejections, alienations, heartbreaks. Each memory sharper, more vivid than the last. The time she had stumbled during a play, the whispers of her classmates, the sting of a harsh word from a friend, the coldness in her mother's eyes after a fight. These memories wrapped around her like strong chains. The world felt like a prison, replaying moments she wished to forget. Her personal demons, refusing to be laid to rest.

Lily's life unfolded like a theatre of shadows, casting her in the role of a clown—either mocked or tormented. She was the reluctant actress in a play she never wanted to act in, forced to relive her missteps under a harsh spotlight. These were reflections in a mirror cracked by her own doing, showing her the uncomfortable truth: she was the heroine of her own misfortunes.

Her life had become a scripted drama in which she had always sought the lead role, craving the warmth of the spotlight. Every word, every action, was played to captivate an audience she desperately needed. Like a flower straining towards the sun, she reached for attention, for validation.

This realization dawned on her, a cold sunrise illuminating a landscape she had painted but never truly seen.

This dance for attention, this never-ending performance, was rooted in a nostalgia for brighter days. A longing for the affectionate embrace of her father. A yearning for her mother's undivided attention. A desire to be among friends, having a sense of belonging. In her quest to recapture these lost echoes of joy, she had become a ghost in her own narrative, haunting the corridors of her past.

The revelations of Lily's journey struck her like a rogue wave, washing away her illusions. It taught her that she didn't need to be the protagonist in every tale. This included her own surreal love story, straddling the realms of both the living and the departed.

Lily came to understand, as Daffy had suggested, that their story wasn't a love story. It was just another ghost story. A narrative woven with vengeance and wrath, interlaced with flowers and blood. It was far from the romantic saga she had imagined. Instead, it was a chilling tale, dealing with the darkest supernatural forces.

The real love of this story was a time long gone. But it was marked by wounds and forbidden desires, and a dangerous path. Now, Lily realized she was the one who had to walk that path gracefully to end this twisted tale. She needed to weave the end of their story, not with anger and vengeance, but with the gentle hues of a gracious farewell and eternal serenity. It was time for her to turn the page; to let the ghostly love story drift away on the autumn breeze. Then, she must relinquish that lover's role back to its rightful owner, not Lily, but Jasmine.

So Lily stopped waiting for the Heartbreaker in the field of gladioli. She stopped closing her eyes in the amaryllis forest, hoping his magic would lift her up. She stopped lamenting in the mansion on the hill, hoping he would come and take her away. She went home, to the Lonely House, which now seemed lonelier than ever.

These thoughts troubled her as she walked home. Each step seemed uncertain. Her journey felt endless, like watching a never-ending scene on a bright, old TV. Every move she made was stark, like stepping from shadow into bright light.

Just when Lily thought her mind could rest, new mysteries surfaced. These puzzles weren't amusing; they were confusing and unsolvable. It seemed they weren't tickling her funny bone; they were trying to tickle a corpse—leaving her perplexed and without answers.

Approaching the Lonely House, expecting it to be as solitary as a forgotten graveyard, she was greeted by a bewildering sight. A horde—yes, a horde—of people had decided to turn the Lonely House into a haunted house as an attraction for a Friday night carnival.

The Lonely House had become a spot for social gatherings, contradicting its name. The sight just didn't sit right with Lily. She decided to rescue the socially awkward Lonely House from the invading crowd. It had pulled quite a crowd, too—dense and daunting, it seemed impenetrable. It stretched out before her as if for miles—a maze of humans packed tightly together.

As she began to weave her way through, Lily tried to be as courteous as possible, softly uttering 'excuse me'. But her words seemed to vanish as soon as they left her lips.

They were lost in the cacophony of voices and movements around her. The crowd, absorbed in their own world, hardly acknowledged her. Her presence, rather than causing a stir or even a glance, seemed to go completely unnoticed. Their indifference to her polite attempts was disheartening.

But Lily was far from discouraged—she took a deep, steadying breath, readying herself to try a different approach. She began to ask the crowd about the event that had drawn them all here. It was as if she was trying to immerse herself in the chain reaction of conversation murmuring through the crowd, hoping to catch the message in a bottle floating on the sea of voices, unravelling the mystery of what had brought them together.

But she hardly got a response; it was frustrating being treated like a child asking a parent about something trivial during a serious discussion and being ignored. Her questions seemed to bounce off the impassive faces without leaving a mark, her curiosity unmet by any meaningful answers.

'Man, I'm feeling nostalgic for our quiet little corner of the world. These news headlines are seriously giving me a headache!'

'Seriously, can you believe the cops are showing up here? I mean, the last time anything remotely criminal happened was like a decade ago, right?'

'I woke up to a police siren this morning! Had me thinking lilies were sprouting out of someone's mouth again!'

'Apparently, they're saying someone's gone missing!'

'You know that girl at the centre of all the ghost rumours? She's the one they're talking about, the one who disappeared.'

'Yeah, maybe the ghost's taken her to his world.'

'I hope so, I hope they're gone for good, and our town's safe from the spookiness of it all, just like the old days.'

It was like Lily was on a Halloween candy scavenger hunt, searching for sweet morsels of information. But instead of dressing up as a ghost, she was a ghost herself. And being a ghost meant she wasn't getting any treats.

It didn't disappoint her, really. It gave her a wild idea, actually. Her invisible form had the benefit of being see-through, giving her the privilege to cut through the queues of these crowds without angering anyone or taking their place, as she was no longer bound by the space and time of the living world.

Lily decided to wade through the crowd like an abstract wind, silent and unnoticed. She managed to glide through the swarm effortlessly.

She finally worked her way to the front of the crowd. Once there, she struggled to understand what was causing the commotion. Everything seemed unclear and chaotic. Then, without warning, the sound of loud crying cut through the noise. It was a familiar voice, one Lily had grown up with, but it was filled with a level of sorrow she had never heard before. She scanned the crowd, and her gaze landed on her mother. Her distress was evident, standing out starkly in the midst of the indifferent onlookers.

The police formed a tight circle around her mom, bombarding her with a flurry of questions that were mostly drowned out by the commotion of the gathering crowd. Amid the jumble of voices, Lily caught snippets of enquiries like, 'Could you provide us with the full name, age, and physical description of the missing person?' and 'Can you tell us when and where she was last seen? What was she wearing at the time?'

Assailed by the relentless questions, her mom's only response was a tearful silence. The police held a photograph, a snapshot from when Lily had been at a flower shop, holding a bouquet of lilies, carnations, and roses.

The crowd grew increasingly rowdy, filled with guesses and confusion. Yet, they could never grasp this bewildering truth: the missing person they were frantically searching for . . . was standing right there, in a different dimension.

Lily had returned home. But, in an eerie twist, her presence seemed to elude everyone's notice. As usual. Classic Lily. Some of them might even secretly harbour a wish that Lily remain eternally undiscovered.

She attempted to capture the police's attention, but they remained engrossed in their walkie-talkie's cryptic update—a breaking news. The lost teenage girl had been discovered. She was dying, clutching a daffodil, its petals fallen and gone.

Lily couldn't wrap her head around this, even as her mom's wail kept echoing through the air. She couldn't bear to watch her mom's teardrops fall like monsoon rain, so she lunged forward, ready to step into action. Just as she was about to offer her mom some consolation, a mysterious voice cut through the air, calling out to her.

'LILY!'

Finally, someone wanted to interact with her. She scanned the crowd but not a single pair of eyes looked back at her.

'LILY!'

It was an unfamiliar voice, soft and sweet, calling out to her like a siren's song. She looked to the left, then to the right, trying to locate the source.

'LILY!'

She hurriedly plunged back into the crowd, scrutinizing every face she passed, searching for the voice. All she found was apathy looking back at her.

'LILY!'

Finally, Lily was at the tail end of the crowd, where there was no one.

'LILY!'

Her hunt persisted.

'LILY!'

Seconds felt like an eternity; the noise around her seemed to fade into the background.

'LILY!'

The voice grew clearer, and her heart skipped a beat.

'LILY!'

And there it was!

'LILY!'

In the tapestry of life's moments, there was a thread that had been tugging at her heart for what felt like an eternity. Every sunrise and every twilight had carried the whisper of its absence, leaving an ache that echoed in the chambers of her soul.

Suddenly, in an almost magical moment, everything seemed to align perfectly for Lily. The chaotic noise of the world around her faded away, and time itself appeared to pause as she finally found the person she had been searching for.

It felt like a special, timeless moment had been created just for her. Lily experienced a rush of familiar emotions, a blend of surprise and a deep, calming recognition. His presence seemed to fill an emptiness she hadn't fully realized was there, and the air around her seemed to pulse with their shared memories.

Amid the crowd, as if woven into the very fabric of life, Lily saw the one person who had always been a part of her. There he was, his presence as significant and awaited as a groom's for his bride on their wedding day.

The Heartbreaker. And he no longer felt like a haunting myth, but a genuine embodiment of a fond memory.

The ache of longing within Lily reached its tipping point. Those sparkling blue eyes beckoned her like the North Star guiding a lost sailor. The radiant glow on his face broke through the surrounding darkness akin to a moonless night.

Yet, amid all the celestial splendour, little did Lily realize that there was a surprise lurking around the corner—something even more wondrous than anything she'd seen so far.

'Hi, Lily!' She'd never heard his voice before. The words fell on her ears like a fragrant breeze on a summer day, bringing familiarity and warmth.

The silent ghost she was familiar with—his voice was a symphony of velvety tones and harmonious notes. A soothing sound with a touch of mischief and charm. It wrapped around her like a cozy blanket on a chilly evening. Each syllable felt like a caress.

With each pounding step, Lily raced toward him. Her heart echoed the rhythm of her footsteps. Determination etched on her face, she pushed herself beyond her limits;

the wind tugging at her hair like a playful accomplice. The ground beneath her seemed to blur as she fought to maintain her balance; but destiny had its own plans.

Just as she was about to reach him, she slipped and the world turned upside down, causing her to fall into his waiting embrace instead.

Lily's gaze lingered on that enchanting face, and she couldn't look away. She felt his charming aura creep up on her like a lavender haze, accelerating her heartbeat, her pupils locked on his, unblinking, frozen in place. Lily found herself spirited away from the noise of reality's commotion, drawn into the embrace of an alternate realm where wonders never ceased. The allure of this newfound world held her in its thrall; the past felt more like an afterthought.

No more did Lily glance over her shoulder at the world she had left behind; instead, she became an adventurer penning her story in the ink of uncharted realms. Within the intricate tapestry of existence, the constraints between the dimension of life and death melted away, helping their love transcend across realms.

But the beginning of her daring journey through this newfound realm came to a screeching halt, disrupted by a poignant cry that pierced the air. She faced her tearful mom, still shrouded in uncertainty, wondering whether her daughter would return or disappear into the unknown forever.

Lily, once again, became indecisive. Her heart whispered a different truth—but the human heart can never be easily deciphered, right?

Her attention then shifted to an empty pot perched on the banister of the Lonely House. She had once planted a sunflower seed in it but nothing had sprouted from it as yet. In an inexplicable twist, right at that very moment, a plant emerged from the pot at a miraculous speed. Astonishingly, it blossomed before Lily's eyes, giving rise to . . . a sunflower? Well, that was how it should have been, but strangely no. Out came a cluster of sweet Williams.

Or could it be that this new bloom held the key to her heart's true message? Sweet William, a flower her dad used to send her as a promise of his return, like a soldier. Lily's hope rested on the possibility of her mom understanding this—even if it meant her reading Lily's diary, where the language of flowers was jotted down.

She wished that her mom would understand that this meant she would come home. Or maybe she never would.

Lily turned her gaze back to the ghost, who began to sing the haunting song. The game had begun, and an unsettling sensation crept over her. It was as if her spirit was solidifying; the promise threatening to bind her to this otherworldly realm, to him, for all eternity.

Garden breeze, blow it all,
who's the fairest flower of them all?

Her soul entwined more with the haunting melody of the song. The sounds of the earthly realm ebbed further away, as if the volume had been turned down. The once bustling crowd now seemed distant, as if she was looking at it from inside a car. The cries of her mother were reduced to mere echoes in her memory; and the birds fell silent, their songs hushed. The trees ceased their rustling.

Lily's entire being was fixated solely on the ghost's lips as he uttered each syllable of the chant. She felt herself freeze in the grip of his otherworldly incantation, disconnected from the world she knew.

In a garden so chic,
which flower to pick?

She felt like she was a hypnotic trance, as if the lyrics of the song had seized control of her. She found herself effortlessly reciting the song, even though she was not familiar with its lyrics. It was as though she was being guided through it, while being drawn deeper into the mystical game that was ensnaring her.

In a garden so chic . . .

Lily's fate was sealed. Her path was now irrevocably intertwined with the eerie melody. The end of her life had been rewritten; she was going to spend the remainder of her spiritual existence bound to her spectral lover in this haunting realm. In his embrace, she found a sanctuary of safety that had eluded her in the living world. Only he could provide her the attention and affection she had longed for, filling the void in her heart.

Here, in his arms, the evil forces and the sorrows of the real world could no longer reach her. In this ethereal realm, their love would flourish without the constraints of mortal limitations, blooming like an everlasting spring in the garden of eternity—a paradise they would now share.

In a garden so chic . . .

She was almost at the last line of the song, a soft smile on her face. The words were coming easily, like they had been waiting to be sung.

She had a mission, didn't she? To fix what was broken, to return the love stories and songs to their rightful places and owners. Her own love story, as haunting and tangled as it was, had to end here. It was time to finish the song.

In a garden so chic . . .

A hand, unexpected yet familiar, gently tilted her chin upward. It was him, his deep blue eyes burning into hers with an intensity that seemed to melt away her resolve for a moment. His gaze held a romantic power, weaving a spell that threatened to crush her fleeting thoughts of rebellion. Lily was captivated.

Yet, deep down, she knew she had to break free from his enchantment. Her mind wandered, seeking solace in the image of a serene lily garden. But the garden that bloomed in her thoughts was different—filled with flowers resembling lilies, she noticed they were smaller, delicate and without big pistils. They were jasmines, pure and white, their beauty untouched.

Known for their sweet fragrance, their scent filled her senses. It was a strong yet soothing aroma that calmed her soul, which was in turmoil, battling for her attention amid the chaos of her heart and the bizarre world around her.

But the jasmine scent wasn't just a figment of her imagination. There stood behind the Heartbreaker the woman from Lily's dreams. She was an embodiment of her native tradition—her skin a rich brown, dressed in Javanese attire, her hair elegantly styled in a bun, adorned with clothes that signified heritage and a different time in history. She was the unmistakable source of the scent.

Lily was perplexed. The chant was not complete yet, the incantation that was supposed to summon this figure from her dreams. So, why was she here already?

The Javanese lady, elegant but haunting, stirred a strange unease in Lily. Despite her calm demeanour, Lily felt a surge of emotions—a mix of anger and jealousy bubbled up within her. The lady, a remnant of her ghost lover's past, stood there like an ex-girlfriend laying claim to what had once been hers.

This unsettling scene brought back painful memories for Lily, reminiscent of Rosy, who had stolen Daffy from her. And the last thing Lily wanted was to be part of another love triangle, to be reduced to just a fleeting summer romance in someone else's story.

No, he must end up with her. That was the perfect ending to this love story.

*No, no, it should be me who ends up with him.*

No, no, no . . .

In a garden so chic . . .

The Javanese lady, in contrast to the tumultuous emotions swirling in Lily, was the epitome of calm. Her presence radiated a tranquil energy, as if she had passed away in peace, not in fear or anger. There was a sense of forgiveness and optimism in her, also a stark contrast to the turbulent aura of the Heartbreaker. She was like the water to his fire, the acceptance to his rejection, the wisdom to his vengeance.

Her silence was powerful, yet her words from the dream resonated in Lily's mind: 'What was wounded in the past must not avenge in the future.' These words struck a chord with her, and as she gazed into the serene eyes of the Javanese lady, she was transported back to her own past, as if she was looking into a mirror.

Visions flooded her mind—painful memories of her parents arguing, the ache of waiting for her father's call, the longing for his return. She relived the moment her mother moved her to the Lonely House, and the crushing realization that she had abandoned her forever. She saw herself, a girl who never grew, always stuck in the past, hoping it would somehow return. This hope led her astray, and the pain of never letting go created an evil curse that haunted her future. A dark voice inside her told her that if hope couldn't restore everything then she would have to do it herself: return her mother's attention and her father's affection, even though they didn't want them. She resolved to make herself loved and cared for again, if not by her parents then by others.

But each time she listened to these dark whispers, she ended up humiliated, the victim of pranks and sabotage. These evil whispers blocked her from hearing her true self, from understanding her true needs.

Now, as she stood there, the wise, forgiving gaze of the Javanese lady helped Lily comprehend the depth of her own entrapment. It was a moment of painful clarity but also one of potential liberation—a chance to break free from the chains of her past, to silence the whispers that haunted her, and to step into a future of her own making.

*We must be healed. To seek a cure, we cannot return to the past, but we can find it in the future.* Healing, as the ghost revealed, was not a journey back through the thorny paths of the past, but a voyage forward, sailing on the winds of change and hope. To let go was to set sail on this journey, leaving the familiar shores of past pains behind and venturing boldly into the uncharted waters of the future.

Lily felt the heavy chains of her past dissolve in the face of sage wisdom. Her own eyes, once clouded with the fog of revenge and longing, now cleared, revealing a vista of new possibilities. This time, she didn't see her own reflection in the Javanese lady's eyes, but the Heartbreaker's past. It was as if their souls were now connected by an invisible thread; a shared understanding of pain and the decision to undertake the journey towards healing.

Through the intertwining of their fates, Lily saw a reflection of her past life's tapestry in the love story between the Javanese lady and the Heartbreaker. Their ghost tale, much like hers, was one of joy and stars, tragically marred by a wound so deep it cast long shadows across the future. The pain of this wound had cursed the Heartbreaker, dooming him to wander on his vengeful quest to fill the void in his heart by inflicting terror and sorrow upon the living.

Lily saw her own self in him, too. She was trapped in the past's painful embrace, desperately searching for something to replace the love she had lost. When the Heartbreaker came into her life, it changed everything. In him, she had found not just a substitute for her lost love, but a path to healing—an unexpected chance to let go of her past.

She, too, had brought light into the Heartbreaker's cursed existence. She filled the void in his heart, breaking the curse that bound him. Her love crossed the barriers between the living and dead, defying the rules that kept their relationship forbidden.

In a moment of profound clarity, Lily understood the true essence of this love story. It wasn't a tale destined to unite those who had been separated in the past; rather, it was a journey to break free from their respective curses. It was not about rekindling old flames or mending what was broken long ago. It was about being free.

And then, in a moment of peace and resolution, Lily watched as the Javanese lady slowly faded away. She felt a sense of closure; her spirit had finally found the tranquillity it deserved. A beautiful, lush garden, a symbol of new beginnings and hope took root in her mind.

In a garden so chic,
Lily's the flower I pick.

The melody, tender and harmonious, blended seamlessly into the peaceful environment around them. But it wasn't Lily who had brought the song to its conclusion. It was the Heartbreaker.

He had changed it, turning it into a song about her; about them.

The haunting aura that once surrounded him had vanished and been replaced by a newfound serenity.

The blue in his eyes, once a stormy sea of revenge, now mirrored a calm, clear sky. The anger that had once contorted his moonlit face had given way to tranquillity, and his smile captivated her heart with its gentleness, free from the shadows of fear.

Then, in a moment as timeless as any fairy tale, their lips met. It was a kiss that pulsed with life; warm and vibrant. It was like a magical revival that breathed life back into her, as if she was Snow White waking from her slumber—just as he had done once before.

The world seemed to spin around her, a whirlwind of emotions and sensations, until everything slowly faded into darkness. She felt herself falling, as if tumbling down an endless abyss, but his embrace steadied her, warm and grounding.

And as the darkness wrapped around her again, it didn't feel cold or frightening; instead, it lulled her into a peaceful, dreamless sleep; safe and secure in the arms of her Heartbreaker.

\* \* \*

'Welcome back!'

Lily struggled to open her eyes.

'How are you feeling?'

Her mind was foggy; her body felt like it had been asleep for ages, almost like she was waking from the dead.

'It's remarkable to see you recovering well after that nasty flower poisoning you got. We're going to do some basic tests to assess your condition.'

The words barely made sense to Lily.

'Everything is good. There are no problems whatsoever.'

'Can you call her family?'

Lily tried to piece together her memories, but they remained elusive.

The door opened with a soft creak. 'Oh, Lily!' The voice, tinged with relief and worry, was unmistakably her mother's.

'Lily, I'm so glad you're awake.' Her mom approached the bed, her steps hesitant yet eager. She reached out, her touch gentle as she took Lily's hands in hers.

'Lily, I need to apologize to you,' she began, her voice laced with a deep sincerity.

'For years, I've been so caught up in my own struggles and challenges that I've failed to see how much you needed me. I was absent when you needed guidance, support, and love . . .' Her eyes brimmed with tears, a tangible sign of her remorse. 'I let you down, and for that, I am truly sorry. You've grown into such a strong and independent young woman, and that's despite my absence, not because of my guidance.'

She squeezed Lily's hands a little tighter, a silent promise in her grip. 'I'm here now, Lily. I want to be the mother you deserve; I want to support you and be there for you, no matter what. I can't change the past, but I can be here for you now onwards. Forever.'

As Lily forced her eyes fully open, words escaped her. She noticed something on the silver table beside her mother—a bouquet of lilies.

It was unusual; her mother had never bought flowers like this before. That had always been her father's job—lilies, specifically for her. But mixed in with the lilies were white clovers and pink camellias; silent symbols of her father's feelings—his longing to see her and how much he missed her.

'I called your father. He's on his way here,' her mother said, her voice carrying a note of reconciliation, an unspoken permission for him to return into their lives.

This revelation overwhelmed Lily. But she didn't know how to react.

The doctor stepped forward, addressing her mother. 'Ma'am, could you please step outside for a moment?'

Her mother shot a lingering glance at Lily, nodded, and quietly left the room, closing the door behind her.

The doctor began a series of checks. They worked methodically, examining Lily, taking notes, ensuring that every aspect of her recovery was documented. Lily, still struggling with the flood of emotions and the weakness of her body, remained silent throughout, her eyes following the doctor's movements.

Once the doctor had finished the checks, they gave Lily a reassuring nod.

'You're doing well, all things considered,' they said gently, before leaving the room, giving Lily some much-needed space to process everything that was happening.

As Lily lay there in the quiet room, a sense of profound peace enveloped her. The wounds and burdens of her past felt as though they had dissolved, leaving behind a strange emptiness. It was like having navigated across a tumultuous storm at sea, only to find herself now adrift in a tranquil, azure expanse. She longed for an island; a new beginning to anchor her new life on.

With a deep breath, Lily closed her eyes, seeking solace in the darkness behind her lids. That's when she saw it—a glimmering light, a distant beacon.

It was a vibrant, ethereal blue, calling to her, promising her a haven, a place to rest.

Then, she opened her eyes, and there he was—the Heartbreaker, standing right in front of her. In his hands was a bouquet of purple salvia, wishing her healing and serenity.

*He was no myth.*

*He was real.*

*He was here.*

His haunting reputation had dissipated. As had the fierce aura and constant supervision, which Lily had once turned to for protection. Her world was now healed, and she didn't need him to save her.

But she wanted him to go on showing her his supernatural love. Metaphysical kisses. Transcendental hugs. Otherworldly dances.

She wanted him to go on showing her a love that challenged logic and norm.

To make her continue believing.